JENNIFER BROWN

PERFECT ESCAPE

Little, Brown and Company
New York   Boston

For Scott
and
for Pranston

CHAPTER ONE

I was six the first time we found Grayson at the quarry. Dad and I had just gotten back from my peewee soccer game, and Mom had met us at the front door, car keys dangling from one hand.

"We won!" I crowed, hopping past her. "And Ashley's mom brought fish crackers!"

But Mom didn't answer. Instead, she muttered something to Dad, whose eyebrows knit together. He turned and peered out the front door into the rapidly approaching night, then stepped outside, cupped his mouth with his hands, and started yelling my brother's name—"Grayson! Graaayson!"—while Mom shrugged into her coat, not even acknowledging that I had gone on to tell her all about the goal I'd scored and the goalie with the freckles who'd gotten a bloody nose when Imogene Sparks accidentally fell on top of her.

Nobody told me what was going on. All I knew was our next-door neighbor Tammy came over and fixed me a cheese sandwich for dinner. We played checkers over and over, and she stroked my braids out with her fingers and didn't make me take a bath so I could go to school with braid-waves the next day.

"Where did Mom and Dad go, anyway?" I asked. "King me."

She shrugged. "To get Grayson. Your move."

"Where is he?" I jumped one of her checkers and picked it up, tucking it into the lap bowl created by my nightgown.

Tammy hesitated the tiniest bit. Her eyes flicked toward the front door, and for a second I thought I might have seen the same worried crease between her eyebrows that I'd seen between Dad's. But she smiled and slid her checker across the board. "They didn't say," she said. "I'm sure they'll be back soon. Your turn."

It wasn't until the next morning when Mom was brushing my hair for school—using the smoothing brush, which destroyed my waves—that I asked again.

"*Ouch*. Mom, where did you guys go last night? *Ow*."

Unlike Tammy, Mom didn't hesitate one bit—just kept pulling the brush through my hair, all business. "Newman Quarry," she said, as if this were something they did every evening. "The place off the highway, with all the rocks." She pulled particularly hard on a knot at the base of my neck, and I sucked my breath in through my teeth. Staticky strands of my hair were floating outward, following the brush; the whole thing was a fuzz-mess. "I really wish Tammy'd given you a bath last night," she muttered. "You're frizzed."

I frowned. "Why did you go there?" I asked.

She set the brush on the counter, wet her hands in the sink, and smoothed them over my hair, meeting my eyes in the mirror. She sighed, then moved her palms down to my shoulders and patted them lightly. "Your brother is having some difficulties, Kendra. Go get your backpack now. The bus will be coming."

I left the room, my scalp feeling heat-pricked and pulsating, wondering what Mom had meant by "having difficulties" and what that had to do with my parents' going to Newman Quarry the night before in the dark.

But that was eleven years ago. Grayson had been to the quarry hundreds of times since then. Sometimes several times a day, walking three miles down the highway in that precise way of his, muttering under his breath, his fingers hooked like claws while he calculated whatever it was he was calculating.

And we'd all had to go fetch him at one time or another. Stand at the top of the pit and call his name out, knowing he wouldn't answer. Stumble down the rock beds, trying not to lose our footing, trying not to get too many pebbles in our shoes, trying not to get angry. Still calling his name, stupidly. "Grayson! Come on! Mom and Dad are going to be mad if you miss therapy again. Grayson! Graaayson! I know you hear me!"

And we'd all had to try to make him leave the quarry before he was "finished." Which always meant tears for someone. Usually everyone.

I'd been to the bottom of that quarry hundreds of times, starting when I was seven and my parents began sending me over the fence to fetch him, always framing it as "an adventure."

But it didn't feel like an adventure. It felt like a chore. He never wanted to leave. I'd end up doing just about anything to get him out of there. Push him. Pull him. Yell at him. Make promises to him.

I'm not finished, Kendra. I have to count them.

But you have therapy. And there are billions. Come on, just go with me, okay, Gray?

No! I can't! Uh-uh-uh!

Okay, Grayson, okay, okay. Here. I'll help you. I'll count the ones in this pile, okay? Don't cry. We'll count them together....

We all knew what Grayson's "difficulties" were. Grayson's difficulties dominated his life. And Mom's and Dad's.

And mine.

Sometimes, like when Zoe left, it felt like *especially* mine.

CHAPTER
TWO

Nobody warned me he'd be coming home today.

I got home from school, dropped my backpack on the floor, and read a text from Shani as I walked into the kitchen.

Then screamed when I bumped face-first into a bony chest. Before my brain could catch up with my reflexes, my phone-wielding hand reached out and punched at the chest with a hollow thump.

"Ouch! Nice to see you, too." My brother, whom I hadn't seen in months, was rubbing the spot where I'd just hit him. He was impossibly skinny, his hair greasy and flopping in his extremely pale face. He always looked like this when he got home from treatment. Probably I should've been used to it, but it's hard to get accustomed to living with someone who looks like an extra in a zombie movie.

"You scared the crap out of me, Grayson. Jeez!"

"I gathered that much when you hit me."

"I'm sorry," I said, pushing past him and heading for the refrigerator, my breath still coming in quick bursts. "Automatic reaction when I think I'm going to be murdered in my kitchen. It is good to see you. I just..." The phone vibrated in my hand, and I glanced at it. Another text from Shani. Major boyfriend issues. "I didn't know you were getting released today. Where's Mom?" I grabbed a slice of cheese out of the refrigerator and unwrapped it, closing the fridge door with my hip, my heartbeat beginning to slow.

"Neither did I. They told me this morning. And the store. She'll be right back."

I tossed the cellophane into the trash, thinking it would have been nice to have gotten some warning, and began folding the cheese slice into little squares, peeling the top square off and shoving it into my mouth. Grayson stood awkwardly in the doorway, staring intently at my hands, his lips moving.

I knew what he was thinking. With Grayson, everything had to be so perfectly lined up. Even if it wasn't his. He was bothered by how I was folding that cheese slice into uneven squares, and I knew by looking at him that he wanted to take a ruler to it before I ate it. I chewed self-consciously, wishing he would stop looking at me like that. Didn't Mom send him to these treatment places to make him stop looking at people like that? "So why the sudden release? Are you better?" I asked, pulling out a chair and sitting. "I mean, is the OCD, you know...?" I trailed off. I didn't know how to finish the question.

I opened Shani's text, pretending that seeing Grayson back in our kitchen was no big deal and that this was a question people asked each other all the time. Pretending he hadn't been in that resident facility Mom had found—the one that was supposed to cure him of his obsessive-compulsive disorder, his depression, the billion anxiety disorders he had, and God knows what else.

Pretending that things hadn't been weird between us ever since his quirks had slowly evolved into full-blown mental illness. Pretending that I could once again overlook his rituals and worries as I had done when we were kids. I wished I could. But the older we got—the worse he got—the harder it was to pretend that he was normal, like the rest of us. People noticed. I noticed. It was impossible not to notice.

How do you not notice someone's mental illness when the whole family constantly revolves around it?

"Yeah, I think so. I guess. Whatever" was his answer. He was probably thinking the same thing I was thinking: *What exactly is better?*

"That's good," I said, and I really meant it, though I wasn't sure if I meant that it was good for him or good for me. Probably a little of both.

There was an awkward silence between us, during which he shifted from foot to foot, mumbling numbers under his breath and knocking the wood frame of the door softly with one knuckle while I stared intently at my phone, as though Shani had written me an engrossing novel.

This was the way it'd been for the past three years.

We couldn't move. We were both trapped by whatever ritual he was struggling with at the moment. Prisoners of the great Obsessive-Compulsive Oppressor.

Who was I kidding? This was the way it'd been for our whole lives.

This is what it's like living with a mentally ill person: everyone afraid to move. Everyone afraid to speak. You don't say certain words like *suicide* or *crazy*, and you do everything in your power to keep the good milliseconds lasting as long as they possibly can. And you don't rush into anything at all, because rushing feels like courting disaster, and you don't even know what that disaster is, because it's never the same disaster twice. A ruined birthday? A scene at a restaurant? Police cars in the driveway in the middle of the night? All of the above?

And you don't ask for attention.

And you get used to it when you don't get any.

And you try really, really hard to forget that not getting attention hurts and that this person—this muttering, shadow-eyed, scabbed patient—was once your hero and best friend in the world. Back when he was just a "weird kid."

And you try to remember that you still love him, even if some days you can't exactly pinpoint why.

After what seemed like forever, he finally moved out of

the doorway, and I could hear his steps, slow and rhythmic, on the floorboards leading to his bedroom. He made it in one try, which meant he must have been feeling better.

Before Mom sent him out to Camp Cure Me, or whatever this one was called, it could sometimes take him two hours to walk from the kitchen to his bedroom, his cries of frustration piercing the hallway. Mom's voice trying to soothe whatever broken part of him told him he couldn't put his foot down until he'd counted every grain in the wood beneath it. Her sobs creeping through the bedroom walls at night. That feeling of fullness behind my eyes all the damn time. And the feeling of resentment that I tried to stuff away because when someone can't even walk through his home normally, resenting him somehow feels mean. Not to mention pointless. Resenting Grayson wasn't going to cure him.

After he was gone, I sat at the table for a few more minutes, taking in deep, even breaths and pressing my forehead into my palms. I could smell the cheese on my fingers, and it made the taste in the back of my throat go sour. I knew I should've been happy that he was back, but all I could think was, *Things have been so calm around here without him.*

I also thought about the night, two months or so before he left, when things had seemed so good. He'd seemed relaxed... or at least relaxed for Grayson. Mom and Dad were really happy, and we'd all spent the evening watching TV together, which hadn't happened in months. We joked with one another. Mom made popcorn. I fell asleep on the couch.

At some point, Grayson had brought in his old alarm clock—the kind that buzzes—set it to go off about thirty seconds later, and propped it right next to my ear. Then sat back and waited for it to go off. When it did, I was so startled and confused, I almost fell off the couch. Grayson laughed until his whole face was red and he was holding his belly and gasping for breath. Mom and Dad, still curled up together on the other couch, were giggling as well.

"Kendra, get up!" he'd said, trying to look serious but gasping too hard to pull it off. "You're late for school!"

I'd punched him in the arm but had laughed, too, because even I had to admit that his prank was a good one. "Paybacks, bro, paybacks," I said sleepily.

The next morning, he'd refused to get out of bed. Said the air was filled with toxins and he couldn't breathe them in or he'd get cancer. And he'd been that way since. I never got the chance to prank him back. He would've been way too anxious to find the humor in it.

Sitting at the kitchen table, I hoped for another evening like the one we'd had before he went away. Only I hoped it would last longer this time.

I sat there until I heard the garage door rumble to life, and then I got up in a hurry, pushing the chair back with my legs, and headed upstairs to my room. I didn't want to deal with Mom right now. She would be in that on-edge place again. No softness. No smile. Forever the woman who had yanked that brush through my hair, saying earnestly, *Your brother's having some difficulties, Kendra,* only not finishing the sentence: *and you've got to make up for them. You've got to be the child with no difficulties at all.*

CHAPTER
THREE

From: Kendrazone@comcast.net
To: zoezo@yahoo.com
Subject: He's ba-ack!

Hey, Zo!

So G is back. Seems better. A little jittery and def way too skinny, but better. I can't help but wonder, though... how many times can a person do the treatment thing and come back not any better? I mean, what's the point of going? Will he ever get better, or will he be like this forever? It sounds brutal, and you know I'll never give up hope, but... Well, sometimes my life seems like... *a lot*... when G's around. You know better than anyone what I mean.

Listen, Zo. Neither one of us has heard anything from you in a long time. And I'm cool with it. Your dad gave you loads of trouble when you moved, and you're probably

super busy with Bible study or something. ;-) But I haven't heard from you in like six months and...I don't know... I guess I think it could really help G if you said hey sometime.
Ken

.■ ■ ■ ■

I hit the "send" key and sat back against the headboard, scooching so my pillow was right in the small of my back, and commenced staring at my laptop screen. My phone vibrated on the dresser, but I didn't want to get up. Shani would have to wait.

Wait for what? For me to stare at my empty inbox, expecting Zoe's reply to pop up? Like that was going to happen. I'd said it'd been six months since she'd replied to any of my e-mails, but it felt longer. Maybe it had been longer. Maybe it had been longer than I'd even want to admit to myself. God, had it been a year?

The phone buzzed again. I ignored it again. I guess that, in a nutshell, was the difference between Shani and Zoe. I liked Shani. Called her my BFF when I was feeling it. Hung out with her and had sleepovers at her house. Shared pizza and locker space and gas money with her.

But she wasn't my best friend. She wasn't Zoe.

Zoe and I had grown up together. Literally. My birthday was July 31 and hers, August 1. Our moms were next-door neighbors and best friends and, once upon a time, did everything together. Including pregnancy. They had morning sickness together, ate loads of greasy food together, talked about epidurals and episiotomies and all that gross-out stuff together, and even went into labor on the same day. But since my mom had already had one baby, I came quicker. Or at least that's how Mom put it.

Zoe and I bonded in the hospital nursery and didn't stop until all the craziness between our parents went down and her family moved away three years ago. As if moving could erase what had happened between Zoe and Grayson. As if moving could kill a lifelong friendship.

In a lot of ways, I blamed Zoe's parents for how much worse Grayson became. When Zoe was around, he was a lot more relaxed. She understood him. She didn't make him feel weird. She didn't make him feel anxious about feeling anxious. She didn't expect him to ever be anything other than what or who he was. She was better than me in that respect. Because, after she left, I had all kinds of expectations about him, none of them anything he could ever live up to.

I also blamed Zoe's parents for the fact that I lost my two best friends for no good reason. But everyone was too busy worrying about Grayson to care about that.

After Zoe's parents left, taking her with them, Grayson's anxiety went through the roof. His OCD spun out of control, like nothing any of us had ever seen before. He could barely function, and all he could think about was rocks and counting and germs and weird stuff that had kind of always been there, but not nearly as bad. Before, he'd been a kid who did some obsessive stuff. Afterward, he was just plain obsessive. And it was totally their fault. It's not like what Grayson did was *that* bad. He was in love with their daughter. So what?

The last time I saw Zoe, she was streaking out the back of her parents' minivan toward my yard, where I was standing, unabashedly watching, hoping that her parents would see how they were breaking my heart, too, and maybe change their minds. Her parents were occupied talking to a guy in coveralls, a moving van rumbling in idle at the curb.

"Here, Ken, take this," Zoe had said, her face slick with tears and her nose plugged. She shoved a tiny rectangular piece of paper into my palm—her school photo, with her new address scrawled across the back. "I'll write as soon as I set up a secret e-mail, okay?"

Her dad had noticed her standing in our yard and began shouting for her. "Zoe! Get in the van. We're leaving."

"Okay," I whispered, nodding, my own chin quivering.

"Zoe! Dammit, get off that lawn!"

Zoe glanced back at the minivan, where both of her parents were staring daggers out the windshield at us, and then quickly wrapped her arms around me in a tight hug. Almost immediately the minivan horn blared, and I could feel her shoulders jump and tense. "Don't forget me," she whispered. "And don't let Grayson forget me."

"Never," I whispered back. "Don't forget us, either, okay?"

"I couldn't if I tried," she said, and then turned and ran

for the van, which had begun pulling away from the curb before she even had the back door all the way shut. I watched as it pulled past our house, Zoe's parents' faces grim and eyes set firmly on the road ahead.

Just after the car passed our driveway, Zoe turned around in her seat, staring at me through the back window. Slowly she held up one hand, her fingers slightly curled in, and waved. I held up mine in return.

And when the van turned the corner and out of sight, I sat on the curb and cried, remembering a million days playing with our dolls under a sheet stretched across Zoe's picnic table. A million afternoons spent painting each other's fingernails, because neither of us was good with our left hand. A million sleepovers. A million board games. A million times we'd promised to go to college together and see the world together and be best friends forever and ever. And even though we had all of that...it still wasn't enough.

My dad had sat on the curb next to me, and I'd leaned into him.

"Maybe you'll see her again someday," he'd said, putting his arm around my shoulder and pulling me in. "You never know."

I'd shaken my head pitifully. "They're moving to California. That's so far away. I'll never see her again."

Dad seemed to consider this, then patted my head and said, "The world gets a lot smaller the older you get. Never say never." And he'd gotten up and gone inside the house to help Mom coax Grayson into a bath, a process that could take hours on a high-stress day like that one.

And I'd stayed on the curb and felt sorry for myself, staring at Zoe's photo and sniffling, repeating under my breath, *I won't forget you, Zo. Never say never.*

My phone buzzed again, jarring me out of my memory, but this time it kept buzzing—not a text but an incoming call. I groaned and set the laptop next to my pillow, then got up and grabbed the phone off my dresser. Shani and her guy problems.

But when I looked, the caller ID displayed a number I didn't recognize. "Hello?"

"Kendra? It's Bryn."

I paused. Why would Bryn Mallom be calling me? Other than in Advanced Calculus class, we never talked. Ever. Bryn was one of those girls you talked to only when you absolutely had to. Her arms were always bug-bitten and her clothes dirty and out of style. She was chunky, and she was always in trouble for something. When we were growing up, the boys called her Bryn Bubblebutt, and Ryan Addleson once made her cry when he told the class that his dad had arrested her mom for drunk driving the night before. Probably being picked on didn't do wonders for her personality, but on top of being an easy target, Bryn was kind of a bitch, so people didn't feel very bad when they were mean to her. And almost all of us avoided talking to her at all costs.

But lately I'd had reasons to talk to Bryn. And they weren't good reasons.

"I got your number from Shani," she said. "We need to talk."

I squeezed my eyes shut and massaged the bridge of my nose with two fingers. I'd have to remember to thank Shani for sharing my number with the most obnoxious girl on earth. "Um, I'm kind of in the middle of something, Bryn," I said. "Can we talk in calc tom—"

"It's important," she said. "It's about the calc final."

"What about it?" I asked, thinking, *I should never have started talking to Bryn in the first place. That's where I went wrong. Nothing good ever comes from hanging out with Bryn Mallom.* "We've still got three weeks."

"I heard Mrs. Reading talking to Mr. Floodsay about it today when I was picking up my tardy slip. They know."

My heart thrummed, one time, hard, in my chest. I swallowed, but it felt like a wad of peanut butter was lodged in my throat. I swallowed again, my mind reeling for something to say, and could almost instantly feel cold sweat prick up across the backs of my shoulders. My eyes landed on my laptop screen, which was still pulled up to my e-mail account. *No new messages.*

"Hello? Are you there?"

"Yeah," I said at last. "I'm sure there's nothing to worry about, Bryn."

"Uh, yeah, actually, there is, *Kendra*. Mr. Floodsay said something about searching lockers tomorrow, starting with

Chub's. I don't know about you, but I find that kinda worrisome."

"So?" Bryn's sarcastic voice was really rubbing me the wrong way. "Chub's not dumb. I seriously doubt he's leaving evidence in his locker." Coming out of my mouth, the words sounded so sure, but in my mind I was freaking out. The truth was Chub was just dumb enough to totally leave evidence in his locker.

"I hope you're right," she said, then sighed, her breath barreling into the phone. "But you're probably not. They're going to figure it out. And when they do, we're all in really big trouble. Especially you."

CHAPTER
FOUR

After my conversation with Bryn, I went downstairs to feel out what Mom knew. Surely if the school had figured something out, they would have called Mom immediately, so if I went downstairs and she was happily making a Welcome Home, Grayson dinner, I'd know Bryn was just being her typical dramatic self and I was safe. If I went downstairs and Mom was canceling my college savings account, I'd know the shit had, as they say, hit the fan. And hard.

She was doing neither. Instead, she was sitting on the couch cross-legged, a book open in her lap and earphones clamped down over her head. She smiled and waved at me with her pencil when I walked by, then announced in a slow, measured voice, *"Dov'é il bagno?"*

My heart slowed down. I wiped my sweaty palms on my thighs. If she was calmly practicing her Italian, there was a good chance I was safe. I peeked into the kitchen and saw a pot of something bubbling on the stove, and Grayson sitting at the table, lining up coins in neat little rows in front of him—one of his two favorite pastimes (the other being looking at, talking about, arranging, gathering, and basically knowing everything there is to know about rocks).

"How long's she been doing that?" he asked. He slid a nickel into the "nickel line."

"It's one of her New Year's resolutions," I said, leaning my hip against the doorframe and watching his hands. *Fffp!* A quarter in its spot. *Fffp! Fffp!* Two dimes, smooth as butter.

I couldn't count how many times I'd watched Grayson do this. When I was little, I used to wait until he was finished and then run up beside him and brush my hand through the lines just to mess them up. It made him cry and his face always got beet-red and I thought it was funny. But by the time we were ten and thirteen and he was spending sometimes four hours a day lining up his coins and pulling out wads of his own hair in frustration because he couldn't get them perfect, it wasn't funny anymore. I spent a lot of those nights sitting next to him with a ruler in my hand, helping him move coins such minuscule degrees I couldn't even see the movement. *Is this good, Gray? Does this make you happy?*

"She's learning Italian," I continued. "Dad told her he'll take her anywhere in the world she wants to go for their twenty-fifth anniversary next year. I guess she wants to go to Italy."

"They're going away next year?" he asked. *Fffp! Fffp! Fffp!*

"That's the plan," I said. "I'll be away at college and you'll be..." I trailed off when his eyes lifted to meet mine, his curled fingers frozen over the coins.

He'd be... what? Cured? Living on his own? Not likely. He'd still be there, moving pennies around on the kitchen table and muttering about feldspars and micas and pyroxenes. And there was no way Mom would feel comfortable leaving for a week, with the thought of Grayson being locked in a compulsion and unable to leave the bathtub or get a drink of water or get out of bed. We locked eyes for a moment, all the things we hadn't talked about since Zoe left fluttering between us like dark and dusty moths.

We used to talk about everything. Nothing went unshared. So why couldn't we talk about this? Why did we pretend that his illness didn't exist? Was it because we were both still reeling over what happened with Zoe? Was it because I was too resentful to let him in again? Or had we just given up?

He shrugged, looked back down, and said, "Doesn't matter," and my whole body froze at the weird, defeated tone of his voice.

"Sure it matters," I said, trying to sound light, trying to protect him, as I had since I could remember, from the humiliation of being himself. The guy who blamed himself for driving a whole family of best friends away. The guy who made my parents cry. The guy who interrupted all our lives and couldn't just hop in the car to grab a burger, ever. The guy who held us all hostage, without even meaning to. I knew he hated being that guy, even as his brain forced him to keep doing it. "I'm sure they'll figure something out. I'll come home from college that week or something. We'll have the place to ourselves. It'll be like old times. I'll make the pizzas; you'll choose the movies." *The only thing missing will be Zoe*, I almost finished, but decided against it, knowing what even the mention of Zoe's name did to Grayson's anxiety level. Like the time I'd asked him if he'd heard from her and he'd spent the rest of the night picking up the phone hundreds of times to make sure the dial tone was working.

"Yeah," he said. "Okay." But he was only looking at his coins, switching two pennies for reasons that would never make sense to anyone but him, and leaning close to the table to gaze at them from a different angle. *Fffp.* Gaze. *Fffp.*

"You still like jalapeños and cream cheese on your pizza?"

He shrugged. "They don't serve much of that in treatment."

I took a breath. Tried again. "Remember that time you and Brock ate that superlarge with triple jalapeños and then Brock drank that entire two-liter of root beer and you and his mom ended up having to take him to the ER because his stomach was burning so bad?"

Grayson didn't look up from his coins, but his mouth

twitched into a smile. "That was pretty funny. I kept telling him I could see an alien head moving around under the front of his hospital gown."

We were both smiling now. "And when they brought you home, Dad gave Brock an ice pack and told him to brace himself for the pizza's reappearance in the morning."

Grayson laughed out loud. "I forgot about that."

Mom's voice floated in from the other room: "*Paria Inglese?*"

I shifted uncomfortably as the moment turned back to awkward, and when the urge to dash over and swipe my hand across the table where Grayson sat got to be too much, I turned and went back up to my bedroom.

Between Bryn's phone call and Grayson's sad coin arranging and my fear of what awaited me at school, not to mention never getting a response from Zoe, I could no more sleep than run a marathon in my bathrobe. Instead, I sat up through the night, listening to Dad close the house up, the soft bumps and creaks of everyone moving around in their bedrooms. Then I just lay there in the silence, until the sky began to lighten again, staring out the window and wondering what I would do if Bryn was right and Chub had been stupid enough to store evidence in his locker.

And the thought must have etched itself into my brain, because morning had come and I'd gone through all the motions of getting myself to school, yet there I was, sitting in Hunka (short for Hunka Junka, the name Shani and I had lovingly given the blue-and-rust Oldsmobile I'd inherited when my grandfather died) in the school parking lot, still wondering. But I knew that even if I sat there and thought about it for the next twenty-four hours, I'd never come up with a good answer. If Chub left evidence in his locker, I was busted. Plain and simple.

The first bell had rung, and then the second. But still my legs didn't want to move. I was so afraid of what awaited me in that school.

But I finally told myself that the last thing I needed was a tardy, because then I'd have to stop by the attendance office on my way in, and Mrs. Reading's office was next to it, which meant Mrs. Reading was usually hanging around right inside, and she would probably take one look at my guilty face and call district security to haul me off to juvie or something.

God, irrational, I know, but I was in an irrational place.

Before the third bell rang, I took two deep breaths, exhaled them with a "You can do this, Kendra," and pulled myself out of Hunka, yanking my backpack by one strap and dragging it along behind me.

There was hardly anyone going into the building now. Almost everybody was already inside, getting last-minute stuff out of the lockers and reporting to first period. I wondered if the others knew. If Bryn had called any of them last night as well. If I wasn't the only one walking in on leaden legs with a brainful of knotted black squiggles.

I pushed through the front doors and stood on the rug inside the school vestibule. My mouth tasted salty, and my palms felt slick, and I could feel every nerve ending in the bottoms of my feet.

This is it, I thought. *This is where I find out how bad it really is. Either everything will be cool...or I might actually die of fear.* And then I had the thought *Is this what Grayson feels like all the time?* That made me wish I'd gotten out the ruler and helped him with his coins last night.

But I had only a second to feel it before panic set in completely: Chub Hartley, his wide face pale and quivering, was standing between Mrs. Reading and Mr. Floodsay in the attendance-office vestibule.

Mr. Floodsay was talking, animatedly waving a sheaf of papers in his hand, frowning so hard his glasses weren't even touching the bridge of his nose. I wanted to keep walking. Willed my feet to move. But I was rooted to my spot, barely even registering it when Artie Morris hit me in the back with the door and shoved past me, saying, "Get out of the doorway, 'tard."

All I could do was watch. And suppose. And worry. And watch and suppose and worry some more. And then some more. A loop of awful.

And when Mr. Floodsay put his hand on Chub's back and turned, guiding Chub into Mrs. Reading's office, I knew it was only a matter of time before all the horrible stuff I had worried about would come true.

CHAPTER
FIVE

Here are the things I thought about during what would probably be the longest day of my life:

1. I really hated Chub Hartley for how stupid he was. But I hated myself for being even more stupid than Chub Hartley.
2. If God somehow got me out of this, I would do something huge, like...I don't know...like put out one of those statues of the Virgin Mary on my front lawn and garden around it, like my friend Lia's family does. Or build a wing on a church someday. Or maybe even both.
3. If Chub somehow kept me from getting in trouble, I would hang out at his house a few times, like he was always asking me to do, regardless of how stupid he was and how much he smelled like

mildew. But I wouldn't go to prom with him, no matter how many times he asked. There was a limit to grace.

I sat through my classes, feeling jumpy and like my palms were vibrating and my eyeballs sweating. My knee pumped up and down nervously under my desk, and I bit my nails. Every time a classroom door opened or a teacher said my name, things got gray and grainy, and I had to remind myself to take a breath.

In calc, everyone was eyeing me. Darian poked me in the back with his pencil eraser when Mr. Floodsay turned his back to us, but I refused to turn around to see what he wanted. I had a pretty good feeling I knew what it was anyway. He wanted what three-fourths of the students in that class (and half of the students in the third-period class, and all but one student in the seventh-period class) wanted: for me to tell them everything was going to be all right, which I, at the moment, could definitely not do.

By the time I got to lunch, I was adding nausea and ringing ears to my list of stress maladies.

Things were only made worse when Bryn stopped by my table, setting her tray down on top of my hand. Her face was set in hard lines.

"Chub got sent home," she said. "Word is he's expelled."

I pulled my hand out from under her tray and used my forefinger to push it toward the edge of the table. "I'm eating," I said by way of response. (I wasn't. I was moving my orange chicken and rice around on the tray and trying to keep from hurling under the table.)

Bryn's eyes went slitty, and she cocked her head to one side. "Well, while you eat, think about this: If they sent Chub home, it's probably because he gave them all the information they wanted."

I picked up my fork and stabbed a piece of chicken nonchalantly, hoping Bryn would just go away...like a dissipating fart. Which, now that I thought about it, was the best possible way a person could describe Bryn Mallom. "Or he gave them none," I said, shoving the chicken into my mouth and chewing, despite the protests of my stomach. I offered her a confident smile, even though on the inside I was thinking, *Oh, God! He told them everything!*

Fortunately, Shani and Lia showed up then, carrying fruit plates and biscuits — an odd combination, even for Shani, who liked barbecue sauce on her waffles and easily had the weirdest eating habits of anyone I'd ever known. They set their trays on the table, glaring at Bryn as they slid into their chairs.

Bryn glanced at them, her face losing some of its cockiness now that we weren't alone. Shani and Lia really didn't have much of anything to do with Bryn, ever, but Lia's boyfriend was Ryan Addleson, and even after all the years since Bryn's mom's DUI, Bryn was still afraid of him.

She picked up her tray and swayed a little, looking as if she couldn't decide whether she wanted to stay or leave or fall through the floor. Finally, she tossed her hair over one shoulder, turned her back on Shani and Lia, and pursed her lips at me.

"Just so you know," she hissed, "I'm not Chub, and I don't have a crush on you."

I rolled my eyes. "Go away, Bryn," I said, and poked another piece of rubbery orange chicken into my mouth. Shani and Lia both snickered. My tongue felt fat and mutinous.

But everything on the inside of me said I probably really could use Bryn on my side.

After Bryn left, Shani leaned across the table. "So it's true that Chub got expelled?" she whispered. "Skylar Tomason was sketchy on the details, but she was saying this morning that by tomorrow half the school is going to be expelled."

Lia was nodding furiously as she poked a strawberry into her mouth. "I heard it, too, in French. Somebody was saying the school called the cops."

"The cops?" I said, looking at Lia amusedly. Even I wasn't scared enough to believe the police would get involved. "Who said that?"

She shook her head and swallowed. "I don't know. I just heard it."

"That's kind of stupid," Shani said, biting into a biscuit. "Unless it's, like, drugs or something. Chub Hartley is hardly a drug dealer." I looked down at my orange chicken and wished I had their appetites. But the two pieces I'd eaten for show with Bryn were sloshing around in my stomach disagreeably as it was. I set my fork down.

"I can't help it," Lia said. "It's just what I heard. And I heard that a lot of really smart students are caught up in it."

You have no idea, I thought, but I didn't say it out loud. I'd never told Shani and Lia what I'd been up to, mainly because they didn't have calc and it didn't really seem like that big of a deal when it started, and by the time it escalated into something way big, I didn't know how to bring it up with them. I would've told Zoe about it, but then again Zoe wasn't answering my e-mails.

Also, Zoe never expected me to be perfect.

But listening to Bryn and then to all the rumors, my earlier thoughts that maybe God or Chub would save me were looking more ridiculous by the moment. I was going to be caught. And then everything I'd worked so hard for would be over.

I took a long sip of my soda, and when I looked up again, Shani was staring at me hard, her fork holding a cube of pineapple an inch or so in front of her lips.

"What?" I asked, attempting a lighthearted laugh to offset my cheeks, which felt like they must have been giving off steam, they were so hot. "Do I have a sesame seed in my teeth or something?"

"You sick?" she asked. "You look weird."

"No."

"She's right," Lia said. "And you're not eating."

I pasted on a smile, my mind racing to come up with an explanation. Anything to throw them off the current conversation. "Grayson's back," I said, offering up my brother as an excuse for why things weren't right with me, a tool I'd learned to use to get out of sticky situations since I was about seven. Of course, most of the time it wasn't an excuse. Brothers like Grayson tended to ruin a lot of school days. And birthday parties. And Christmases (especially Christmases). And good moods.

"Oh," Shani said, turning back to her lunch. "Is he still nutso?"

Lia smirked. "Yeah, does he still count his cereal?"

"Did he bring home any of the little green germ monsters who lived in his closet at Camp Crazypants?"

I tensed.

Over the years, I'd vented to Lia and Shani about Grayson more times than I could count. And, sure, I'd made some pretty snide remarks about him behind his back. Sometimes it was the only way to keep from blowing up at him at home. Sometimes it was just a way to clear my own mind. Sometimes it was just a way to break the tension and get a laugh.

But even though I know they only thought it was okay because I'd done it so many times before, I kind of hated it when Shani and Lia made fun of him. I could do it because he was my brother and I was the one who had to deal with him. When they said mean things about him, it just felt mean. But I tried not to act upset by it. I didn't need that battle on top of everything else.

And I guess some part of me believed he deserved it in a way. Like, people wouldn't make fun of him if he'd simply act normal every once in a while. If he'd just be the Grayson who played CSI with Zoe and me down in the creek behind Zoe's house. Or the Grayson who ate superlarge jalapeño-and-cream-cheese pizzas with Brock and who stuck an alarm clock under my ear.

But, honestly, I didn't think *that* Grayson even existed anymore. I hadn't seen that Grayson in so long. That Grayson had fallen into the black hole Zoe left behind. For three years he'd been scrabbling at the sides of that hole — sometimes coming oh-so-close to getting out — but he always fell back in. It was like watching someone you love be buried alive.

I waved my hand dismissively at Shani's and Lia's questions. "I haven't really talked to him since he came back," I said. "I've mostly been avoiding everyone."

"Speaking of avoiding," Lia said, holding up her left hand to block that she was pointing to something at the far end of the cafeteria with the fork in her right hand. Both Shani and I looked toward the doors, where Tyson, Shani's belligerent boyfriend, was entering with his muscles-for-brains crowd of friends, including Tommy, my jerk ex-boyfriend.

Shani made a face. "Whatever. Idiots."

"You guys still fighting?" I asked.

"Hello, check your texts every now and then," Shani answered, wadding up her napkin disgustedly and tossing it onto her plate. "Ew. I can't look at him. I just lost my appetite."

"They broke up last night," Lia said. "Again."

"Oh," I said. "Sorry. I didn't know."

"Duh. Because you don't read your texts, like, ever." Shani glared at me and then took a deep breath, her face softening. "Don't worry about it. I know you've got family issues right now."

I let out a puff of air. "When don't I?" I murmured, even though I knew that my "family issues" were the least of my worries. For a change, my life wasn't being dominated by Grayson's problems. But it was just easier...and safer...to let my friends believe that was what was going on with me.

All three of us were silent for a minute—Lia scraping the last bits of fruit from her plate, Shani tearing little pieces off her napkin and dropping them into her soda can, and me gazing at the muscles-for-brains gang. Three of them— including Tommy and Tyson—could be in big trouble, too, if Bryn was right.

When Tyson caught my gaze and nodded in my direction, his face serious and determined, my hands seized the sides of my tray.

"I should go," I said. "I've got to turn in a paper."

And before either of my friends could say a word, I was gone. My uneaten orange chicken and rice were at the bottom of the giant gray wastebasket by the kitchen conveyor belt, and the two pieces I had eaten were floating in the toilet water of stall three in the science hallway before Tyson could even get to our table.

CHAPTER SIX

It happened right after the final bell rang. I rounded the corner by the library, my plan being to grab my jacket and get the hell out of Dodge and put an end to this rotten day. Go home. Try to eat something. Get some sleep, hopefully. Figure out how I was going to get through tomorrow. How I was going to stay under the radar.

But Mrs. McKinley, my English teacher, was pegging something to the bulletin board by the library entrance and caught me.

"Oh, hey, Kendra," she said around a mouthful of thumbtacks (*"Oh, fey, Fendra!"*). She pulled them out and dropped them into a pocket on the side of her flowy brown skirt, which looked as though it had come straight out of the back of a Volkswagen bus. "I was going to talk to you about tonight's NHS meeting."

"Oh," I said, inwardly cursing. I'd totally forgotten about this month's National Honor Society meeting, which couldn't be at a worse time.

"I was thinking," Mrs. McKinley continued, which must have meant that my fear wasn't visible on my face, "as head of the community outreach committee, maybe you should do a little presentation at tonight's meeting about your plans for the rest of spring semester. Nothing fancy or formal, of course, but I know you have that program with the preschoolers coming up and—"

"I can't," I blurted out. And then I tried to paste on my best goody-two-shoes smile. "I'm sorry, Mrs. McKinley, but..." I paused, feeling a brief pang of guilt for using my brother twice in one day, but then figured I had nothing else. I couldn't tell her I had to stay away from the school because I might find myself in huge trouble by morning. For the first time, I realized that if I was found out, I would definitely be kicked out of National Honor Society. Worse, Mrs. McKinley would know what I'd done and would be so disappointed in me. And she wouldn't be the only one. Probably the whole world would be disappointed in me. The thought made tears spring to my eyes, but I cleared my throat and said, "My brother came home from treatment yesterday, and I want to be home for him tonight. I'm going to miss the meeting."

Her face fell momentarily, but then she smiled understandingly. Mrs. McKinley had had Grayson for American lit his sophomore year. She used to let him file papers for her in the back of the room while she was lecturing; filing calmed him. Anything regimented calmed him.

"Of course," she said. "I'll have Alison Wells do it, then."

"Thanks," I said.

"And tell Grayson I said hello and I hope he's feeling better."

I nodded and moved around her, heading for the science hallway, where my locker was.

The crowd in the hallways had thinned out. Locker doors were slamming, and the squeak of the west entrance opening over and over again filled the air. I turned the corner, looked toward my locker, and stopped dead in my tracks.

There, at my locker, was the custodian everyone called Black Lung, his giant key ring jingling and clanging, metal against metal. He poked a key into my combination dial and pulled the door open, then stepped back.

Mrs. Reading, who had been standing behind him, stepped forward and began pulling things off the shelves, letting them drop with echoing slaps onto the floor. Mr. Floodsay, down on one knee, sifted through my stuff as it landed.

For a minute, it was as if nothing existed in this world but those three people and the *slap, slap, slap* of my books and notebooks on the tile. Everything else just sort of faded away—the squeak of the west entrance door, the chatter of people on their cell phones, the metallic rattle of lockers shutting, and the shuffle of feet going up and down the stairways.

My arms hung slack at my sides, and my mouth opened as I tried to catch my breath. Someone had sold me out. Chub, probably. Or maybe Bryn. Could've been anyone, really. I knew they wouldn't find anything—I wasn't that stupid—but the fact that they were even looking meant I had reason to worry. Okay, to panic.

This is it, my mind kept repeating. *This is where you get busted. All they have to do is turn their heads and they'll see you here. You'll get dragged into Mrs. Reading's office, and it'll be all over.*

But before any of them could turn their heads, I was suddenly slammed back into reality. Literally. By Bryn, who came barreling out of the ladies' room so fast she rammed into me, knocking me backward onto my butt with a resounding "Oof!"

Bryn had also fallen to a knee, and she glanced back at me over her shoulder while she got up, glaring at me reproachfully. Neither one of us said anything. We didn't need to.

I told you so, her eyes said.

I know, mine said back. *I know you did.*

She got up and raced for the west entrance. I heard the door squeak, and then it was just me and maybe six other students in the hallway.

And them.

I couldn't face them. No way. I was one of Mrs. Reading's "star pupils." Whenever she wanted to make an example of how well her school was doing, she'd inevitably turn to Macy Nastrom, Ralph Storius, and me.

Facing Mrs. Reading right now would somehow be worse than facing Mom and Dad. Because Mrs. Reading had never seen me do anything wrong before. She would be more than shocked and angry—she would be confused.

Hell, I was confused. How had I even gotten into a mess this big?

I scrambled to my feet, as quickly as Bryn had done, ignoring the sore spot on my butt where it had struck the tile, then darted back around the corner and down the stairs to the lower science hallway. I took the U of hallways as fast as I could without running, and plowed my way through half a dozen cheerleaders up the stairs at the other end of the school.

And then I really did start to run. Right out the east entrance, around the front of the building, and over to the side where Hunka waited for me. I was barely in the seat before I had the car started and was speeding away from the school.

I didn't realize until I was out of the parking lot and halfway down the highway that I'd left my backpack on.

CHAPTER
SEVEN

I pulled over on the side of the outer road and parked. Not next to the highway, of course. If you parked on the highway side of the quarry and a cop drove by and saw your car, he'd come get you and threaten you with trespassing ("This time I mean it, you two. I won't come out here again!").

But if you took the outer road around to the far side of the quarry, where the road was nestled between the enormous piles of rock and a grassy, untouched hill, nobody would bother you. You could leave your car there, climb the tall chain-link fence, and drop to the edge of the pit on the other side with nobody ever being the wiser.

I'd done it enough times with Grayson to know.

When we were little and the quarry owners threatened to sue my parents if they had to come out one more time to unlock the gate after hours so we could retrieve my counting brother, my parents began parking on the secluded side of the outer road and lifting me so I could climb over the fence instead. I was nimble, and they knew Grayson would come with me, even if they didn't know what it took for me to get him to leave.

As soon as my feet hit the ground on the other side of the fence, I'd always stand at the top of the pit, feeling like the queen of the world, hearing the swish of unseen cars on the highway and feeling the chalky breeze blow my bangs around on my forehead. I'd stand there and close my eyes, inhaling the earthy scent of the quarry, tinged with motor oil and exhaust emanating from the bulldozers padlocked in their sheds, and for that brief period of time, I totally understood my brother. We were one, both of us wanting to capture the perfection and beauty of the earth's crust around us—both in our unique ways. There was something exciting about the quarry for both of us. I wanted to own it, to master it; Grayson wanted to dissolve into it.

My parents would let me stand there for a minute before they'd begin hissing at me to find my brother.

Only then would I open my eyes and begin searching the piles of rocks for a familiar scrap of clothing or the glint of the dying sunlight off a pair of glasses somewhere deep in the shadows below.

And the spell would be broken. I was no longer queen of the quarry. I was the parent, tugging on his shirt and promising him things if he would come up to the top with me; my older brother was the child.

For me, Newman Quarry always felt like broken spells

and frustration and harsh, ugly reality. Our family's personal hiding place.

Which, I guess, was why it made so much sense for me to go there, even though I never had gone on my own before. My backpack was still strapped on and pinned between my back and the driver's seat, the image of Mr. Floodsay rifling through my writing journal and history books fresh in my mind.

I don't think I was intentionally going there. Probably, had you asked me, I would have told you I was going home. And then, when I passed the turnoff into my neighborhood, I might have said I was "going for a drive."

I don't even think I realized I was pulling off the highway onto the outer road until I'd rolled around to the hilly side of the quarry, my tires crackling on the dirt, which got rockier and rockier as the road became more secluded. I hit a pothole and Hunka's glove compartment door dropped open. I reached over without even thinking—Hunka's glove box opened on its own a hundred times a week—and closed it.

I pulled off the road, right in the same spot where my parents had parked the minivan a million times before.

And I sat there. I squeezed my eyes shut, hard, then opened them wide. No tears. Just... numbness.

Weird. I was expecting tears. Expected my eyes, like Bryn's, to be tired and swollen and red, maybe a hitch in my breath as I berated myself over and over again for how stupid I'd been. I expected... something, at least.

I unsnapped my seat belt, leaned forward, and shimmied out of my backpack, tossing it into the backseat. I reached into my front pocket and palmed my cell phone, which had buzzed three times while I was driving. I glanced at the screen—it was Shani—and then tossed it, too, into the backseat with my backpack. Then I opened the driver's door and got out.

For a few minutes I stood, my fingers laced through the holes in the chain link, resting my face against the inside of my right elbow, which hung at face level.

"What now?" I breathed into the hollow of my chest. Here I was, three weeks before finals... four weeks before *graduation*... and I was about to lose everything. "What do I do now?"

No answer came to me, but the gooseflesh that popped out on my arms spurred me to action anyway. Ignoring the spring chill creeping in around me, I moved my fingers from the holes they were in to holes much higher, gripped tightly, stuffed a toe into a hole at about knee height, and leaped up, pulling myself most of the way to the top of the fence in one motion.

Even though it'd been months since I'd last been here, the climb was like second nature to me. Fingers here, toes there. Watch the sharp, clipped edges of the fence at the top. Swing over the right leg, balance, swing over the left leg, balance, and then push off. But not too far—you didn't want to tumble, ass over teakettle, as my dad always used to say, down the quarry wall.

Once inside, I stood at the edge of the steep decline,

watching the toes of my shoes kick loose gravel over the edge and down, down, down, taking more rocks with it as it went.

I closed my eyes. Turned my face to the sun. Felt the breeze, always blowing at the top of Newman Quarry, muss my hair. I let my arms hang limp at my sides. I took a deep breath. Queen of... nothing. Just like always.

Queen of less than nothing now.

I stood there for a long time. The earth did not split and swallow me up. No lava burbled out and melted me, eyeballs and teeth and hair, into a red river. Sediment did not cover me, pressing me into a sad fossil. I was just a girl, standing on a pile of rocks. No superstar to see here, people. Move along.

When I opened my eyes again, I was almost surprised to find I was shivering. The sun had started to set, and the shadows in the quarry were growing longer. The highway noises had picked up. The birds settling along the quarry's fence top had flown.

I wrapped my arms around myself and squatted, looking out over the rocks. Billions. There must be billions of them. How could Grayson have thought he'd ever count them all?

As if in answer to my thoughts, the breeze gusted suddenly, carrying a small noise on top of it, right to where I huddled over the rocks, my teeth chattering.

It was a small cough. Not a *cough* cough, but a short, nervous burst, almost half throat-clearing, half cough. One I recognized well. I'd heard it my whole life. It was one of

Grayson's tics—a little noise in the base of his throat. He made it when he was getting to a crisis point. When he was overwhelmed.

Like a shot, I stood up again, squinting over the quarry. Grayson was in there somewhere.

I saw it—a tiny glint of sunlight reflecting off his glasses, and when I squinted harder, I saw his dirty white T-shirt and blue jeans. He must have been freezing. Even though the breeze didn't reach the bottom of the quarry, the shadows were so much deeper down there.

Again I heard the cough. And some murmuring that sounded like numbers being chanted.

Stepping sideways down the steep wall of the quarry, my shoe sinking into the gravel, I began trotting toward him, just as I'd done a million times before.

"Grayson?" I shouted. He didn't respond. Of course not. He never responded when he was counting. It would make him lose track of where he was. "I'm coming down!" Half jogging, half sliding down the steep embankment, holding my arms straight out to keep my balance, calling my brother's name.

Saving him.

On a day when I needed to be saved, once again I was saving him.

CHAPTER EIGHT

Grayson was standing ankle-deep in stones, his pointer finger extended out in front of him and bouncing along in the air as if he were touching each one individually. I knew in his mind, he probably was doing exactly that. Touching each rock and marking it. Counted.

He was up to 4,762. He'd been out here a long time. When I touched his arm, it felt cool, even under my fingers that were practically numb from my run down the pit.

"Gray," I said softly, tugging at his arm.

He pulled away sharply. "Four thousand, seven hundred sixty-*three*."

I tented my hands over my mouth and blew into them to warm them, then reached out and pulled his arm again. "Gray, come on. You're cold. We should go."

"Four thousand, seven hundred sixty-*four*," he responded, his voice louder. This time he didn't jerk away, though.

"Gray," I said, pulling a little harder, getting frustrated. I tried so hard to be sympathetic. Really, I did. But I was sick of the song and dance. Why couldn't this ever be easy? I'd come here for myself. Why couldn't it ever be about me? "Come on. You're on an even number. Just quit now."

Grayson liked even numbers. When he was forced to quit counting, he always held his ground until he got to an even number. He told me about a year ago that if he stopped counting on an odd number, it meant that someone he loved would die. And if he ended on an odd number, even accidentally, he had to count backward from where he'd been, all the way back to zero, and then start all over again, not stopping until he reached the next even number above the number he'd stopped counting on.

"I know it's stupid," he'd mumbled when he first told me that he'd been counting every time a family member left the house. We sat side by side on the bumper of Dad's car in the driveway. "But it makes sense to me, you know? Like, as long as I kept hitting even numbers, you were going to get home okay."

I shook my head, flexed my toes so my flip-flops would stay on as my feet swung back and forth over the driveway. I'd just gotten home from a date with Tommy and had found my brother standing by Dad's car, counting. I shook my head. "No, it doesn't make sense. You can't stop something horrible from happening by counting. How long have you been doing this?"

He'd shrugged. "A while. It started with me just saying,

'Kendra will be all right,' or 'Dad won't get in a car crash,' or 'Mom will come home,' and that used to be good enough, but then I started having to say it a bunch of times. And then...you know, it turned into I had to say it an even number of times. And then it got to where I could just count and it did the same thing. Which is better. Takes less time."

We sat in silence for a few minutes.

Oh my God, my brother has really gone crazy, was all I could think. It scared me. And it broke my heart.

"I know," he said, as if he could hear my thoughts. "I can't help it. I'm sorry."

"It's okay, Gray," I'd said, and put my hand on his shoulder. "But you really should stop. You're not keeping everyone safe by counting."

Still, some days Grayson did nothing but sit on his bed and count, forward and backward, to really high numbers, just to keep us all alive. I always felt like I should have been more appreciative of his efforts. Like I shouldn't have thought it was so stupid or something he could just stop doing. Like I should have thanked him that night instead of telling him it wasn't working.

"Four thousand, seven hundred sixty-*five*," he said, then shook his head and gave one of those little coughs that I'd heard earlier. "Four thousand, seven hundred sixty-*six*..."

Even though it was still late afternoon, the bottom of the quarry was fully engulfed in shadows. My fingers were starting to hurt, no matter how many times I blew on them to warm them up, and my ears were starting to sting, too.

"Gray," I said again. "Come on. Mom's going to get all worried when she realizes you're gone." He kept counting. "She'll probably cuss you out in Italian," I tried, smirking, hoping he'd get the joke. He coughed again and kept counting.

I bowed my head, knowing what I needed to do. I hated it when I had to do this — and Grayson really hated it — but sometimes it was the only way.

"Grayson! Stop counting and listen to me!" I shouted, and jumped in front of him, using my feet to kick at the rocks he was staring at. I shuffled my feet like I was doing a dance, sending the rocks flying everywhere.

"No!" Grayson gasped in his raggedy been-counting-all-day voice. "Don't...Kendra..."

His face looked pale and terrified, his fingers jerking as he tried to follow the scattering rocks with his eyes. As if he could keep track of them, keep counting them.

Normally this would have been enough to stop me, but today was different. Today, turning Grayson's world into chaos felt justified somehow. It felt right. It felt...good.

"One-two-three-four-oh-God-Grayson-look-at-them-go!" I shouted, jumping up and down and doing side kicks into the rock mound. Rivers of rocks swirled at his feet. He gazed down at them sickly, that cough coming in rapid fire: *Uh...uh-uh-uh...uh...* I bent over and picked up two handfuls of rocks and slung them high into the air over our heads. They rained down on us and I laughed, blinking every time a rock pelted the top of my head. "Oh, no, Grayson, you better count them quick!" I yelled. "They're getting away!"

"Stop it!" he shouted, and before I could even react, he lunged forward, both arms outstretched, planted his hands on my shoulders, and pushed me backward. For the second time that day, I found myself flat on my butt, only this time I was laughing too hard to feel the fall. "I made you stop," I sang, pointing up at him. "I made you mo-o-ove." Grayson looked at me, his eyes slits behind his glasses, and reached down with his left hand, scooping up a handful of rocks.

He cleared his throat a few times. "You don't know what you're doing!" he shouted, flinging the rocks at me. They hit me, hard, drying up my laughter. I covered my face with my forearm.

"Ouch!" I yelled, struggling to get up. "That hurt, you jerk!" And this time I pushed him. He barely moved, but produced a rock out of nowhere and tossed it straight at my forehead. "That's it!" I shrieked, and body-slammed him, knocking him down and pummeling him with my fists, the way we used to when we were kids and would fight over who got to sleep in Zoe's tent at backyard campouts or who got the last Oreo in the bag or whatever stupid stuff kids argue about.

We rolled around in the rocks for a few minutes, arms and legs flailing and rocks scraping white lines onto our cheeks and scalps. Grayson was older, taller, but he'd gotten so skinny, and I easily matched him, my muscle tone making up for the years between us.

After what seemed like forever, we finally stopped, panting and rolling away from each other. Truce. I wiped my nose with the back of my hand, then noticed how red my hand was from the cold that I didn't feel anymore.

"Come on," I said to the sky. "It's freezing out here." I pulled myself up, looking down at the dent we'd made in the rock bed and giggling despite myself. "They're going to know we were here," I said. "Mom and Dad will be getting another phone call." I reached down toward Grayson, whose eyebrow was seeping a little blood right above his glasses. He took my hand and let me help him to his feet.

"If Mom's smart, she'll tell them to *vada ad inferno*," he answered, taking off his glasses and wiping them with his shirttail. He grinned at me. "Go to hell," he explained.

"Since when do you know Italian?"

He smirked, made that *uh* sound again, twice, and stuck his glasses back on his face. "I know a lot of things," he said. "I'm sort of a genius, in case you don't remember."

I rolled my eyes. Of course, we all remembered. Like any of us could forget. Our Grayson had an IQ of roughly nine billion. The elementary school guidance counselor had actually called him a "genius." Until he'd gotten so sick with his OCD that he couldn't go to school anymore, it was all we ever heard. Grayson-the-genius this, Grayson-the-genius that.

I was the one who brought home straight A's. I was the

one who'd wear the honor ropes at graduation. I was the one who *would* graduate. But I was never a genius. Of course, I could go to the bathroom without counting the bumps on the ceiling, too. I guess there's a good and a bad to everything.

"Well," I said, tromping through the rocks ahead of him, across the bottom of the quarry. "I'm not a genius, but I do know one thing." I flicked a glance over my shoulder at him. He was following me, eyes firmly glued to the quarry floor. His finger was up in front of him again, bent like a claw. He was counting steps. "I can still kick your ass."

When I looked over my shoulder again, he was still counting, but I could see the corners of his mouth twitch with a grin. Barely detectable, but there nonetheless.

We hiked up the steep quarry wall, our feet raining down rocks behind us, and soon were standing at the top, looking out across the basin, as I'd done when I arrived. We paused, shoulder to shoulder, our bellies rhythmically stretching for breath.

"How'd you know I was here?" he asked. I could feel him shiver next to me. The motion was contagious; soon I was shivering again, too. "Mom send you?"

I shook my head. "I heard you."

He glanced at me, then kicked a rock off the edge and watched its path down the side of the quarry. "Why were you here, then?" he asked.

I chewed my lip. Considered his question. "I don't know,"

I said. And, in truth, I didn't. I mean, I knew why I didn't want to go home. I just didn't know why this was the only other obvious choice. "Let's go," I said, before he could ask any more questions. "I'm cold."

We scaled the fence and climbed into Hunka, which blasted hot air on us as soon as I turned it on. We held our fingers directly in front of the vents, flexing and bending them, trying to get the feeling back.

"So what's the deal?" I finally said when we'd warmed up. I put the car into gear and began creeping around the outer road back out toward the highway. "I thought you were better."

He turned his body away from me, almost curling into a fetal position, and faced the window. "I thought I was, too," he said.

"So what happened?"

He shrugged. "Life, I guess. My brain. I don't know." Then he murmured, "It's bullshit. Can we just drive for a while? I don't want to go home yet."

"Okay." Little did he know, I didn't exactly want to go home yet, either.

I pulled onto the highway, driving in the opposite direction of our house, and started speeding up. My limbs were tingling now, and I was beginning to feel the bumps and pricks where the rocks had dug into my skin. I rubbed one elbow absently, then my knee, and then a spot on the back of my shoulder.

"I won't tell Mom I found you at Newman if you don't want her to know," I offered. "But you've got to stop going there, Grayson. You've got to stop...all this. Mom and Dad need a life without worry, you know?"

I felt a pang in my stomach. As if I had any room to talk. As if they weren't about to have a whole bunch of worry heaped in their laps in just a matter of hours courtesy of yours truly.

When my brother didn't answer, I bumped his shoulder with my fist, playfully. "I'm going to be leaving for college in a few months, and you know you don't want to see Mom trying to climb that fence in her bathrobe."

Grayson turned to face me. There were tear tracks on his cheeks, carving clean lines in the mineral dust that had gathered there. "You think I don't know that?" he said.

"It was just a joke."

"No, you think I don't want to stop doing this?" His voice had escalated, and his words bounced against the windows sharply.

I took a deep breath. Clearly, he wasn't in a joking mood. But it's not like I was, either, and it only further irritated me that everything always, *always* had to be about how Grayson was feeling. Why did it feel like I was always the only one trying? "I don't know, Grayson. You're supposedly a genius. How is it you can understand everything there ever was to know about metaphoric rocks—"

"Metamorphic."

"Whatever! See, that's my point! You're so smart—why can't you figure this out? Why can't you just figure it out and stop it?"

"I don't know!" he practically roared, his chin wrinkling and his cheeks bright red. I flinched. Grayson wouldn't do anything to hurt me, but when he shouted, it was loud. "I don't know," he said again, more softly. "If I knew, I'd fix it."

We drove along in silence for a few minutes, the only sound in the car the hum of the heat blowing on us full-blast.

"I know you would," I said.

He turned his body back toward the window again and took a few hearty sniffs. "I wish I could get away from it, Kendra. Just run away and leave it here and never have to deal with it again. Run away and be normal."

We drove along, through rush hour and through sunset, and into evening, when I flicked on my headlights. Grayson hadn't said anything else, and after a while I began to hear soft snoring rattling against the window. It was no wonder—he was always exhausted after a counting trip to the quarry. I could only imagine how tiring it was—standing in one spot, afraid to move at risk of rearranging the rocks at your feet and having to begin again. Standing in the shadows and counting, counting, knowing that your efforts were ridiculous, but hoping they'd work anyway.

I didn't blame him for wanting to get away from it.

Most of the time, I wanted to get away from it. Sometimes I thought even Mom and Dad wanted to get away from it. Especially Dad, who never really understood, I don't think, that this was something out of Grayson's control. He got it on an intellectual level. But he was forever telling Grayson that all he needed was "a skill to fall back on" and shouting at him sometimes to stop it, exactly as I'd just done.

Only Zoe had ever seemed to really understand it. She'd never tried to get away. How ironic that, in the end, she was the only one who did get away.

I heard my phone vibrate against the seat behind me. I glanced back but didn't reach for it. I had a feeling that, no matter who was calling, it wasn't going to be good. Either it was Bryn, telling me that I'd been wrong about Chub and he'd turned on me, or it was Shani, wondering if what everyone was saying about me and the calc final was true, or maybe even Mom, reeling from a phone conversation with Mrs. Reading.

I couldn't answer any of them right now. Like Grayson, I just wanted to get away. I needed to get away. I needed some space to figure out what had gone wrong. To decide when I'd turned into this person who needed to be perfect all the time and was willing to do just about anything to keep it that way. Mistakes? Not me. Control, control, control. Perfection and control. But when did that happen? Was it when Zoe left? Was it when Grayson started getting really sick? Or was it the day I was born, and I was only just now realizing it?

I knew exactly what would be waiting for me at school tomorrow. What devastation I'd brought onto my college plans. God, did I still *have* college plans? Could I still go to college if I got expelled, like Chub? I never, in a million years, thought that would be a question I'd be asking myself.

What's worse, I knew what was awaiting me at home. What betrayal I'd brought down on my parents. How disappointed even Shani and Lia would be.

I wanted to get away from it all.

Just like Grayson.

I was coming up on the interstate exit, the green signs telling me to get into a different lane or I'd end up heading west. I turned on my blinker and peered into the rearview mirror. The headlights behind me were thick. My phone lit up in the backseat as it buzzed again.

We could, I thought. *We could get away. The two of us.* Neither of us could go home and pretend life was wonderful. Both of us knew it never would be, even if it was for entirely different reasons. I could help Grayson escape his OCD. And I could get away, too.

Away from all of it.

The more I thought about it, the more it not only seemed like the best choice.

It seemed like the only one.

I turned off my blinker and eased the car onto the exit ramp. At the bottom of the ramp I pressed the gas pedal. Grayson's body rocked as Hunka accelerated onto the interstate.

I settled back in my seat and took a deep breath to steel myself.

Grayson didn't know it yet, but we were running away.

CHAPTER
NINE

I needed gas. I'd punched through rush hour, crossed the state line into Kansas, and made good time on the other side of it, blowing past towns I'd heard of in passing conversations over the years between my parents—Bonner Springs, Basehor, Tonganoxie, Lawrence—without even noticing the miles that stretched between them. Funny how when you had no idea where you were going, really, it seemed as though you would get there really fast.

It was totally dark outside now, and the rumbling in my stomach told me it was well past dinnertime. Also, the rumbling in the backseat. I knew from the insistent buzzing of my cell phone that Mom had been trying to call.

I didn't want to ignore her, but I couldn't reach the phone from the driver's seat, and I didn't want to stop. Something told me that if I stopped too soon, I'd probably chicken out and go home. And I couldn't do that. Not until

I'd had some good, solid highway time to think this over, to get a good grip on what exactly I was going to do.

The plan was starting to make sense to me. What I was doing was for the best for everyone. Really. Grayson would get away. Get better. Somehow I knew it. If I took him away from his comfort zone—away from Newman Quarry, away from Mom, who wanted so badly for him to feel secure, away from his bedroom with the perfectly lined-up coins and the geology books and the even-numbered rock collection on his windowsill—he would get better. He would see that it was possible to be safe and be okay and be unplanned.

Exposure therapy. That's what Dr. St. James had called it. I'd heard Mom and Dad talk about it more times than I could count. Well, fight about it, really.

You've got to make him get out there and face his anxiety, Linda.

But he suffers. I can't watch it. Who is he hurting, really?

Himself! He's hurting himself, Linda! Dr. St. James says it's the only way. You have to put him in the situations that make him anxious and force him to cope.

No. I won't watch my child suffer. I'll get another opinion....

Mom was tough. Always calm and assured when she needed to be. But there was one spot where she was weak, and it was my brother. She babied him.

But I could be tougher than Mom. I could watch him struggle. It would hurt and I'd feel bad, but I could hold the line and not give in and not coddle his compulsions. I could do it, and then she wouldn't have to. I could do that for her, and then maybe what I'd done wouldn't look so bad anymore.

And if it worked, Mom and Dad would get some time off. Mom could learn her Italian, and Dad could come home from work without first having to stop and drag his son out of a pile of rocks, and they could spend some time being with one another, relaxed and happy.

And, yeah, I knew I was using Grayson as an excuse for the fact that I was running away from my own troubles. But as far as I could see, at this point I didn't have a whole lot of options. The music was too tough to face. I knew I'd have to face it eventually, but right now I needed some time—some space—to figure out just how I was going to do that.

Grayson stirred as I pulled off the highway and crunched into the pothole-riddled lot of a tiny gas station. Hunka's glove box popped open and bounced against Grayson's knee.

I winced and slowed down, rolling up to a pump so slowly it was almost as if the lot was moving rather than my car.

Right now the last thing I needed was for Grayson to wake up. He'd obviously want to know where we were—where we were going. And, well, really, I didn't know. We'd gotten past towns I'd heard of and had started seeing much longer stretches of field and shorter stretches of town.

But he only shifted his weight, brought a hand up to sleepily swipe at his nose a couple times, and then snuggled his cheek against the seat and sighed back to sleep. I shimmied out of the car, grabbing my purse and cell phone off the backseat along the way.

I ran inside and headed first for the restroom, a stinking hole in the back corner of the store, which also housed a crusted, empty mop bucket and rolls of paper towels on a shelf. On my way out, I grabbed a pack of beef jerky and two sodas, then handed the guy behind the counter the fifty Mom had had me stuff in my wallet on the day I got my driver's license. *Just for an emergency*, she'd warned. *You never know when you'll be in a bind.*

I figured this is what she meant by "bind," even if she probably never in a million years had thought my "bind" would be gas and grub out in the middle of nowhere while running away and kidnapping my mentally ill brother. I chuckled, thinking about it that way.

The fifty would pay for the food and drinks and partially fill the tank, and I figured that'd buy me at least another couple hours on the road. By then, we'd have enough distance to really make a decision.

I jogged back out to the car and stuffed the gas nozzle into Hunka's tank, and then pulled the cell phone out of my purse, turning my back to the wind, which had me gazing at Grayson's sleeping face in the side mirror on the car door. He looked so peaceful there, and my gut twinged.

He was probably going to hate my plan. Probably, he was going to demand I take him home immediately. Play the "I'm the older sibling and you have to do what I say" card.

But maybe not. He was fresh out of treatment, after all. He was feeling better. Maybe he'd be open to it. See that my idea was for his own good. It would be uncomfortable at first, but I had faith he would eventually see what a good plan it was, my kidnapping him.

I'd missed nineteen calls and at least as many texts. I didn't have to scan the numbers to know that at least eighteen of those calls were from Mom.

I knew I couldn't ignore her any longer, but I also knew she wouldn't agree with my plan, either. She wouldn't see the genius in it—not in a million years. And she might already also know about the calc final and be super pissed. And if I even gave her a little bit of time to argue with me, I might not see the genius in it anymore, either. I might wimp out.

First, I had to call someone else.

I dialed the number I knew by heart and pressed "call."

"Yuh?" a familiar voice said, deep, husky. I could hear video-game music in the background. Super Mario Brothers. Real earworm stuff.

"Brock?"

"Yuh."

"It's Kendra."

The music in the background came to an abrupt stop. He'd paused the game. The phone rustled a bit. "Hey, Kendra, what's up? G-Man still at crazy camp or whatever?" Brock was Grayson's best, and only, friend. They'd met in ninth-grade P.E. class—Grayson's OCD making it impossible for him to dress out; Brock's extreme obesity making it impossible for him to do pretty much anything else. They spent a lot of time on the bleachers together, watching everyone else be normal. They were tight. I didn't even mind, really, when Brock called Grayson crazy, because I knew that, like me, Brock loved my brother, and sometimes calling him a nutcase or making fun of his quirks was the only way to keep from hating him.

I remembered the first time Brock had Grayson sleep over at his house. Grayson's compulsions had been getting worse, and Mom was a nervous wreck, sure that he would embarrass himself or have a breakdown of some sort. She'd sat by the phone all night, waiting for him to call, in tears, begging to be picked up.

When he still hadn't called by morning, she packed me up in the car and we drove over there to make sure Grayson hadn't slipped out and walked to the quarry.

Instead, we found Grayson and Brock in Brock's front yard, tossing a football back and forth. Brock was lounging back in a lawn chair, eating potato chips, the folds of his stomach drooping down between his legs; Grayson was wearing a pair of green, elbow-length dishwashing gloves, a pile of discarded gloves on the ground by his feet.

Mom pulled to the curb and rolled down her window. "I hadn't heard from you. Everything okay?"

"It's all good, Mrs. Turner. G-Man cleaned my room for me. Totally arranged my video games."

Mom's eyes got moist and she kept swallowing, and for a second I thought she was going to bawl. "Good" was all she said.

"We've got four more pairs of those gloves," Brock shouted. "My mom'll bring him home after that."

"I'm good, Mom," Grayson had called, and the feeling of happiness that swelled through the car almost made me feel light-headed. Mom and I went home and baked cookies together, and I decided right then and there that Brock was a really great friend for my brother. Like Zoe, Brock never expected my brother to be anything other than who he was.

Just hearing his voice over the phone as I stood in a gas station parking lot somewhere in Kansas brought that feeling back. I knew I could count on him. "No, he's home from treatment now."

"Cool. Tell him to come on up. I got the new Zombie-splosion 5 game. It rocks. You should see what happens when you blow their heads off."

"Okay, I'll tell him. But, um, Brock? I have a favor to ask you."

"Sure. What's up?"

"Um, I need you to cover for me. Well, actually, for Grayson. For both of us."

"Okay. How?"

"My mom is probably going to call there in a few minutes. Can you tell her that Grayson is at your house and he can't come to the phone? Just make something up. Tell her Grayson will call her later. I'll take care of that."

There was a pause. I could hear his trademark heavy breathing whistling into the phone. Grayson never made fun of Brock's weight, and neither did I, but everyone else did. "What's going on?" he said, his voice laced with suspicion. "G-Man okay?"

"Yeah," I said, trying to keep my voice breezy. The nozzle *thunk*ed and the pump switched off. "Yeah, of course. We're going...we're taking a little trip. And Mom will get worried. You know how she is."

"Huh. A trip." He sounded skeptical. "Where?"

The wind gusted across the Kansas plain behind me again, and I stiffened against it, wishing more than ever I'd gotten my jacket out of my locker before Black Lung had opened it up. *Good question. Where are we going, exactly?* "I don't...just...just tell her he's in the shower, okay?" She'd believe it; Grayson went through phases when he showered twenty times a day.

"And everything's okay? You wouldn't bullshit me, right?"

I took a deep breath. "I totally wouldn't bullshit you, Brock. Can you do this or what?"

"Yeah," he said. "Yeah, I guess so."

"Thanks," I said. "I owe you."

"No problem," he said, and the music started up again. Brock's attention span only went so far. "But have G-Man call me, okay?"

"You bet," I said, then hung up and leaned back against the car. Step one, done. Step two...coming up.

And then I didn't even want to think about step three: convincing Grayson that this was a good idea.

CHAPTER
TEN

I tried to keep my conversation with Mom short, partly because I didn't want the lack of motion in the car to wake up Grayson, and also partly because I didn't want Mom to figure out yet what was really going on, and I figured the longer I talked to her, the more time I had for it to dawn on her that there were highway noises in the background.

Fortunately, luck was on my side, and I took it to be a sign that I was doing the right thing. Mom was ticked, sure, but easily calmed, which meant she hadn't heard from the school yet.

"Kendra! For crying out loud, I've been calling you for hours. Where on earth are you? Where is Grayson?"

"Sorry, Mom," I mumbled. "I had to turn my phone off for a science quiz, and I forgot to turn it back on. But everything's cool. Did Gray forget to call you?" I made a frustrated grunting noise for authenticity. "He was supposed to call you and tell you I gave him a ride to Brock's. I'm at Shani's house. We're working on a psych project. Do you mind if I just crash here tonight?"

"On a school night?"

"Mom, seriously. We're working on homework. And if I'm sleeping here I won't have to get up early to pick up Shani on the way to school. This way I get more sleep. You can talk to her mom about it if you want." I was bluffing, but I knew it was a risk I could take. Mom didn't talk to anyone else's mom, ever. Not since Zoe's mom went away.

When Zoe left, Mom lost her best friend, too. I remember Mom standing on the deck behind our house, shouting across the yard at Zoe's mom, who was having some sort of party with some moms I recognized from school. Mom was screaming, "You changed his diapers, Rachel! How could you treat him like some sort of danger? I thought you and Rob were better people than that!" and Zoe's mom was sitting with her back to our house, but I could see the faces of the other moms looking uncomfortable around the patio table.

It went on for months, the feud between our families, until finally Zoe's family gave in and moved out. But even after they were gone, the grudge had affected Mom so much that she went into a deep depression and had to get medication. Even after three years, Mom still didn't trust other parents. She was polite but separate.

In a lot of ways, Dad was all Mom had. Dad and Grayson and me. But given the grief Grayson had always brought her, and the grief I was about to bring her, we were little consolation.

Mom paused over the phone. "No, no. It's fine. And your brother is at Brock's?" Her voice had gotten much calmer. Mom still loved Brock, even if he couldn't help my brother with a pair of elbow-length dishwashing gloves anymore.

I started to relax. *See? Everything is going to be fine. Great. By the time they get the call from the school, I'll be too far away for them to make me come home. And by the time I actually do come home, Grayson will be normal, and things will look so much better to all of us. We'll all be so happy to have a normal family, we won't even care about the damage I've done at school.*

"Yeah," I said. "I saw Gray walking when I was leaving school, so I picked him up and took him to Brock's. I figured it would be good for him. I can't believe he forgot to call you. I reminded him, like, a billion times."

"I'll call him," she said. "I'm glad he's seeing Brock again. That'll be good for him. Did he seem relaxed to you at all, Kendra?"

"Sure, Mom," I lied, and then I felt really, really horrible for all the lies. Mom wanted nothing more than for Grayson to be happy. And she was always trying so hard to make him that way, even though Dr. Sellerman, Dr. Houston, Dr. Fantaglio, and especially Dr. St. James had all warned her about enabling his OCD. Poor Mom couldn't deny him. "He seemed really happy to see Brock. When I left, they were playing some video game. Blowing up zombies or something." I tried not to think about Grayson counting the rocks at the bottom of Newman Quarry a couple hours before, or about him crying, telling me to just drive, and saying he wished he could run away from it all. Mom would want to know those things. Mom would *need* to know them.

I promised her I would call the next day and told her I loved her, then hung up and turned my phone off completely.

There was no turning back now.

I got into Hunka, shutting the door as softly as I possibly could, and pulled out of the gas station parking lot. I turned the vents to blow hot air onto my fingers as they were wrapped around the steering wheel. The headlights carved little tunnels out of the extreme dark of the Kansas highway. Grayson snored steadily, the glove box door tapping against his leg.

I opened my soda and the bag of jerky and headed west, imagining all my lies dropped unceremoniously on the ground by the gas pump. This was going to be a new beginning, where none of that old stuff would matter anymore.

All that mattered was what was ahead of us.

Even if I wasn't certain what exactly that was.

Or how I'd know it when I found it.

Or if any of this would work at all.

I couldn't think about those things. I took a deep breath, popped a piece of jerky into my mouth, and focused on the highway ahead.

CHAPTER
ELEVEN

To understand how I got into the mess I got into, you first have to understand what it's like to be born under the shadow of a sibling's extreme failed potential.

Grayson was everything to Mom and Dad. Their first, a boy, just as they'd hoped for. He was sweet and cuddly and rough-and-tumble and smart and what they saw as the culmination of everything good about themselves. Of course, this was back when they thought that only good could come out of their children. Only perfection.

He was gifted. Of course he was. He could throw a tight spiral on a football by the time he was five, and by the time he was six could explain the physics behind it. Science was his thing, and, they figured, math was, too. Before he could even walk, he could count to ten and seemed to be stacking blocks in a particular order. Before he went to school, he would melt down if a puzzle piece went missing under the

TV or if Mom picked up his toys from their permanent perch on the piano bench.

They figured he was just precise. And when he began counting—sometimes to astronomically high numbers—they figured he was just quirky. So many geniuses are.

But at some point it became obvious that Grayson's eccentricity was going to be a problem. And a genius with a problem was a "waste." A "shame."

Suffice it to say, I was never a genius. Not even close. And of course they noticed. I wasn't even as smart as Zoe, something I had heard Mom say to Zoe's mom on more than one occasion—not bitterly, but simply as a statement of fact.

But my parents really didn't seem to mind that I was just normal. Grayson needed more attention. Because he was Grayson. And I was self-sufficient. I was self-reliant. I had a good head on my shoulders, and I didn't cause trouble. Those things were important. When there's someone needy in the house, everyone else has to be need-less. It's nothing personal. Even if it sometimes feels that way.

Mom and Dad were good parents. They loved each other. They loved us both. They wanted good things for us. And they were heartbroken that Grayson wasn't perfect after all.

After a while, the fact that I was just a regular kid was a really good thing. Mom and Dad could rely on my steadiness. If I worked hard, I could do well in life, maybe even great. They had replaced their high hopes for Grayson with even higher hopes for me. I brought in good grades. I was involved in things. I smiled and laughed and got dirty and played, lounging on my belly on the carpeted living room floor with my toys strewn everywhere around me. Orderless. Childlike.

I don't know exactly how being normal turned into a need to be perfect, but at some point it did. For every time my brother dashed my parents' hopes, I ratcheted my performance up a notch. Maybe I wanted to distance myself from him. Maybe it was the only way for me to get some attention, too.

Maybe I was trying to forge an identity other than "poor Grayson's little sister."

Whatever the reason, that's exactly what happened: I shifted from normal Kendra to Kendra the star. While Grayson's grades and attendance fell, mine got better. While Grayson threatened suicide and went into screaming tantrums when his life didn't feel right to him, I blossomed. And when Grayson quit school midway through his junior year and spent two holidays in various residential facilities, counting his brain into oblivion, I vaulted to the top of my class.

I wanted Mom and Dad to have something to be proud of. And I wanted to prove that I could do it.

So when, at the beginning of my senior year, I pulled Mr. Floodsay, otherwise known as the worst calc teacher in the whole school, I got scared. And when, halfway through the first semester, my grade had dipped into the C range, and then to a low D, I saw it all begin to slip away from me. Everything I'd worked so hard for. All the pride I'd stocked up in Mom and Dad. All the hard work, all the sports, all the projects, all the nights trying to study while Mom stood sobbing in the hallway to Grayson that if he didn't calm down, she'd have to call the police. All of it, gone.

I tried going to tutoring. It didn't work. I tried staying after with Mr. Floodsay. It didn't work.

I was embarrassed. And frustrated. And hopeless. And I was petrified over what failing calc would do to my college plans.

I needed that math credit to get into the college I wanted to go to. I begged Mr. Lloyd, my guidance counselor, to put me in another class, but all the other classes were full, so I couldn't transfer out. So I had no choice. Fail the class or drop it entirely. Either way, I would lose the math credit I needed. I would go to a second-rate school. I would be status quo—*almost* perfect, *almost* amazing. And I was scared to death that the whole rest of my life would be defined by that, by an *almost*. I'd have come so close but never quite gotten there. This wasn't about me losing everything; this was about me losing the only thing I'd ever gotten attention for. This was about me losing the most important thing.

I had to do something. I couldn't let one lousy teacher take it all away from me. Make me just one more child who had *almost* lived up to her potential. Make me the one who couldn't overcome that she wasn't born great.

I didn't realize until a car's headlights on the other side of the median had streaked by that I was silently crying. I didn't know what time it was, but we'd been on the road for hours, it seemed, and Grayson's stirring was becoming more and more frequent.

I had no idea where we were. For miles, I'd seen almost nothing but darkness. The only sign of a "town" was an occasional diner or defunct gas station perched at the top of an exit ramp.

"What's...?" was the first thing Grayson said when he finally woke up for real. He pulled himself up straighter and blinked, looking around. He licked his lips repeatedly. I reached over and picked up the warmish soda out of the cup holder and held it out to him. He looked at it as if he'd never seen such a contraption before.

"Good morning, sunshine!" I said, way too cheerily. I could feel the tears hanging off my jaw, but didn't make any move to wipe them away. "Jerky?" I put the soda back in the cup holder and held up the open bag of beef jerky instead. "Dinner of champions." Again he stared, so I shook the bag a little. A meaty waft of air clouded the car.

He didn't take the bag, but looked out the window instead. "Where are we?" he finally asked, his voice still foggy from sleep.

"Dunno." I folded a piece of jerky into my mouth and began chewing, chewing, chewing. "Somewhere in Kansas," I said around the meat.

"Kansas?" he repeated, then peered out the window

again. He began methodically touching his fingers to his thumb, the way he likes to do when he's nervous. Back and forth, back and forth, forefinger, middle, ring, pinkie, ring, middle, forefinger. It made me want to burst out in song: *Where is Thumbkin? Where is Thumbkin?* "Why are we in Kansas?" His voice was getting clearer now, and his fingers were speeding up.

"You told me to drive," I said. "So I drove."

"Into the middle of Kansas?"

I nodded, smiling around the wad of beef jerky that didn't seem to want to be broken down. "Why not?"

"What time is it?" he asked, peering at his watch, but it was too dark for him to see its face.

I shrugged. "We've been on the road for a few hours, so maybe eight o'clock or so?"

His face whipped around to me, startled. "Eight o'clock? At night?"

"Well, it isn't morning, Genius Boy."

"You've been driving through Kansas for four hours?"

"Yeah," I said. "Give or take. Here, have some beef jerky. It's dinner."

I held out the bag again and gave it another little shake. I could feel the tension build in my brother as it began to dawn on him what was going on. He'd stopped touching his fingers together and instead had started balling and relaxing his fists in his lap. *Squeeze. Relax. Squeeze. Relax.* Faster now. *Squeezerelax. Squeezerelax.* I wondered if this was a new coping technique he'd learned in treatment, and then it occurred to me that I'd never really asked him about what went on in treatment. I'd only asked if he'd gotten better. There was a whole part of him that I didn't know. I resolved to ask him about it at some point while we were on the road. I was guessing there'd be plenty of time for talk.

I wiggled the beef jerky bag again. He frowned and pushed it away; it fell out of my hand, the meat spilling out onto the floor at his feet. "I don't want beef jerky. Kendra, what is going on?"

"Hey, I was eating that!" I said.

"I asked what's going on."

"I said I was eating that. Pick it up."

"Not until you tell me what's going on."

"Fine," I said. "If you must know, you're running away."

He squinted behind his glasses, as though he'd heard what I'd said but the words didn't compute. "What are you talking about?"

"You said you wanted to run away from your OCD. So you are. I'm helping you. Simple."

He let out an exasperated laugh—just one little breath of air, really—and looked forward, cocking his head to one side. I leaned over and grabbed for the bag of jerky, but had to sit up quickly as the hum of the car veering onto the shoulder jarred me.

"Stop the car," Grayson said, a little too calmly.

"No," I said. "Give me the jerky." I even sounded stupid to myself, fighting so hard for a bag of stale gas-station beef jerky. I don't know what came over me, but all of a sudden everything I believed in, everything I wanted, was wrapped up in that bag. And I wasn't going to let it go. "I said give it to me!"

"Pull over," Grayson said, his measured voice slipping, his left hand reaching for the steering wheel.

"No! Stop it! You want to kill us? Just give me the beef jerky!"

"Stop! The! Car!" he shouted. He yanked the steering wheel and we crossed over into the shoulder, bumping into a little ditch on the other side. I screamed, pulling the steering wheel to get Hunka back under control, and stomped on the brake. We came to a stop, halfway on and halfway off the shoulder of the road.

For the briefest moment, there was nothing but silence. No other cars on the road. Nothing but fields around us. And in that silence, I heard my heart pounding. *Ka-thunk-ka-thunk-ka-thunk*. I tasted the jerky, salty in the corners of my mouth. I heard my brother's breathing, quick and angry.

And then the moment broke around us, as if we'd been suspended in a filmy, iridescent soap bubble and it had given, spilling us out into reality.

"You could've killed us!" I screamed, and pounded my fist into Grayson's shoulder. "You could've wrecked us out in the middle of freaking nowhere!" I pounded his shoulder again, but when I reared back to hit him a third time, he yanked his door open and launched himself out into the black fields. "Get back here!" I yelled, but he kept walking as though he hadn't heard me. "Dammit," I cursed under my breath. I checked my side mirror—no headlights, of course—and jumped out of the car, then raced across the field after him.

"Grayson!" I shouted. "Grayson, stop!"

He walked for a few more feet and then stopped, allowing me to catch up to him. He turned abruptly and faced me. "I can't believe you're this stupid. Running away? You really think I meant you should drive me out all the way to a Kansas soy field?"

"You said you wanted to run away from it," I argued, trying to catch my breath. "You said you wanted to run away from the OCD."

"You really think coming out here is what I meant?" he asked, his eyes bright, his voice breaking. "Are you really that stupid?"

"Stop calling me stupid," I said. "I'm helping you."

"No, you're not!" he yelled, his face furious. "And we're not going another five feet. Turn the car around and take us home."

He turned and walked back toward the car. I stood where I was and watched him go. He was so angry, he ended on an odd number of steps, but got into the car anyway. But I noticed, once he shut the door, that his fingers crooked in front of him and his lips were moving. He was counting, probably backward, to make up for doing it.

I stood in the field and looked up at the sky. It was totally clear, and in the dark, the stars stood out like Christmas lights. Had it not been cold and my eyes not been blurred from tears, it would have been beautiful. I could imagine Grayson and Zoe and me, lying on our backs in a circle, the tops of our heads touching, trying to identify the constellations. Grayson would know them all. Zoe and I would purposely mess up the names, just to frustrate him. But it would make him laugh.

"What's that one again?" Zoe would ask, pointing straight up. "Ursula Major?"

"No, dummy," I'd say, laughing. "That's Ursula Minority."

Grayson would growl exasperatedly. "It's called Ursa Major, and no, that's not it. You're pointing at Betelgeuse, and it's in Orion."

"Yeah, Zo," I'd say, tapping her foot with mine. "You're thinking of the Big Dipstick." And we'd both laugh while Grayson pretended to angrily pound his head backward into the grass, groaning, "Big Dipper, you guys, Big Dipper!"

I would've given anything to have Zoe with me tonight. Grayson sure wasn't pretending to be mad this time.

"Well, Zo," I said aloud, peering into the sky. "I wasn't expecting that. What do I do now, huh? You know him as well as I do. Help a girl out a little. I need my best friend."

And just like that, I knew where we were going.

CHAPTER
TWELVE

I was right—Grayson was counting backward when I got into the car. He was only on number ninety-seven, so the goal number must have been pretty low. I had a frightening second where I wondered how high Grayson could count, and if I would find out on this trip. I was pretty sure if I had to listen to it for hours on end, we'd both end up mumbling numbers to ourselves and opening and shutting our car doors 100 times each to ward off bad omens and cruel accidents.

I couldn't think that way. I had to have hope.

I turned onto my knees and leaned over to the backseat. I pulled my purse off the floorboard, where it had fallen during our little trip into the field. I unzipped it and pulled out my wallet. I thumbed past my student ID, my driver's license, and two used-up gift cards and worked my way into the pocket section of the wallet. There, tucked away by itself, was a little rectangle of paper. Zoe's eighth-grade photo. The one she'd pressed into my palm on the day she left. The day we promised not to forget each other. I studied the photo, my finger tracing the heart-shaped jawline of my best friend. Did her hair still flow to the middle of her back, or had she gotten it cut? Had she lost baby fat or had her teeth whitened? Would I even recognize her if I saw her in a crowded mall? I turned the photo over. Scrawled on the back were these words:

Zoe
555 Clark Street
Citrus Heights, CA 95611
"BFFs 4 Ev!"

I ran my finger over the letters, feeling the raised bump of the ink, then stuffed the photo back into its hiding place and zipped the purse shut, dropping it onto the floorboard behind me.

I buckled my seat belt, put the car in drive, and thumped over the grass and onto the highway. A whine was coming from the tire on Grayson's side, but otherwise Hunka seemed to have taken the rough ride like a champ. I stuck my hand through the hole of the steering wheel and patted the dash appreciatively.

After several minutes, Grayson turned to me, back at zero, and said, "Just drive over the median."

"No."

"The next exit's probably ten miles away. Nobody'll know."

I was silent for a beat, sizing up my words. Grayson was thumping his thumb against his knee rhythmically. I fought the urge to mess up his rhythm, but knew that would be a bad idea. It would only serve to make the counting start up again.

"I'm not turning around," I finally said. My voice was steady, even, sounding much more confident than I felt. Honestly, after that mini-crash we'd just had, I was feeling pretty shaken up, and I wasn't so sure going home was a bad idea after all.

"Yes, you are," he said. "I'll pull the wheel again."

"Fine," I snapped. "Go ahead and pull the wheel. You break us down out here and we're not getting home at all. Nobody would even think to look for us here."

"Mom and Dad—"

"Mom and Dad think you're at Brock's and I'm at Shani's," I said. "They aren't even going to be suspicious until tomorrow morning when the school calls to…" I trailed off. My mouth still couldn't form around the words. Called to what, exactly? Called to tell them what I'd done? Called to tell them that their perfect daughter was getting expelled and wasn't going to be going to college after all? "To find out why I'm not in class," I finished, thinking, *You wish that was the worst of your worries, Kendra.* "By then," I continued, "we'll be almost out of Kansas." I flicked a glance at the gas gauge and added silently, *I hope so.*

Grayson straightened. "Out of Kansas? Have you lost your mind? We can't just go driving across the country."

"Why not?" I asked, shrugging. "Huh? I mean, here we are...we're driving...and we'd be fine if you'd just chill out. It's a road trip. Have fun."

He shook his head and gave a sardonic laugh. "Fun," he muttered. "You're insane. I don't know why they keep locking *me* up. *You're* the crazy one."

"Yeah, fun," I said, choosing to ignore his little dig. He was unhappy, but at least he wasn't shouting at me and reaching for the steering wheel. Or counting, which, to me, seemed like progress. Maybe even seemed as if my plan would work exactly as I'd wanted it to. Like Dr. St. James was right, and all we had to do was make Grayson face his anxiety. "Remember fun? You used to have it sometimes?"

"Ha-ha-ha," he deadpanned.

"Okay. Remember the time we made the woods behind Zoe's house into a haunted forest for Halloween?"

He made a noise in the back of his throat but didn't comment.

"And we invited all the little neighborhood kids, and you were the headless ghost, and you were so good you made that Ian kid cry?"

Grayson's mouth twitched. "Yeah."

"See? That was fun. And remember last summer when we snuck out at midnight for that twenty-cent taco sale at Jose Grande's? And we bought, like, twenty dollars' worth of tacos? And we both forgot our house keys and we couldn't get back in?"

Grayson laughed. "And you had the brilliant idea to throw your shoes at Mom and Dad's window because they didn't hear the doorbell."

I cracked up. "And they called the cops instead and there we were, holding all these giant bags of tacos on our own front porch."

"And your shoes were stuck in the gutter."

We both laughed. Mom and Dad had been so mad at us, but we hadn't gotten into any trouble, because they were also both so thrilled that we were doing something normal. Together.

"See? That was fun, too. And you didn't die from it," I said. "Loosen up, Stuffypants. Enjoy."

His face got serious. "Enjoy," he repeated. "It seems to me that you haven't been in the mood for much fun for a long time yourself."

"What? I have fun all the time," I said, though in the back of my mind I was scrounging to think of a recent example to offer. "Shani and Lia and I have lots of fun."

He rolled his eyes. "If you call standing around trying to impress everyone fun, I guess," he said.

I opened my mouth to argue, but nothing came out.

Whether he was right or wrong, I was mostly floored that he'd even paid attention. I'd thought Grayson only paid attention to Grayson. And rocks.

"It doesn't matter," he said. "What are we going to do when we hit Colorado?"

"Keep driving," I answered. Again, my eyes cut to the gas gauge, which was down to just under a quarter of a tank now. I was still trying to shake off his accusation that I didn't have fun. I had yet to think of an example of something fun I'd done recently, and that was just depressing.

"Just drive forever?"

"No," I answered, taking another sip of my soda. I picked up his and offered it to him again. Surprisingly, he took it. "We're going to California."

He let out a bark of a laugh now. "California!" he repeated. "What the hell is in California?"

I thought about it. I couldn't answer him truthfully. I couldn't tell him there were lots of things in California. My redemption, for instance. Distance, during which maybe the school, or Mom and Dad, or maybe even I would figure out what to do next about the mess I'd left behind. Or Grayson's redemption, maybe. His cure from OCD, finally really putting to the test that cognitive behavioral therapy and exposure therapy crap all those docs had been talking about for years. The stuff that Mom wanted everyone else to do but couldn't seem to make herself do.

And I definitely couldn't tell him truthfully what was really waiting for us in California: help.

Zoe.

So I told him the next best lie I could think of instead.

"The Hayward Fault," I said matter-of-factly.

Grayson paused, his soda perched below his lips. He looked at me, stunned.

The Hayward Fault was one of Grayson's longest-running obsessions. His second-grade teacher talked about it in science one day—this 100-kilometer fault in the San Francisco Bay area that some people believe will cause a seven-plus magnitude earthquake any day. Most of the kids in his class blew it off as more boring junk to memorize, but it became Grayson's world.

He had nightmares. Would wake up sweating, screaming for Dad. Dad would run into Grayson's room, only to hear, "The Hayward had the big one, Dad!"

And when we'd go outside to play, Grayson always wanted to play Hayward Fault rescue. Zoe and I would pretend the ground had shaken us off the swing set and would lie buried under an overturned wagon or empty box and Grayson would flit about the yard, pretending to use superhuman strength to free us from our prisons.

He used to tell us he wanted to see the fault for himself someday. A pilgrimage for the geologically devoted. He wanted to touch the ground, to see if he could detect any tremors from deep within the earth. He wanted to scoop up a handful of gravel and bring it home as a souvenir—more priceless than the snowflake obsidian Grandpa had brought him from New Zealand. It would be his most treasured piece of geology: pebbles from the fault that last rocked the earth in 1868 and would most certainly rock the earth again.

But sitting on Hunka's bench seat next to me, he didn't say anything about the treasures of the Hayward. Instead, he silently lowered his soda into his lap and stared out the passenger-side window.

"We'll go to the...where was it again? The football stadium?"

He cleared his throat. "Cal Memorial Stadium. At Berkeley."

I snapped my fingers and pointed at him. "Yeah. That's the one. The fault is under it, right?"

He nodded, numbly. "Directly. From..."

"Goalpost to goalpost," I said excitedly, having heard him say those very words so many times growing up. "See? I was paying attention. Cal Memorial Stadium, here we come! See, Gray? Fun! This will be fun!"

My brother sat still, looking dazed. I was hoping for more excitement from him. Maybe it would come. Yeah, that was it. He just needed time. The excitement would come.

"Gray," I said softly. "This is important to me."

A long time passed before he moved again. I watched the highway roll by, every now and then glancing back at my brother, who seemed to be mesmerized by something he saw out his window. But I knew what he saw wasn't out the window at all. What he saw was something out of the past. Or future. Or maybe both.

"Okay," he said, very quietly. He gently placed his soda back in the cup holder. "I can't believe I'm going to go along with this, but okay."

CHAPTER
THIRTEEN

I was already sick of being in the car. We hadn't seen any-thing for what seemed like forever. Just miles and miles of darkness and shadowy fields on both sides. I knew people lived out there somewhere, and I spent some time wondering what it must be like to be so isolated all the time. Was it wonderful, never having to worry about parking or sales on paper towels? Or was it horrible and restless? After so many hours in the car, with nobody to talk to but my brother, who wasn't exactly talking, I was feeling horrible and restless.

"We've gotta stop," I said, craning my neck to look for a highway sign that might give some indication of a town somewhere ahead. "My butt's numb. And we need gas. Bad."

Grayson nodded and peered out the window. The *uh-uhuhuh-uh* sound had crept back into his throat. I wanted to stuff something into my ears to drown the sound out. I didn't know about him, but it was making me feel twitchy.

For the past hour, I'd been ignoring the noise and the pressing need for gas as best I could, entertaining myself by envisioning what it would be like to see Zoe again. I imagined running up the driveway to meet her, her parents beckoning us into their house, all forgiven. I imagined Zoe and Grayson and me, shoulder to shoulder, twining our fingers together once again, walking hand in hand, as we'd done so many times throughout our childhood. Grayson was smiling in my imagined scene. He was relaxed and smiling. And I wasn't running away from a mess at school. We were both having fun.

Just how we used to be, before.

Funny how a couple lousy sentences can ruin everything.

Listen, Linda. We need you to keep Grayson away from Zoe, okay? We don't want her dating a kid with mental problems.

I'd never forget my mom's reaction to Zoe's dad when he said that. How she'd physically recoiled from him, clutching a margarita glass to her chest, her back brushing up against a little paper lantern she and Zoe's mom had hung earlier that day for our traditional end-of-summer luau. I'd never forget the way Mom's eyes clouded with shock, and how she'd glanced over Mr. Monett's shoulder, peering in embarrassment at the other guests, who had just begun to arrive.

And I'd never forget her response to Mr. Monett: *How dare you say such a thing, Rob? You with your Thursday afternoon mistress and your Sunday binge drinking, acting like you're better than my son? Get out of my yard. And keep your daughter away from my son, while you're at it! He doesn't need some trampy little preteen giving him any pointers.*

And I'd never forget how my mom's drink had stained the tops of Mr. Monett's shoes as she threw her cup with a hollow plastic *thunk* down on the deck. Or how Zoe had cried, curled up in the hollow of Grayson's arm on the edge of the sandbox underneath our old swing set. How she'd bitterly cursed my mom for calling her trampy and how she swore she'd marry Grayson someday because he was her soul mate. That she'd been in love with him since she was a toddler, and how could my mom and her dad not see that?

And I'd never forget any of the little scenes that followed — Mr. Monett showing up on our front porch, clutching Grayson's elbow so hard Grayson's face was crumpled in pain; Zoe's mom calling mine, screaming that she'd caught Grayson kissing her daughter again; Dad and Zoe's dad almost coming to blows when Mr. Monett shoved Grayson off their porch after finding Grayson and Zoe studying rocks out of their landscaping there; Grayson moaning and pacing and rubbing the sides of his head through the night, the hardwood floor of his bedroom strewn with fly-away, frizzy tumbleweeds.

And me, fighting for my brother. Standing by my friend. Holding her hand. Stroking her hair. Until they did that last stupid thing and Mr. Monett said it was the final straw and announced they were moving and took everything away from me. Zoe, away to California. Grayson, away inside his head. I was the one who did everything I was supposed to do, yet I lost my two best friends. It wasn't fair. All of them were so wrapped up in their own pain, they didn't even think I might be in pain, too. My best friend was gone, and nobody even bothered to ask if I was okay.

But in my mind, as I drove toward Cali, I got it all back. Zoe would take me into her bedroom, and it would be pink and have butterfly decals on the walls, just like her bedroom back home. We'd eat soft pretzels on her bed, and she'd tell me about her school—about how she'd found friends but, like Shani and Lia, they weren't the same. She'd take me to the beach, maybe. Let me borrow a halter top. Introduce me to boys. She'd spread her hands on Grayson's chest and absorb the anxiety that had eaten him up all these years. She'd embrace him, and we'd even drive to Berkeley and look at the football stadium, and we'd marvel at the irony of how the fault we'd always worried would destroy us all had actually saved us. Brought us all back together.

Maybe even our parents would reunite. Maybe they could forgive one another. They would see that Grayson was fixable. They would see that Zoe wasn't trampy and that Grayson wasn't crazy and that we were all exactly what they'd always wanted us to be—happy.

No, not maybe.

Definitely.

It had to be.

"Is that something up there?" Grayson asked, pointing

out his window toward a dim light, an oasis in the middle of nothingness.

I eased up onto the exit and followed the dusty road toward the light, which, as we drew closer, looked like a small motor lodge at the edge of an even smaller town.

I pulled into the parking lot as Hunka sucked down almost the last bit of gas in the tank.

CHAPTER
FOURTEEN

"You're kidding, right?" Grayson asked, as I put the car into park and practically jumped out onto the cracked asphalt. I stretched greedily, my muscles feeling drained and weak after so long sitting still. "This place is...God, Kendra, they probably have bugs...."

I held a finger out toward him, schoolmarm-style. "Uh-uh. No you don't. This place is fine." I stepped up onto the curb and gazed at the office, which sat at the end of a dilapidated statuary-lined path. There was a cow skull lying in the grass by the walk. This was no Holiday Inn. I tried not to think about horror movies and dead hookers and crazy diseases on sheets. This was fine. It had to be fine. For my brother's sake, I had to pretend that I thought this motel was the finest motel ever.

Grayson stepped up on the curb and down again. Then up again. Then down again. I turned.

"Stop it," I hissed. "Come on. I'm going in, with or without you."

He followed, hesitantly, his head jerking back toward the curb as though he wanted to step on and off it a few more times. "I won't be able to sleep in a place like this," he said, edging around a large bird dropping on the ground. He crouched and touched the clean ground next to the dropping, over and over again. "One, two, three, four..."

I'd reached the door. A McGruff the Crime Dog sticker on the window was faded and peeling off. A broken wind chime lay crumpled on the concrete stoop. A chewed-looking Tupperware bowl filled with about half an inch of filthy water sat nearby, along with an open and mostly eaten can of cat food. A muddied, skin-and-bones cat peered up at me from behind a half-dying bush off to my left. It meowed and scooted back into the bushes as I reached for the door handle.

"...sixteen, seventeen, eighteen, nineteen, twenty. I can't do it. I can't sleep here."

"Fine. Sleep in the car," I said, trying on my best exposure therapy voice. Or at least what I imagined an exposure therapy voice to sound like. I actually had no idea what a therapy voice would sound like. I'd spent so much of the past three years trying to ignore it all.

"We're going home," he said. "This isn't a game, Kendra. I appreciate what you're doing, but you can't just put people like me through this kind of exposure all at once. Mom wouldn't...."

I turned, my hand still on the door handle. "I'm not Mom," I said. "I'm not going to baby you. You're fine. Either come with me or sleep in the car. I'm tired and I don't care which you choose. I'm going in."

"You're being ridiculous," he said, rushing up behind me. I caught him casting a worried look as the cat jumped deeper into the bushes and disappeared. "This is the most ridiculous idea you've ever had. I'm not nine. I don't even want to see the Hayward Fault anymore. I'm sick. I should be home."

I ignored him and pulled open the door. Immediately I was hit by a cloud of incense that nearly knocked me over. It reminded me of the time I went to church with Grandma on Easter Sunday. I'd come home wheezy and succumbing to a terrible cold, and Mom had refused to let Grandma take me to church with her ever again. Grandma couldn't convince her that the incense hadn't caused my respiratory distress.

The top of the door knocked against a little metal bell, which clanked our arrival to the empty lobby.

I stood awkwardly in the middle of the room, taking in the mishmash of decor, which seemed to be a cross between Native American, commercial cowboy, and Woodstock. There were dried soda can rings caked on a scrubby coffee table, yellowing magazines with curled corners on the couch, and a pervasive fluorescent feel to the atmosphere, like we were fleas under a microscope.

On the other side of the counter, far back in an adjoining room, a white-haired man in a stained tank top sat in a recliner, his feet pointing toward a teeny television set, which blared out a reality show. He seemed to either not notice Grayson and me standing in the lobby, or not care.

I shuffled to the counter and timidly tapped a bell next to the cash register. No sound came out. I glanced back at Grayson, but he was staring at a stain of something brown and once liquid that had been splashed and then left to dry on the wall. I could only imagine what was going through his mind. He was probably wondering if it was possible to actually die of grossed-out-ed-ness in a nasty motor lodge lobby. I grinned despite myself, because this place probably ranked as the number one worst place on earth I could take Grayson to spend the night. Not that it was funny. But, yeah…it kinda was.

"Dare you to lick it," I whispered.

He looked horrified. "No!"

"Come on. I'll pay you ten bucks."

"You're crazy, Kendra. I'm not licking the wall. Here or anywhere else."

"Chicken."

"Okay, fine. I'm a chicken. A chicken who'll live to see tomorrow."

"Bawk-bawk-bawk," I whispered, making little wings out of my arms.

Grayson rolled his eyes and shook his head. "Unbelievable. I'm being held hostage by a three-year-old."

"A three-year-old who isn't afraid to do this." Quickly,

without thinking about what I was doing, I stuck out my tongue and grazed the wall with it, leaving behind a wet streak.

"Oh! God!" Grayson screeched as I laughed and stuck my tongue out at him.

"Mmm...certain death," I teased.

"That's just...disgusting," he said, but the conviction was gone from his voice, and I almost thought I heard an amused tone behind it.

I wiped my tongue off on the back of my hand and turned to face the check-in desk again. "Um, excuse me?" I called out. The man glanced at us, and then turned back to the TV again. Not a word. I shifted my weight. "Hello?" I said, louder this time.

"Rena!" the man shouted, still not looking away from the TV. He scratched his belly. "Re-NA!"

A baby cried somewhere off in the distance, there were some stumbling noises, and then a curtain next to the cash register swished to one side, and a blonde stepped out of the darkness behind it, blinking in the light, her long, shiny hair in sleep-tufts around her head. She looked about my age.

"Chill, I was feeding Bo," she said, closing a ragtag robe around her middle. The baby protested some more in the background. "Hey, there," she said to me, stepping up to the counter. She yawned. "Checking in?"

I nodded.

The baby's fussing crescendoed, and she cinched the

robe shut with a belt. "Okay," she said. "It's um, forty a night for the basic, fifty-five for a double, and we have, uh, one lovers' suite for eighty dollars. That one has a two-person Jacuzzi."

"We'll take a basic," I said, resisting the urge to add "ew" about the lovers' suite. I pulled out my wallet and handed her my credit card. Actually, it was Mom's credit card, but she let me carry it for the times she needed me to pick something up for her.

The blonde took the card. Her fingernails were filed blunt and painted pink, a shiny spot in this place that so needed a scrubbing.

"Do you have ID?" she asked, again glancing at the curtain as the baby's cries turned to hiccups.

I pulled out my driver's license and handed it to her. She squinted at it, looked up, then squinted at it some more. Finally, she looked up at me, scratching her neck and leaving ragged red lines down her throat.

"Um, you have to be eighteen," she said.

"Oh." I gestured behind me at Grayson, who was now staring at a stain on the shabby carpet. For one wild moment, I had the urge to lick that, too, just to see what he'd do. "He is."

"I have to see his ID, then," she said, handing me back my license.

"Gray, give her your ID," I said. Grayson didn't have a driver's license. He never could get over his anxiety enough to take the test. Instead, he carried a state ID, which was hard enough for him to get, given he had to stand in a line at the DMV, *where people bleed and vomit and spit all the time*, he'd said, as if he'd survived an acid rain shower or a swim in a porta-potty or something.

His eyes grew wide, and his hands instinctively went to his back pockets. "I don't have it," he said.

"What do you mean you don't have it?"

He turned in a circle, holding his arms up at shoulder height, as if this proved something. "I don't have my wallet with me."

"You left without your wallet?" I said incredulously.

"I'm sorry. I didn't realize we were going to be sleeping in a dumpy no-tell motel in the middle of nowhere tonight. If you'll recall, this was not my idea."

I had nothing to say. I turned back to the girl at the counter, my mouth hanging open. Grayson had no wallet. Which meant Grayson had no money. And which also meant we couldn't stay in any hotel anywhere, because I was too young and he couldn't prove that he wasn't.

And we'd be stranded here in... wherever we were... with no money, no gas, no sleep, and no Zoe.

And Mom and Dad would get here and find Grayson stepping on and off a curb over and over, which he hadn't done in a year, by the way, so don't think I hadn't noticed he was actually getting worse instead of better, and they'd be so pissed.

The baby had stopped crying, and this fact seemed to disturb the blonde girl more than his crying had. "Archie," she said over her shoulder. "Would you check on Bo? See if he went to sleep or something?"

But the white-haired man ignored her as soundly as he'd ignored us.

She slumped. "Look," she whispered. "I'll give you a room for one night. But don't tell Archie, okay?"

"Thank you," I said through the lump in my throat. My vision had gotten grainy, and now I felt supercharged, like I'd gotten my first lucky break. Like this was a sign that I was doing the right thing after all. Like someone "up there" was on my side. "I really appreciate it."

"No problem," she said, flashing a weary smile. The baby started a watery cry in the back room again while she ran my card through a machine and copied some information from my driver's license down into a notebook.

"Sign here," she said, pushing a clipboard at me. I signed, and she handed me a key—one of the old-fashioned kind stuck to a big plastic paddle with the words HAPPY HOUR INN etched in faded silver across the front. "You're in room nine," she said, pointing, the bell of her sleeve knocking over an aluminum can filled with pencils. It clattered and the baby cried again, even louder than before. "Go out this door and take a left. You're almost on the end there. I just cleaned it today, so it's good to go."

I gave Grayson a pointed look—*See? She just cleaned it today! Another sign of luck!*—and took the key from her hand.

"Thank you," I said.

She smiled again, her face lighting up the gloomy room. "No problem," she said. She gestured to the back room. "I'll be here if you need anything."

She stacked a few papers together, picked up the pencils, and disappeared behind the curtain again. The baby's cries softened and then stopped completely. I could hear her crooning to him back there, a soft song that sounded like sunshine.

"Come on," I said, pulling Grayson's arm. "Let's get some sleep."

Grayson gave one more worried look at the carpet and then stumbled along behind me. "Yeah," he said in a ragged voice. "Maybe you will, but I already know I won't."

I started out the door and then turned to him. I put my hands on his face, spreading my fingers out over his cheeks. "You will," I said, looking deep into his eyes. "I know it."

Because luck was on our side, and I was nothing if not determined to make this work.

I had to.

CHAPTER
FIFTEEN

Our room was decorated like the lobby. Thick, stained curtains on broken and duct-taped rods, orange-and-rust-colored bedspread decorated with cow skulls and cacti, and old, cracked brown vinyl chairs, one of which Grayson was crouching on.

"What are you doing?" I asked, coming out of the bathroom and standing with my back to the discolored dressing room mirror.

"Trying not to touch anything," he answered. I noticed his fingers were clawing the air like they always did when he was flowing with anxiety.

I grunted and tromped to the bed, turning down the dusty bedspread and exposing the blanket below, which was riddled with cigarette burn holes. Grayson wasn't counting, but his breathing was high and whistly. He didn't say anything, but I could hear the creak of the vinyl beneath his feet as he shifted his weight.

I took a deep breath. "Just get down, okay? The bed smells really clean. You can have the other side. Come on, Grayson."

Nothing. Just breathing and creaking.

I flopped back against the pillow. "Come on, Gray. Just give it a try."

But, even though I waited up as long as I could, he never did. And when I woke up in the morning, he was still crouched in the chair, his head dangling between his knees, his breathing soft and even. The small of his back kept him propped against the chair back. He'd managed to sleep without touching anything.

The clock beside the bed flashed twelve o'clock repeatedly, so I had no idea what time it was. All I knew was that the orange parking lot lamplight had been replaced by white morning light, and the thump of the people on the other side of the wall packing up their things and leaving had stirred me.

I sat up in bed and stretched. It felt weird not going to school. Part of me wished I was waking up in my own bed right now, grabbing a granola bar on the way out the door, meeting Shani and Lia at the school café for our real breakfast—caramel iced coffees. Part of me wished I was sitting on the bench outside the front doors of the school, laughing with the girls about something stupid. Going to class, feeling good. I'd never so much as ditched an hour of class before, and the pangs of anxiety washed over me briefly, before the realization of why I wasn't there dawned on me full-force. If Mom hadn't already gotten a call from the school, she soon would.

What would Mom think when she found out? What would she say? I was so humiliated by it all, I didn't see how I would ever look her in the face again.

Nothing you can do about it now, I told myself. *All you can do is go forward. Find Zoe. The music will still be there when you get back—you can face it then. Zoe will help you figure out how.*

Quietly, I pulled myself out of bed and padded to the shower, glancing at Grayson as I shut the door. He looked cold, but I was afraid of draping a blanket over him. His wallet wasn't the only thing he was without on this trip. He'd also left his medicine behind—something I hadn't even thought of before now. His antidepressants. They calmed him. I didn't know what would happen if he stopped taking them cold turkey, but it probably wouldn't be pretty. The last thing I needed was him waking up in full freak-out, which I'd seen too many times and would really prefer to never see again.

I remembered Grayson's first full freak-out. I was maybe nine; Grayson, twelve. We'd been headed to our grandma's house for Christmas. This was a big deal because Grandma and Papa lived on the other side of the state, and it was the closest thing we ever had to a family vacation. Grayson's fears made travel nearly impossible, but usually the thrill of Christmas morning, paired with a knockout dose of Dramamine in the afternoon, made it so Grayson could sleep most of the way there. While he was out, Mom and Dad and I would play word games and sing road trip songs and play license plate bingo and the alphabet game, and it sometimes even felt like we were a normal family.

But this time, Grayson didn't sleep. And, over the previous few months, he'd developed a serious fear of overpasses. He feared that Dad would drift and we'd plummet to the road below and die a horrible and grisly death. He feared another driver would drift and push our car off the road. He feared it would collapse. He feared it would crumble. It would explode. It would end abruptly. Didn't matter how silly or far-fetched it sounded; in my brother's mind, overpasses meant certain death.

So at first he counted and muttered phrases under his breath hundreds of times ("We're fine we're fine we're fine we're..."), but then he started rocking and shifting, and tears sprang from the corners of his eyes; and halfway through the trip, as Dad approached an overpass, Grayson started shrieking.

"Stop!" he cried out, his voice squeaking with strain. "Stop, stop, stop, stop!"

Dad looked in the rearview mirror, his eyebrows knitting together. "Buddy?" was all he got out before Grayson began flailing against the back of Mom's seat, hitting his head against the window, and clawing at the door handle.

Mom's eyes grew wide as she turned to look over the top of her seat, then she reached out and grabbed Dad's forearm. "Pull over," she said in a gruff voice I'd never heard from her before.

Dad whipped the car to the side of the road and jumped out, running over to Grayson's side and ripping Grayson's door open. Grayson, sobbing, coughing, shaking, spilled out of the car and scrambled to his feet, bending down to touch the ground with his fingertips repeatedly.

"We're fine," he whispered as he pressed his fingers into the gravel. "We're fine we're fine we're fine...."

Only we were anything but fine, because we were halfway across the state—dozens of overpasses in front of us and dozens of them behind us—and we sat by the side of the road like that for hours until Mom finally squeezed into the backseat with us, pulling Grayson's head into her side and stroking his hair until he finally fell asleep.

"Go home," she whispered to Dad, and we did. We never went back to our grandparents' house for Christmas again.

I leaned into the hot water, hoping Grayson wouldn't revert to that person on our trip to California, then fought off butterflies in my stomach when I realized that whether or not Grayson cried on an overpass was the least of our worries. How could I be so stupid to not even think about his medication?

I got out of the shower and dried off, pulling my clothes back on and shivering against the rough material on my skin. I brushed through my wet hair with my fingers, then stepped out into the room to put on my socks and shoes.

Grayson was still sleeping, his head cocked to one side and his cheek resting on one knee now.

I shuffled through the room quietly, my stomach growling loudly. It dawned on me that all I'd had yesterday was the lunch I'd thrown up and half a bag of beef jerky. I had no idea what Grayson had eaten. I needed to find some food, and sooner rather than later.

I slid my feet into my shoes, grabbed my purse, scratched out a note for Grayson on the back of a receipt, and slithered out the door, holding the handle so it wouldn't click and wake up Grayson when it shut. Maybe if he got some more sleep, he'd be less anxious today.

Outside, I stood and blinked in the sunlight. It was another chilly but beautiful spring day. Not a cloud in sight. I would hang on to that as another sign of good luck. I needed every sign I could get.

"Oh, hey," someone said over my shoulder. I jumped. Like a fugitive. Which I kind of was, I guess.

It was the blonde from last night. She was coming out of the room next to ours, emptying a trash can into a cleaning cart. She had a baby strapped in one of those cloth carriers on the front of her, facing out.

"You need something?" she asked.

"Hey," I answered. "Yeah. You got any vending machines here? I'm starving."

She shook her head and pulled off a pair of rubber gloves, tossed them into the cart, and rubbed her hands on the front of her jeans. The sun glinted off her lip gloss. She was so pretty, in an undiscovered sort of way.

"Used to," she said, "but it broke down and Archie didn't want to pay to have it fixed, so..." She shrugged.

"That's okay," I said. "I'll find a McDonald's or something." I rooted through my purse for my car keys.

"Yeah," she said brightly, walking toward me. She'd slipped her forefingers into her baby's fists, making him look like he was flying. He struggled to bring his fist to his mouth. "There's no McDonald's here, but Edwina's has some great pancakes."

"Edwina's?"

She pointed with the baby's fist. "That way. Toward town. You'll see it."

"Oh. Yeah. Okay. Thanks," I said, unearthing my keys and plugging one into Hunka's door.

"But you aren't gonna get too far with that," she said. I looked up and she was pointing—with her foot this time—at the front of Hunka. I walked around the front of the car to where she was pointing and looked down. The front passenger-side tire was completely flat.

"Son of a..." I muttered. "How'd...?"

But then it dawned on me how. Grayson yanking the

steering wheel hard to the right, Hunka jumping through the ditch, the whining sound that had accompanied us for miles after that.

"You got a spare?" the blonde asked.

I shook my head. "I don't think so. I've never seen one."

"There's a garage not far that way," the blonde said. The baby started to struggle, and she pulled him out of his carrier and began bouncing him on one hip. "They can probably fix it. I can walk it with you, if you want."

I chewed my lip and thought it over, staring at the tire, as if it would change if I looked at it long and hard enough. Great. Now I needed gas *and* a new tire. What other choice did I have? I couldn't afford a tow. We couldn't stay here forever. And we couldn't leave here on that tire.

"Okay," I said.

The blonde beamed as if I'd just said I'd be her best friend or something, and hopped on her toes. The movement made her look even younger than she already did. "Great!" she exclaimed as the baby twisted his sticky fingers into her hair. "Let me put Bo down for a nap first."

She took off toward the office, practically skipping, her hair swinging behind her as she cooed to the baby. I sat on the curb, thumbing through the ratty car manual that had a permanent curl from being crammed into the glove box since God knew when.

I'd never changed a tire before. Had never even seen anyone else do it. But it couldn't be that hard, right? After all, I was supposed to be relatively smart, despite my obvious shortcomings in calc. You definitely don't need to know calc to know how to change a tire. This was doable.

I fumbled in the trunk until I found the jack, then followed the directions, black tire marks streaking down the front of my shirt and covering my hands. Sweat trickled over my eyebrows as I muscled off the lug nuts and pulled the flat tire off.

Once it was off, I sat on the curb and brushed my hands together. *See, Kendra? You did it*, I thought. *You're not a total failure. You made one mistake, that's all. And if you can do this...who knows what you can do. For yourself. For Grayson.* As if changing Grayson was going to be as easy as changing a tire.

I heard, emanating from the office, Bo's cries, escalating, escalating. I heard a booming voice that sounded like the same voice that had boomed "Re-NA!" last night when we arrived, and then the baby's cries died down. I scowled. Archie seemed like one heck of a dad. The thought made tears spring to my eyes. I didn't want to admit it, not even to myself, but I already missed my dad so much. He would've changed the tire for me. And he would've been proud of me for doing it on my own.

Both of my parents were pretty awesome, in that traditional, stuffy TV-family kind of way. We didn't have the most normal family in the world, but somehow they made it seem like our version of normal was good enough. Or at least they tried. We had game nights and movie nights and the occasional stilted extended-family gathering where we clung to one another like life preservers. They knew what their parents and siblings and cousins thought about our family's situation—how people gossiped—and they didn't care. They stood their ground when it came to Grayson— he was fine. We all were fine. We loved each other and we were good people. So what?

They didn't deserve what I was doing to them. I wasn't even sure if I still qualified as "good people" anymore, with what I'd done.

But maybe if I helped fix my brother, they would forgive me eventually.

At that thought, I pulled my cell phone out of my purse and turned it on. Immediately, it vibrated. I had dozens of messages.

First, I looked at my texts. I had about ten from Lia and at least as many more from Shani. They all said pretty much the same thing:

Where R U?
Why rn't u @ school?
Why rn't u answrin ur texts?
Where R U?
Where R U?
Ur mom called my house this am. Where R U, "friend"?

Where are you, Kendra, when we all want your hide? *Where the hell are you?* The question of the day. Even I didn't know the answer to that.

And then there was a message from Bryn:

OSS for rest of yr. I did not protect u.

And a very similar one from Darian, with a combination of Lia and Shani thrown in for good measure. I had no idea how he even got my number:

Busted. Can't play in the Truman game 2nite.
Where r U? Everyone's looking 4 u.

I'll bet they are, I thought, and closed my eyes. I didn't want to read any more. I hit "delete all" and watched them back off, one by one. I would text Shani and Lia later. Explain to them what had happened.

Maybe.

I heard the door to the office open just as I looked at my voice mails. There were three, all from Mom. I listened to the first one.

"Kendra? What's going on? The school called and said you haven't shown up yet. I'm worried. Call me."

I hit "delete," feeling like the rottenest daughter on earth. It never occurred to me that lying to Mom about where I was would make her think something had happened to me. It never occurred to me that she would trust me so implicitly.

Who was I kidding? Changing a tire didn't make me smart. How could someone supposedly so smart be so stupid? I hadn't thought about Grayson's meds, hadn't thought that Mom and Dad would think I was lying dead in a ditch somewhere, hadn't thought what the calc final could do to my life. I kicked at a rock with the toe of my shoe. Idiot.

In the next message, her nose sounded plugged up, and worry seemed to be laced with panic in her voice. "Kendra? It's Mom. Where are you, honey? I called Shani's house, and her mom said you were never there last night. And I called Brock's house to see if Grayson knew where you were, and Brock's mom said she hasn't seen Grayson since before he went to Oak Meadows. I'm worried sick. I'm about to call the police. Call me back immediately."

My hands were shaking when I hit "delete" on that one, but I never got to listen to the third one because the blonde was back.

"Okay," she said brightly. She'd changed into a baby-blue sweater, which made her eyes look amazing. I wrapped my arms around myself. The sun was warm, but there was still a chill in the air, and I was cold. "Bo should be good for a couple hours. Let's go."

I stuffed my phone back into my purse, grabbed Mom's credit card, wiped my eyes with the back of my hand, and opened the passenger door. I tossed my purse into the backseat and locked it in there. I missed Dad. And I felt bad for Mom. But right now I had more pressing business to take care of.

I had to get Hunka fixed and back on the road.

"Yes, let's," I said, more brightly and confidently than I

felt. If faking confidence was what would get me to California, so be it.

Besides, in a way I'd been faking a lot of things for a lot of months now. It was old hat for me.

What would faking one more thing hurt?

CHAPTER
SIXTEEN

About fifteen minutes into our journey, I decided that the country definition of "not far" and my definition of "not far" were two different things. We started walking down the shoulder of a barely-more-than-dirt road toward a yellow-and-orange road sign: A SLOW DRIVE GETS YOU HOME ALIVE! There was nothing ahead of us but more road and some hills. Definitely not "not far."

I still hadn't shaken off Mom's phone calls, so I was silent, walking along, bent over to roll the flattened tire with my hands, which wasn't easy. *Just like they did in the old days*, I thought. *Except in the old days it was all for fun, not to get the runaways back on the road to California.*

"What was your name again?" the blonde finally asked. "Kenzie?"

"Kendra," I mumbled. "It's kind of an old-fashioned name."

She scrunched up her forehead. "I think it's pretty," she said. "I'm Rena, by the way."

I nodded. At least I wasn't cold anymore. Moving that tire had me sweating. I was already breathing hard, too.

"I hope you weren't planning on getting married this morning, what with the flat tire and all," she said.

I glanced at her. "Married?"

"Sure," she said. "Aren't you on your way to Vegas? That's pretty much where everyone who stops here is headed. Everyone like you guys, anyway. We get a lot of young couples. Eloping is pretty popular. Makes cleaning the rooms kind of disgusting sometimes, though."

I let out a bark of laughter. "We're not going to Vegas," I said. "That's my brother. He didn't even sleep in the bed." I laughed again, imagining anyone having to clean up after Grayson, ever. "We're going to California. To visit an old friend."

Rena's face clouded a little. "Wow," she said. "California's a long way. Must be a good friend."

"My best friend," I said softly, then realized I'd stopped walking and, with a start, set the tire in motion again. "We haven't seen each other in a while. I miss her."

It was an awkward thing to say to someone I'd just met, and Rena seemed not to know how to respond. We walked along in silence for a long time. I felt sweat trickle down my back, and then when the breeze ruffled my shirt, I shivered. Cars and trucks occasionally blasted past us, breaking the middle-of-nowhere silence. I winced and squinted against the kicked-up gravel every time one passed, but Rena didn't seem to even notice. After a while she took over rolling the tire, and I was shocked at how much faster we walked. She didn't struggle at all.

Finally, at the top of a hill, she stopped abruptly. The wind had picked up, and our hair whipped around our heads. I could see the "town" splayed out below us—a few houses, a couple lots full of farm equipment, a restaurant, or maybe two.

"Are you a runaway?" she asked, so point-blank that my mouth dropped open, but nothing came out. She looked deep into my eyes for a long time, ignoring the strands of hair that were sticking to her eyelashes and lips. I didn't answer. Just stood there, shivering, my blood feeling as if it'd been replaced by icicles. After a while, she looked out over the town and then back to me. Her face was grim. "I'm not gonna bust you," she said quietly. "Just...you act like one." My mind was reeling with all the possibilities of what could happen if I admitted to being a runaway on my first day out. She must have taken my silence as an answer because she eventually started walking again.

The sun ducked behind the clouds, and that, combined with our brisk pace and Rena's question, made the whole world feel cold and gray. It was one of the things I hated about spring—it could never decide if it wanted to be warm or cold. I reached over and started rolling the tire again, if for no other reason than to see if the work would rid me of my goose bumps.

"It's down there," she said at last, pointing at a falling-down garage about fifty yards away. The lightness had sneaked back into her voice again. "Mechanic's name is Buddy. I used to be down here all the time, back when me and Archie had a car. It was a real piece of crap. But I kinda liked coming down here. Buddy's a hick, but he's cute. Got a dimple right here." She touched her chin with her finger, leaving a black smudge there. On me, it would have looked like I needed a bath. On Rena, it looked cute. "Buddy tried to kiss me once," she said. "If Archie found out, he'd kill him." She giggled. "But I didn't mind so much." She sighed heavily. "Ahhh, I'm just a married old hag now, I guess."

I was stunned. "I thought Archie was your dad," I said.

She shook her head. "Old enough to be. We got married last June. Two months after I turned seventeen, and three months after I got pregnant with Bo."

"Your parents let you get married when you were seventeen?"

She shook her head. "I left home when I was fifteen. They don't even know about Archie. Or Bo."

The tire slipped out of my hand and rolled a few feet away, then toppled into the grass beside the road. Pushing the new tire up this hill was going to suck. I jogged for it.

"That's kind of sad," I said, bending over to pick it up. "Don't you miss them?"

She shrugged. "Sometimes I miss my mom, but Archie takes good care of me and Bo. He can be kind of mean sometimes. And he wasn't too happy about Bo in the beginning, but as long as I stay out of his hair, he doesn't give us too much trouble."

"Wow," I said, because that's the only thing I could think of to say. Had I known Rena a little better, I may have told her how wrong that was. That a man his age getting a sixteen-year-old girl pregnant was disgusting and a crime. That a good marriage isn't one where you have to stay out of your husband's hair in order to stay out of trouble. Had it been Shani, I would have said all of those things. Had it been Zoe, I would have packed her things for her and dragged her out of there. I'd have tied her in the backseat and stolen her if I had to. But I didn't know Rena. It was none of my business. So we just kept walking.

"Is that my girl out there?" a voice called, and Rena laughed. A guy in gray coveralls was standing out in the gravel lot in front of the open bay door, twisting a blue rag in his hands. He wore a greasy baseball cap, little brown curls snaking out from under it. From where we stood, his smile was very wide, and very bright.

"That's him," she said, then called out, "The one and only!" She took off running down the hill. When she reached him, she wrapped her arms around his shoulders. He kept his hands at his sides, looking like a stunned little boy receiving his first hug from a girl. When she unwrapped herself, I could see, even from a distance, pink on her face. Not like she was embarrassed; more like she was finally alive.

Slowly, I made my way down the hill and across the parking lot, shoving the tire along in little bursts, every so often losing my grip on it and having to step off the road and retrieve it from the grass and gravel on the side.

When I finally caught up with them, Rena and Buddy were giggling and slapping at each other. Rena looked even younger than she had before. And she was right—Buddy was hot.

"Hey," he said when I hit the lot. He jogged over to me and took the tire, picking it up against his chest as if it were no heavier than an envelope. "Need a fix, huh?"

I nodded, out of breath.

"Well, come on inside and get a Coke. I got an oil change ahead of you, and then we'll get this squared away."

"C'mon," Rena said, joining us. "I know where he keeps the keys to the Coke machine." She gave him a wicked grin.

"Aw, c'mon now, Rena," Buddy said, his tone exasperated, but the dimples blooming on the corners of his mouth giving him away. "You're not s'posed to tell anyone 'bout that."

She giggled. "You shouldn'ta told me, then," she said, and stuck out her tongue. Then she grabbed my hand and pulled me toward the grimy little shack off the garage.

I couldn't help liking Rena. I knew I didn't know her at all, and she could've been a terrible person, but at the moment, her hand was warm and felt like friendship, and I really, really needed that.

"I have to tell you about this one time that Archie came down here with me," she whispered, "and Buddy locked him in the bathroom. It was so funny."

I smiled at her.

"I'm dying for a Coke," I answered, and let her pull me into the building.

For the next hour, we drank sodas and chatted, giggling whenever Buddy came into the room, all shy and flirty, and for that one hour everything was relaxed and happy. Rena didn't know me. And she didn't know Grayson, either, which meant I could be whoever I wanted to be. Not perfect. Not the girl who goes down into the quarry to fetch her brother. Not the girl who can't have fun, or the girl running away from her problems. In some ways, it felt like no matter how long our time at Buddy's lasted, it would end too soon. Like I'd never get enough of just being me.

And, as awful as it sounds...for that one hour, I didn't even think about Grayson. I didn't worry about what he was doing back at Rena's motel.

I didn't even stop to think that he might wake up alone and start worrying about me.

CHAPTER
SEVENTEEN

Something told me that Buddy wasn't exactly hurrying on that oil change. He kept coming in and out, every time wiping something off on that blue towel, a distant, happy look in his eyes. He had it bad for Rena, even if she was "a married old hag."

It seemed that the two of them had a thousand stories to tell. Funny ones, sad ones, ones that seemed kind of private to me, and I found myself sort of missing Shani and Lia. It occurred to me that I never gave them enough credit. They were good friends, even if they weren't Zoe. They cared about me.

After Zoe had left and my brother began the great downward spiral that landed him in hospital after hospital and treatment program after treatment program, I really felt as though I had nobody. Zoe gone to California; Grayson just gone. I latched on to Shani and Lia a few months later, and it all felt so easy. We didn't talk about anything depressing or serious. There was no fighting or crying or counting going on. We hung out at the mall and ate a lot of French fries together and did normal, non-dramatic things.

And when I got sick of spending my weekends visiting my brother in the hospital, I could go to Shani's house, no questions asked. And I'd vent about my brother for a few minutes, and then we'd do something stupid to take my mind off it, and eventually it was almost like he didn't even exist.

I felt a twinge of guilt over having ignored their text messages, and resolved that I would call as soon as we got on the road. Try to catch Shani in between school and dance practice. Tell her I was okay and that, yeah, it was true. *I did what they're all saying I did. I'm a horrible person. But you don't hate me, right?* Somehow I knew Shani would forgive me anyway, which made me miss her all the more. And made me feel all the more guilty for holding out on her just because she wasn't Zoe. I'd never given her the chance to be.

I was so lost in my memories, I barely even noticed that Buddy and Rena had stood up and were standing outside the garage, talking, my tire reinflated and propped up against Rena's leg. I hurried out to join them, my stomach growling.

Buddy wouldn't let me pay for the tire. Said he was doing it as a favor for "his girl." She kissed him on the cheek and we were walking again, heading back to the motel.

"You and Buddy are really cute together," I told her.

She blushed. "Yeah?"

I nodded. "I think so." We walked a few paces. "So how'd you end up with Archie, anyway?" I asked, as we worked together to push the fixed tire up a hill.

"Just happened, I guess," she said. Our feet scuffed against the pebbles on the road, and the sounds of rocks clicking against one another made me think of Grayson. I wondered if he was awake yet. "I was sort of homeless when I came through here. My boyfriend Sal took off one day. Gone. And his roommate Jonah kicked me out. Real easy, you know? Like I never existed. He was all, 'Rena, you're hot and all, but I ain't gonna pay for your ass,' which didn't surprise me because Jonah spent most of his paychecks on meth, anyway." She stopped, stood up straight, placed her hands on the small of her back, and stretched backward, looking off into space, like she was seeing Jonah's face out there somewhere. Or maybe Sal's. After a while she shrugged and bent forward, and we started rolling again.

"What a jerk."

"I know. I really loved Sal, you know? So I was, like, crushed. And I didn't have anywhere to go. I wasn't going back to my mom and stepdad's. No way. So one night I ended up at the motel and...I don't know...Archie let me stay there for free. It was really nice of him. He was a lot nicer then. Or at least I thought he was. He talked to me a lot back then."

"So it was like love at first sight?"

Rena laughed. "Uh, no. Archie isn't much to look at. It was more like love at first missed period." She giggled again, but I kept my head down and kept pushing the tire. "So what about you?" she asked, and I nearly tripped.

Of course this would come up. Of course she would ask me why I was running away. And since she'd shared her story with me, of course she'd expect me to share mine with her. I was so stupid for asking.

"What about me, what?" I asked, practically choking from trying to keep my voice light.

"Do you have a boyfriend?"

My legs actually tingled with relief. "No," I said. "I did. Tommy. He was great for a while, but he turned out to be a real jerk. One of those football hero kinds of guys that like to pick on pretty much everyone else. Total stereotype." *Also*, I didn't add, *the kind of guy who blackmails his girlfriend*. "I dumped him a few months ago and kind of swore off guys for a while."

"Smart girl," she said.

Smart. I thought about the mess I'd left behind at school. "I don't know about that," I said. "I've done some pretty dumb things."

"Haven't we all?" she answered. She hesitated, then continued. "So, your brother. Is he, like, messed up or something?"

How many times in my life had I been asked that? *What's wrong with your brother? What's the deal with your brother? What happened to your brother?* And every time I was asked, I always thought of my mom holding down the dampened sides of my hair, looking at me earnestly in the mirror.

"He's got some difficulties," I answered. "He's a good guy. This trip is really going to help him. But don't say anything to him about us going to see our friend in California. That part's a surprise." Then, desperate to change the subject, I said, "You know, you and Buddy would make a cute couple."

She smiled wide and glanced at me. "You think?"

"Definitely. He's adorable. And he likes you a lot. You should go for it."

Her face clouded up. "Nah. Not here. Archie would never give us any peace. You have no idea what Archie…It doesn't matter. It's nice to daydream about it, though."

We crested the hill and stopped, both of us panting. Our hair lay limp with sweat and we had road dust on our backs, so only wisps of it took flight when the wind gusted. I sat on the tire. Rena crouched, pulling her finger in circles in the dust.

"I'll bet California will be amazing," she said.

I looked out toward the horizon, as though I could see California from there if I just looked hard enough.

"Yeah," I said.

"I would love to go to California," she said. "Maybe Archie'll take me and Bo someday." She traced a heart shape with her finger, then scooched her foot forward and obliterated it. "Hey, maybe I'll look you up when we get there, huh?"

"Yeah. Okay," I said, pushing away the obvious thought, which was that I had no earthly idea where we'd be by the time she got to California. That was the part I still had to figure out. That was the part I needed Zoe for.

She drew a sun, childlike, with rays poking out of it at all angles, then stood up and wiped her hands on her jeans again. Somehow the jeans managed to still look clean, despite all the grime she'd wiped on them throughout the day. It was as if Rena couldn't not look shiny.

I stood up and took a deep breath. "Ready?" I said.

"Yep!" she said. "I gotta get back before Bo wakes up. That boy does nothing but eat."

We started down the hill toward the motel, which was sprawled out below, talking about babies and Buddy and the beach and pretty much anything else we could think of.

And, even more important, *not* talking about school and rocks and the Hayward Fault and OCD.

CHAPTER
EIGHTEEN

When we got back to the motel, Rena ducked right inside the office while I rolled the tire to our room and leaned it against Hunka. I decided Grayson could help me put it back on. He would balk, of course. It would be "too dirty" or "too dangerous," and if I were Mom, I'd give in and do it myself. Which was exactly why I was going to make him help me. It would help him get better, just like I'd told Rena this trip would do. Just like I'd been telling myself.

But when I opened the door, Grayson wasn't there.

"Gray?" I called, glancing around, trying to let my eyes adjust to the dark room. I checked in the bathroom. No Grayson. I checked in the closet. No Grayson. "Grayson?" I called again, like he could be hiding under the bed or in the night table drawer with the Bible or something.

I practically flew out of the room, my heart racing. Where on earth could he have gone? It wasn't as if he could have driven anywhere. Maybe he called a taxi and was headed back home right at this moment. Did they have taxis in this town? Doubtful. Plus, Grayson couldn't handle germs when he was anxious. There's no way he'd sit in the back of a taxi for however many hours it would take to get home.

I raced to Hunka and peered in the back window. No Grayson.

It didn't make sense. He had to be around here somewhere.

Oh, God. If something happened to him, Mom and Dad would never forgive me. Forget my stupid school troubles. I'd kidnapped my brother and lost him. That was way worse than failing any stupid calc class.

I practically sprinted down the sidewalk to the office, my sneaker accidentally connecting with the cow skull and sending it skittering in two pieces across the mud patch that was meant to be lawn. My throat felt tight and I was totally panicked.

Just as I was about to pull open the door, Rena stepped out of it.

"Bo's still asl—Hey, what's wrong?" she asked.

"Is my brother in there?" I asked, gesturing at the office door behind her.

"Your brother? Uh-uh. Why?"

"Are you sure?" I asked, trying to press down the panic creeping up my throat.

She looked startled. "Yeah. Positive," she said. "Archie's

asleep in the recliner and Bo's still napping. Your brother's missing?"

I nodded miserably. "Omigod," I whispered. I put my hands on my hips and paced up and down the sidewalk.

"Maybe he got hungry and went to look for something to eat," she said, which seemed entirely possible, since it was the first thing I'd wanted to do after waking up, too.

"Maybe," I said. "But he doesn't have any money. And besides, Grayson never leaves the house. Not unless it's to go to the hospital or to the qu—" I stopped in my tracks. "Do you have any big rock beds around here?"

Rena's face crinkled curiously. "Rock beds?"

"Yeah," I said. "Rock beds. Like, landscaping. Or a ... I don't know ... a pile of rocks. Or a place that sells rocks or something. Just ... any place where there are lots of rocks?"

She thought it over, clearly confused, then brightened. "The gazebo," she said. "C'mon."

She led me around the side of the office, past an old, defunct ice machine and a stack of mattresses riddled with holes, and through a gate, half torn off its hinges.

"Back here," she said.

We walked through what once must have been a little courtyard, formed by three buildings that looked identical to the ones facing the highway, only these rooms were mostly boarded up.

In the courtyard was a tire swing and slide, an empty and severely cracked swimming pool, and a gazebo with holes the size of doughnuts in the roof. All around the gazebo was what must have once been landscaping—a rock bed dotted with dead shrubs and crumbling statuaries.

We circled the gazebo, and there, on the back side, squeezed between two shrubs and a creepy-looking angel statue, sat my brother.

"There he is," Rena said, pointing. "What's he doing?"

"Counting," I said, relief flooding me. "And sorting."

Which was exactly what he'd been doing. There weren't that many rocks left in the bed. Grayson had created four or five mounds of them in front of him, his lips moving feverishly.

I sat down on the grass a few feet away from him, my legs crossed, Indian-style, and rested my forehead in my hands, trying not to cry as the stress melted off me. He glanced up at me and then went right back to work.

"You okay?" Rena asked. Her voice was soft, and I suddenly felt bad for getting her into my family's mess.

"Yeah," I said, rubbing my hands down the sides of my face without even thinking about the grease and grime that had accumulated on them from rolling the tire. "I'm not sure..." I didn't know how to finish the sentence. What I'd wanted to say was, *I'm not sure I'm doing the right thing.* But I couldn't say it aloud. Because the truth was, it'd been so long since I'd been doing the right thing, I wasn't even sure if I knew what the right thing was anymore.

She stood there for a long time, very still. Grayson had stopped mumbling, but I could still hear the rattle of the rocks hitting one another. Finally, I heard a scrape of fabric on the ground and looked up to see Rena lowering herself to the ground, facing Grayson.

He ignored her. Probably didn't even realize she was there. But unlike most people, Rena didn't seem bothered much by Grayson being in Grayson's own world. She didn't get squirmy or insist on small talk or make fun of him. She just sat there, cross-legged, and watched him. She was very still and her head was cocked to one side, almost like she thought she might be able to figure him out.

After a long while, she picked up a rock.

"This one's pretty," she said. "I wonder what it's called."

"That's gypsum," Grayson mumbled, so quietly it was almost like he hadn't spoken at all. He didn't look up, either, which made his words seem all the more ghostly.

"Huh?" Rena asked, leaning forward.

"Gypsum," he said, louder, glancing up at her. And then when she still didn't seem to understand, he added, "You know, the stuff they make fertilizer out of."

"Ew," Rena said, and dropped the rock.

"It's not poop," Grayson said, giving his eyes a condescending roll. "They also make plaster of paris out of it."

Rena sat still for a minute, then picked up another rock. "What's this one?" she asked.

Grayson pushed his glasses up on his nose and peered at the rock in her hand. He seemed to think it over, whether or not he wanted to get into this conversation. Talking about rocks was something he loved to do, but he would have to stop counting and sorting them in order to do it. It would be a tough choice for him. Counting and sorting was his comfort, and he loved it. "Well," he said, taking the rock from her gently. "It's a sandstone. But look here— there's some feldspar in it. Ever heard of sunstone?"

Rena shook her head.

"Hmm. Well, feldspar is sunstone. And moonstone. You know, like jewelry. Sandstone is a sedimentary rock, mainly created in, you know, deserts and stuff, and usually it's got quartz in it."

"Whoa. How do you know all this?"

"He's a genius," I said, my head still in my hands. I could only imagine what Grayson was thinking. Rena was nice but didn't seem to be that smart, and sometimes my brother had a low tolerance for people who weren't as smart as he was.

"And I found this one, too," he said, pulling a rock out of the bottom of one of his piles, not even seeming to notice when the rocks on top of it came tumbling down. He handed it to Rena.

"That's pretty. What is it?"

"Mica," he said. "See those lines in there?" He reached out and pointed at the rock. "Those are cleavage lines. If you were to hit one of those planes, the rock would break along the line. Micas have perfect cleavage, meaning they break into perfect sheets."

Rena giggled. "I used to have perfect cleavage before Bo was born." But when Grayson didn't respond, her smile faded. "Joke," she muttered, pink creeping up into the tops of her ears. "Sorry."

But Grayson acted the way Grayson always acted—as if he hadn't heard a thing. Everything in his world was centered on the rock piles in front of him. He was happy, even if for just a few minutes.

After a while, Rena turned around to face me. *He okay?* she mouthed, turning her palms up in her lap. I nodded wearily. *Yeah, he's okay.* As okay as he'd ever be, I guessed.

"I've gotta get that tire back on," I said to nobody in particular. I pushed myself up off the ground and wiped my palms across the seat of my jeans, flicking off dead leaves and little bits of spring grass. "Soon as I'm done, we're leaving. We'll get some breakfast." I craned my neck to see around Rena, but Grayson didn't look up. Even though I'd told myself I wasn't going to do things Mom's way, I just didn't have the energy to make him help me. Better to just do it myself and leave him to what he was doing rather than fight with him.

"I'll help," Rena said, hopping up. "If..." She let the sentence unravel but gave a lingering look behind her.

I nodded. He would be fine. As long as he had rocks, he'd be just dandy.

As soon as we turned the corner of the building, she said, "Your brother's difficulties...is he, like, retarded or something?"

I shook my head. I'd gotten this question a lot. Also, *Is*

he autistic? Is he a serial killer? And the ever-popular *Dude, what's his problem?* "He has OCD," I said. "He's fine. He didn't used to be this bad. He's been worse...lately. He relaxes around rocks."

No sooner had we turned the corner into the parking lot than Bo's cries started to float across to us from the office.

"Oh," Rena said, startled. "Sorry."

"Not a problem," I said. "Thanks for helping me as much as you did. And thanks for, you know...for not laughing at my brother."

She made a confused face. "He's nice."

She had me there. Sometimes I got so wrapped up in my frustration with Grayson that I forgot he was actually a really nice guy. He hardly ever said anything mean about anyone, probably because he knew what it felt like to be on the receiving end of insults. I'd known people with brothers who were horrible. Brothers who would torment them. Brothers who would call them names, embarrass them in front of their friends. Grayson would never do any of that. I was really lucky.

Would he be able to say the same about me?

"Well, thanks anyway."

"Sure. No problem. If I don't see you before you leave, have fun in California. It was nice meeting you."

I smiled, squinting up at her from my crouch beside the tire. "Yeah. Same here," I said.

Bo's cries increased in volume and intensity, and as

Rena started to jog toward the office, Archie's voice blared out, "Dammit, Rena, shut this kid up! He woke me up. Where are you, you stupid bitch?"

Rena didn't look back. I felt a pang of regret for her. In a different life, who knows, she might have made a really great wife and mother.

I lifted the tire onto the car, fitting the screws through the holes in the rim, and then stood, fumbling the lug nuts out of my pocket, ignoring the nagging feeling in the back of my mind that I knew she was in a really crappy situation and I was going to walk away and leave her there.

I tightened the nuts quickly, trembling with guilt about doing nothing to help Rena, and with hunger, and with worry about what would happen if Archie suddenly came bursting outside and came after me. That's the bad thing about running away—the only person keeping you safe is yourself.

As if to punctuate the thought, a crash sounded from the office, followed by the baby's cries. My fingers worked double-time.

It was definitely time to go.

CHAPTER
NINETEEN

"You hungry?" I asked, standing on the little walkway across from where Grayson now sat, a few feet away from where Rena and I had found him earlier, the piles of stones multiplied and neatly stacked around him. My shadow fell over him, long and lean, as if I were far more formidable than I was feeling.

"Not really. Thirsty, though."

"We'll get sodas when we get gas."

Nothing.

"We need to go, Grayson."

"I'm not done."

I tried to wait. I really did. I stood there quietly, listening to the click of the rocks as he placed them in piles. I listened to him murmur each time he dropped one where it was supposed to go. But I was starving. And thirsty. And tired. And impatient. And I could hear Archie and Rena still fighting. I wanted to leave, and as much as I wanted to be patient for my brother, this time I couldn't do it.

I reached down and grabbed him under the armpit, pulling upward. For such a skinny guy, he did seem to pack a bunch of weight into that body. He barely shifted, even when I gave it all my strength. "You'll never be done. Get. Up." I pulled again, this time jiggling his arm up against one of the rock piles. The rocks tumbled down in a mini-avalanche.

"Kendra!" he complained, scrabbling with his fingertips to get the rocks back in place. "You can't just..." But he was too busy grabbing and stacking, grabbing and stacking to finish his sentence.

I wiped my forehead on the back of my hand, feeling wobbly and sick to my stomach. Why had I thought this would be easy?

"Come on," I whined. "I'm so hungry I'm gonna throw up. Let's just get on the road, get some food and gas, and..." This time it was my turn to trail off, because I didn't know what to say next.... *And get to Zoe?* I couldn't say that. Grayson would flip out.

He didn't get up, but his hands stopped digging through the rock bed, and I saw his eyes flick up toward me briefly.

"Please?" I asked, crouching down so we were face-level. "I need you to do this for me, Grayson," I said. I felt tears coming, and I knew my low blood sugar was going to start making me emotional. "I know it's hard," I practically whispered. "But you can do it."

He sighed and opened his fingers, the half dozen or so

rocks he had in his palms trickling to the ground with little clicks. I closed my eyes and smiled, said a hasty prayer of thanks.

We could hear Archie yelling in the office—calling Rena names, with little metallic bangs and crashes as punctuation. Bo's cries got louder with every crash, and Rena's voice ratcheted up, sounding thin and shaky over the boom of Archie's rage. I glanced over my shoulder, as if I could see into the office from the dilapidated courtyard. I wanted to run into the office, dive behind the curtained area, and yank both Bo and Rena out of there. But I could only save so many people at once. Starting with myself.

When I turned back to Grayson, I noticed his eyes were turned toward the office as well, his face grim. "We should go," he said, and slowly stood up.

Relief washed over me and I jumped up, wrapping my arms around him and leaning my cheek into his chest. He felt stiff and awkward beneath my hug, but I didn't care. He'd listened to me. He'd broken his spell of counting.

Even if it was only this one time, at least I had this once.

I released him, then hooked my arm through his and led him down the walkway, back toward the parking lot. But after a few steps, I stopped.

"Take your shirt off," I said.

He wrinkled his nose. "What? No. Why?"

"Just do it," I said, holding my hand out and bouncing it impatiently. Something broke in the office and we both glanced that way.

142

"No. I'm not giving you my shirt," he said. He crossed his arms over his chest.

"Why does everything have to be difficult with you?" I grumbled. "Fine. You won't take yours off? I'll use mine. Look away or prepare to be grossed out." I crossed my arms at the wrists and grabbed the hem of my shirt and started lifting. Grayson looked panicked.

"Okay, okay!" he shouted. "Stop! Here." He whipped his shirt over his head and handed it to me, then quickly crossed one arm over his chest, his hand tucked into the armpit of his other arm. "You have really lost it, Kendra."

I took the shirt and jogged back to the gazebo. I laid it out on the ground and bent to one knee. Quickly, before Grayson could start freaking out about his half-naked state and how that could most certainly equal some sort of freakish skin disease that would lead to his death if he didn't count to eleventy bazillion, I grabbed handfuls of the rocks he'd been organizing and tossed them into the middle of his shirt. Two, four, six big handfuls, and the rocks were overflowing. I stood and folded the edges of the shirt in, making a pouch for the rocks, and picked it up.

"Come on," I said, breezing past him, dribbling rocks onto the ground in our wake. One broke when it hit the ground, and despite myself I glanced back to see if it was one of those rocks with the perfect cleavage he'd been talking about.

Grayson didn't say a word. He followed me to the car, where I opened up the passenger door and let one end of the T-shirt go, raining rocks onto Hunka's floorboard.

"There," I said, shaking the dirt off his shirt and holding it out to him. "You can take them with you."

Grayson stood immobile for a few minutes, looking at the shirt in my hand as if he didn't recognize it. For a second I worried that his germ fixation would kick in and he'd refuse to take it from me. But he seemed to be more amused than anything, the corners of his mouth twitching toward what might have been a grin for a normal person.

"Rena won't mind," I said.

Finally, he reached out and took the shirt, wriggling into it. "Let's eat," he said, easing his feet into his new portable rock bed and pulling the door closed behind him.

For the first time in forever, I finally felt like I had things under control. I'd changed a tire myself. I'd gotten Grayson out of the rocks. I'd even gotten him to smile.

I'd gotten us through a whole night and most of a state, and I'd get us through a whole lot more before this trip was over.

Because I'd done it my way, and my way was working.

CHAPTER
TWENTY

I took the road back into town, remembering the couple of restaurants I'd seen on the way to Buddy's. At the time, the lots had both been pretty full. Even people who farm all their groceries must like a place to grab a sandwich every now and then.

We pulled past the garage—Buddy standing out front, twisting a car part between two blue towels, as he had been before—and past an old trailer converted into some sort of used lawn mower store. The place looked cluttered and filthy, as if a wet rag hadn't been taken to it in years. Grayson would have a meltdown if I even so much as pulled into the parking lot.

We kept going, passing a warehouse-like building with farm equipment displayed on the lawn in front, and a tiny house with antiques crowding the front porch. A faded flag was nailed to the beam framing the front porch: OPEN.

"Hash and Dash or Edwina's?" I asked, slowing as we neared the only stoplight in town—a flashing yellow light.

Grayson frowned. "They both look disgusting. Look at the front windows on that one. They're so greasy you can't see through them."

My stomach growled. "They're food, Grayson. We've got to eat. So which'll it be? Hash and Dash has more cars in its parking lot. Maybe it's better than Edwina's."

"Or the customers were so sick with botulism they all left in ambulances."

I snorted, glancing at my brother. He was smiling, too. A full-on smile. I hadn't heard Grayson crack a joke in a long, long time.

"Edwina's it is," I said, and swung Hunka into the gravel parking lot.

Edwina's smelled even greasier than the windows suggested. The scent of burger grease made my stomach growl so hard it cramped. I hugged myself as I slid into the first booth.

Grayson kind of hovered by the edge of the table. To a passerby, he might have looked like someone who was lost deep in thought, but my trained eye caught the tapping— one finger against the sticky Formica tabletop. I could see his lips moving as he silently counted to whatever number was the one that would let him sit down.

I pressed my lips together and looked around the restaurant as though I didn't notice, giving Grayson room to preemptively save our lives in his head. After all, he'd left the rock bed for me. He'd taken off his shirt for me. He'd even smiled. I owed him a moment. Was this how Mom felt every day, dealing with my brother? Like she owed him moments with his disorder because he had tried to get better for her? I ignored a thought that was trying to edge its way into my brain—that by not asking him to help put the tire back on and letting him bring the rocks and letting him stand next to the table and count, I was being just like Mom, and if I was going to give in to him, this was never going to work. I couldn't think that way. I'd give myself a few minutes to rest, and then I'd get right back on the program with him.

There were a handful of diners peppered throughout the cafeteria, mostly old men in snap-front shirts and base-ball caps, their bloated and cracked fingers gripping coffee mugs as they talked about politics and weather. A single waitress stood back behind the cash register, scratching her ankle with the toe of her other foot and leaning over the counter to whisper to a woman on the other side. The woman was holding a toddler's hand but was totally unaware that the little boy was using a crayon to draw all over the front of the counter.

Nobody seemed to even notice us, and for the first time since leaving school, I felt like I could relax a little bit. Our problems couldn't follow us here.

After a while, Grayson sat down, skewed over to one side, like he didn't want his whole butt to touch the booth. He gazed at his hands.

"I need to wash my hands," he said. He held his fingers

up for me. The undersides of his fingernails were caked with dirt from digging in the rock bed.

I pointed toward the back of the restaurant. "Restroom's over there."

He started to get up and hesitated. I knew what he was thinking. He couldn't make himself use a public restroom. He hadn't used one of those since he was nine. Even at school, he'd go all day long without going into the boys' bathroom. This meant, of course, that he couldn't eat lunch, because he couldn't wash off the *billions of microscopic germs that you can't see but will kill you as dead as any gun will kill you, Kendra.* One of his favorite germaphobe lectures.

He didn't say anything. But he knew that I knew exactly what was going on in his mind. He was probably waiting for me to say something first, but I was determined to act as though everything was fine and normal. This is what Mom needed to do more often. See? I wasn't acting like her at all. Momentary lapse, that was all.

I reached over and grabbed a laminated menu from behind the napkin dispenser, as if I were clueless. I held it up in front of my face. It was still early, but I really wanted lunch. "Mmm," I said, "grilled cheese..."

After a few seconds, Grayson slowly slid out of the booth. I peeked over the top of my menu, just in time to see him pull open the restroom door.

Good job, Gray, I said to myself, going back to my menu. Mom would've been bawling with pride. I was just hoping I was doing the right thing and wasn't messing him up even worse than before.

"You decide yet?" I heard, and looked up to see the frizzy-haired waitress standing over me. "You eatin'?" she said, raising her eyebrows at me. She held a coffeepot in one hand, and had it propped against her hip, which looked soft under her worn checkered dress.

"Oh, um," I said. "Yeah. Bring us a couple grilled cheese and some fries? And two milk shakes. Chocolate."

She nodded but didn't say another word. She wandered to the table of farmers across from me and started filling their cups. "So, Darrell, I heard them cows got loose ..." she said, and I hoped by the time she got done gossiping about livestock, she didn't forget my order.

My stomach growled again, and I ripped open a pack of sugar and tipped it up into my mouth. The taste was so sweet and wonderful, my jaw tightened up, making it almost painful. I closed my eyes and pushed the sugar up against the roof of my mouth with my tongue, feeling it grind along the ridges of my palate.

"Kendra," I heard, and opened my eyes again. Grayson was making his way across the restaurant, holding his pink wet hands up so they were dripping onto his shoulders. I tipped the sugar packet up over my mouth again, emptying it. "Kendra. We need to go."

"What? No. I already ordered. Why?"

He dropped one hand and pressed his fingertip onto the corner of the table. And then again. And again. "There's no hot water in the restroom," he said. "We can't eat here. And I saw a bug on the tile under the urinal." *Press. Press. Press.*

I laid my hand over his finger, pressing it down hard enough to make him stop. He recoiled from me—I'm sure my germy hand had undone all of his hand washing in that one touch.

"Sit down," I said as calmly and slowly as I could. Zoe had a way of talking to Grayson when he was ramping up into a panic. Very soft, very slow, very matter-of-fact. It always worked. Though maybe it only worked because it was Zoe doing the talking. But it was worth a try. "People are going to start looking at you."

"I can't," he practically whined. "There's no hot water in the restroom. You should never eat at a restaurant where there's no hot water in the restroom. That's basic. The cooks' hands are probably teeming with bacteria. We could get hepatitis."

"Thank you, Professor Poop, for that information. My mouth is really watering now," I said. "Look. We could eat here or we could starve. And I swear I'm about to. I can't drive until I get something to eat. So hot water or no hot water, I'm eating."

As if on cue, the waitress brought our milk shakes—two empty glasses and two frosted metal containers. Her hands were still on my milk shake when I started to pick it up. She left, eyeing Grayson cautiously, just like everyone always did, and I poured myself a glass.

I remembered the time Grayson had made Zoe and me milk shakes. It was summer break, and our moms had gone shopping together, leaving Grayson in charge. By then Grayson and Zoe had already declared their love, had already kissed (once, in the garage, crouched behind Dad's riding lawn mower so I wouldn't see, though Zoe told me all about it later when I spent the night at her house), but our parents didn't know it.

They'd spent most of the afternoon being inseparable, for once not having to hide their feelings for each other. Zoe sat on Grayson's lap while we watched *Full House* reruns, and I watched, feeling totally alone, as Grayson used his finger to draw little invisible designs on Zoe's shoulder, which was bare except for where the spaghetti strap of her tank top cut through her tan. They giggled. They whispered. They'd built a whole little world that no longer included me, and were spending the day immersed in it.

And I couldn't help myself. I got jealous. I pouted, sitting on the couch, ramrod-straight, my arms crossed and my legs crossed and a scowl on my face. I hoped that our moms would walk in and catch them together, and that they'd get in trouble and they'd regret leaving me out.

So eventually when they noticed I wasn't talking and they asked what was wrong, I told them. "When our moms get home, I'm going to tell them that you two were making out the whole time." I gave them a haughty little smile, my head tipped to one side.

Zoe's face clouded, and I knew she was instantly mad. She and Grayson exchanged looks.

"But we haven't been," Grayson said.

"So?" I shot back.

"So why would you do that?" Grayson asked.

Zoe cocked her head to one side to match mine. "Because she's jealous."

"No," I shouted, standing up. "Because you're acting disgusting. I don't want to see my brother with his tongue shoved down your ear."

Zoe jumped up off Grayson's lap. "He wasn't!" she yelled. "You're lying!"

"Practically!" I yelled back, but before we could get too out of control, Grayson stood between us.

"You guys, stop. Ken," he said, putting his hand on my shoulder. "You're right. We've been ignoring you. We're sorry."

Zoe made a noise and rolled her eyes. I glared at her.

"Don't be mad," he said.

And we all stood there, the air thick with silence around us. It was the first time—the only time—there were two of us against one. And the realization had hit me. If we were forced to pick one person to be with now, I would be the one to be alone. They would choose each other over me. Which seemed so unfair. I was the one in the bassinet next to hers in the hospital nursery, not Grayson. I was the one who played card games with her and hung out at the slides with her on the school playground and shared my markers with her. Not Grayson. But I knew if it ever came down to taking sides...it wasn't my side that either of them would ever take.

I let out a breath. "I won't tell," I said. "But stop ignoring me, okay?"

Zoe still looked put out, but Grayson brightened. "I can do better than that," he said. "I'll make milk shakes."

And we'd gone into the kitchen and Grayson had gotten out the chocolate ice cream and the milk, and even though we had to wait for nearly half an hour for him to wash his hands properly, and even though he sweated and worried and took forever to get scoops that were the same exact size and an even number, it was good. He'd laughed along with us when we teased him for having to press the button on the blender over and over again to get to the right number of presses. He'd smiled as he turned his glass in his hand over and over again, wiping smudges away with a towel.

He was sick, even then. Sick as he ever was. But he was still somehow relaxed. He was still somehow okay, as long as Zoe was there to overlook those things.

Back in the booth, I remembered that day, and remembered how he was with Zoe. That was exactly why we needed to get to her. Zoe was able to do something for Grayson that nobody else could: accept him for who he was. Laugh and have fun with him. Love him. Make him relax. She was able to do what I only wished I could. She would never try to cure him. She'd only try to make herself understand him better. I was his sister. I was his blood. So why couldn't I do that?

"Mmm," I said, feeling the shake slide all the way down into my belly. "You should sit down. This is delicious." But Grayson continued to stand by the table. *Press. Press. Press.* Again. Like he hadn't just done this a few minutes ago. But I told myself I was too blissed out on my shake to care. I needed this.

I gulped some more, feeling the pang of brain freeze behind my right eye. I knew I was making slurping and moaning noises, but I couldn't help myself. It felt like it'd been days since I'd last eaten. My stomach started to feel squishy on the inside, as though if I didn't slow down I was going to bring it all back up.

After a while, Grayson's finger-pressing slowed down, then stopped, and he slid into his side of the booth again. I didn't say anything, didn't call attention, even when he lifted his metal cup and drank directly from it.

A few minutes later, the waitress brought our sandwiches, and I dove into mine, taking huge bites and closing my eyes while I chewed. Grayson counted his French fries, tearing the last one in two, and lining them up in order of smallest to largest on his plate. He picked up his napkin and used it to shield the sandwich from his fingers, then took a tentative bite. And then another. And another. And soon we were both tearing into our food, a comfortable silence stretched between us.

"Do Mom and Dad know where we are?" Grayson said at last, as I leaned back against the booth, little greedy burps escaping me. I felt my face grow hot. I didn't answer him. "Tell me," he said.

"I had Brock lie," I answered. "But she figured it out right away."

Grayson stopped chewing. "You had Brock lie?"

I nodded. "I needed time to get us some distance. It was all I could think of. He wants you to call him, by the way. Something about Zombiesplosion."

My brother looked down at the sandwich in his hand, his expression grave. Then, slowly, the gravity gave way and he chuckled. "Oh my God," he said. "They are freaking out right now. You know that, don't you? You have to know that."

I belched again, this time feeling icky grease sliding up and down my throat. I swallowed uncomfortably and nodded. "I know. I'm trying not to think about it. Which, by the way, you're not making easy."

"Maybe we should call and tell them we're okay."

I shook my head, my throat straining against the food now. "I can't."

He leaned forward, his grease-stained napkin shivering above his plate. "We could go home."

I shook my head again. "Listen, I don't like lying to Mom, either," I said. "But I can't go home. Okay? I can't. You're just going to have to trust me."

"Why not? You think you're going to save me or run away from my OCD or whatever, but...I don't get it,

Kendra. I've been this way my whole life. Why is it so important to you all of a sudden to make me better?"

"It's not all about you," I said miserably, and the rest of the words piled up in my throat, threatening to spill out in one big yell if he didn't stop pressing me. I wanted to beg him to stop asking. To leave it alone. To please just go along with this one thing. Instead, all I could do was hold it back as well as I could and let out a strained, "I can't."

"Yes you can. Just turn the car around and go back the way we came. Every day that we're out here and Mom and Dad are freaking out, you're going to get into more trouble, and—"

The more he talked, the more I felt pressure build up in me. He didn't know why I couldn't go back. He didn't understand that there were parts of this trip that weren't about him. He couldn't have known, couldn't have understood, because I hadn't shared those things with him. I couldn't share them. And knowing that, in a sense, I was in this all by myself was too much. Panic rose, beating behind my eyeballs, until I couldn't hold it back any longer.

I tossed my napkin onto my plate. "I just can't, okay? I can't! Because I'm already in trouble," I shouted. Grayson sat back against the booth, surprised, and several of the old men looked up at me, their coffee mugs suspended in mid-air. "Excuse me," I said, feeling tears crowding my eyes. I scooted out of the booth and raced toward the restroom, leaving Grayson at the table alone.

I suppose a part of me knew that I wasn't going to be

able to keep my secret forever, but I wished I'd gotten to keep it for longer than this.

But there was no doubt in my mind...after that outburst, my brother was definitely going to have questions for me.

And I was going to have to answer them.

CHAPTER
TWENTY-ONE

I felt much better after splashing a few handfuls of cold water on my face. The food had settled in my stomach, and I no longer felt like I was going to burp up an entire grilled cheese sandwich every time I opened my mouth.

I could only imagine what Grayson must be thinking back at our table. Nobody ever yelled at Grayson — it was part of the benefit of being "perpetually sick." People don't yell at you because yelling might make you sicker — so I'm sure blowing up at him in the middle of a diner really rocked his world. God, I was so screwing this up. I wasn't an expert or anything, but yelling at and then ditching someone with OCD in a strange, grubby restaurant booth was probably not what anyone ever meant by exposure therapy.

I scooted into an empty stall and sat down on the toilet, holding my head in my hands and taking some deep breaths. I'd told him I was in trouble. Of course he was going to have questions. But was I ready to answer them?

"Okay, Zo," I said, my voice echoing off the metal stall walls. "Remember that time in seventh grade we decided to sneak into the country club swimming pool after it closed? And someone saw us and called the police?"

I chuckled. When the cops had rolled into the parking lot, we knew we were in deep trouble. Our parents had thought we were upstairs in Zoe's bedroom watching movies. We were sure the police officer would make us go back and tell our parents and we'd be so busted. Probably grounded for life.

"But you talked your way out of it, Zo, remember? You convinced the police officer that we had been in the bathroom when the pool closed and that we got locked in. You even cried." I wiped my face, grinning. "God, you were brilliant."

And she was. We'd simply walked back home as if nothing ever happened, our swimsuits balled up and dripping in our purses, and none of our parents ever found out.

"So how do I talk my way out of this one?" I asked the empty stall. I strained to hear an answer, even though I knew none would come. "Yeah. I didn't think so."

After gathering my thoughts, I washed up and wandered back out into the dining room. Grayson was actually still eating, pushing fries into his mouth one at a time, taking each in exactly two bites.

There was a slip of paper facedown on the table. I

flipped it over, trying not to notice that the waitress was eyeing me intently. She chewed a thumbnail while she watched me, her eyes slitted as though she expected me to make a run for it.

I rummaged through my purse, feeling a pang of guilt when my hand brushed against my turned-off cell phone. I could only imagine how many messages and texts were on there now. I'd promised myself I would listen to them. That I'd text Shani and apologize and give her answers, tell her why I'd used her. But the more time that went by without my acknowledging that the world I'd left behind was buzzing angrily, the harder it would be to say anything at all. The idea of talking to Mom made my heart beat faster. The thought of texting Shani the truth about what was going on made my palms sweat. It was so much easier to continue pretending that I was the good girl when I wasn't getting a front-row ticket to how I'd ruined everything, courtesy of phone and text.

When did this happen? When did I turn into this person who runs away? Had I always been? I'd always thought of myself as someone in control. But maybe that wasn't who I was at all. Had I gotten so used to letting Zoe do the talking and letting Grayson get the attention, that the only thing I knew how to do was not be there? Or was it that I was always so busy being perfect, things never got tough for me?

I pulled out my wallet and slipped Mom's credit card out, then took the slip of paper and the card to the checkout. The waitress took both without saying a word, and peered at the card.

"You got ID?" she asked. She turned her head to the side and spit a fingernail onto the floor.

"Uh, sure," I said. "Hang on." I took the few steps back to our table and grabbed my purse, pulling out my driver's license as I made my way back to the counter. I held it out, trying my hardest not to touch the waitress's hand while passing it to her. She had chewed a hangnail and it was bleeding. Grayson was right; this place was disgusting. But I wasn't going to tell him that. If he survived eating at Edwina's, he'd survive pretty much anything I could throw at him during this trip. At least that's what I was hoping for.

She peered at my license, and then shoved it back into my hand. "The names don't match," she said.

"That's my mom," I answered, pointing at the card.

She held the card out as well, and I noticed another of her fingernails was bleeding. Gross. "We don't take credit cards unless you got the right ID." She dropped the card onto the counter. "Sorry. Policy. Cash only."

I looked around. "I don't see a sign saying that," I argued. I could feel my ears get hot. All of a sudden it seemed as if nothing was going to go right on this trip, and I wanted to stomp my feet and pout and cry and demand what I wanted, even though I knew it would get me nowhere.

"I'm saying it right now," she said, and I noticed that her ears looked red, as if they were hot, too. "Cash only."

"Fine." I sighed. "Why not? It's not like it ever has to be

easy," I grumbled, and, as if to punctuate my fury, I heard Grayson's telltale *uh-uh-uh* in the background. I threw up my hands exasperatedly. "Of course!" I grabbed the card off the counter and turned on my heel.

"Grayson," I whispered, slapping my purse down on the booth seat. "You sure you don't have any money?"

"Positive," he said, looking alarmed. "Why? We can't pay for this?"

"You're positive?" I grilled him. I rooted through my purse, even though I knew there was almost no cash left in there, as if some miracle might have happened overnight and my emergency fifty might have reappeared.

He turned his hands, palms up, on the table. "Where would I be hiding it?" *Uh-uh-uh.*

I zipped my purse shut with such force, the zipper pull came off in my hand. I tossed it onto the table and held my face in my hands, thinking.

"We can't pay for this?" Grayson repeated, and when I didn't answer, his voice notched up and got a little squealy. "What're we gonna do, then, Kendra?"

"Let me think, okay?" I said into my palms. I could feel eyes on me, coming from all corners of the restaurant. Especially from behind me, where the waitress stood at the register, no doubt ready to call the police if Grayson and I bolted.

"This was such a stupid idea," Grayson muttered, then followed it with *uh-uh-uh-uh.* "I can't believe you would just run away across the country without any money."

"Say it a little louder next time," I hissed, pulling my hands away from my face. "I don't think they heard you next door."

"This was a stupid plan," Grayson hissed back.

"Well, do you want the police to know we're runaways?"

"Actually, yes. They'll make us go home like I've been trying to get you to do since I woke up halfway across Kansas."

"This isn't just about you, Mister Center of the Universe," I said. "Just. Shut up. Count. Or something. I have money." I couldn't believe I was encouraging him to count, but I needed him to stop talking for ten seconds until we got out of this place.

And I did have money. Lots of it. In my backpack. But I didn't want to use it. I couldn't use it. That cash was the last thing that might save me when we went home again. As long as I still had all the cash in my backpack when we got home, maybe I wouldn't be in quite as much trouble. Without it, I would probably manage to be in even bigger trouble.

But I had no choice. I had to pay for our lunch, or Mrs. Cash Only would definitely call the cops. And I'd have to go home and face the music anyway, and Grayson would still be sick. Maybe sicker. And then this whole thing would've been for nothing. Actually, for worse than nothing, because I'd have only served to make everything worse. I took a deep breath and pulled Hunka's keys out of my pocket. "I'll be right back," I said to Grayson, then said it louder and jiggled my keys at the waitress as I walked past the counter. "I'll be right back."

She didn't answer. Instead, she glared at me, her mouth working a fingernail between her front teeth.

I unlocked Hunka and leaned into the backseat, pulling my backpack to me and unzipping the small front pocket. Inside, curled up in a tight roll, were bills. Tens and fives, but mostly ones. More than three hundred dollars' worth. Just looking at the money sent a wave of guilt over me, but I squashed it down. I ignored images of Bryn and Darian and Tommy pressing the bills into my palm at my locker. Ignored the memory of me standing in a closet and stuffing money hastily into my pocket, my palms sweaty with nerves. I couldn't think of those things right now. I needed to pay for lunch and get back on the road. That was all that mattered right then. Nothing else. I pulled a couple bills off the wad and clenched them in my fist, then turned and walked back into the diner.

"Here," I said to the waitress, shoving the money at her. She held up the bills to peer at the light through them, as if they might be counterfeit, then started pushing buttons on the register. "Come on," I said to my brother. "Grab my purse." He slid out of the booth and walked toward the door, my purse held out in front of him like a sack of garbage.

The waitress crammed my money into the drawer and counted out the change. She dropped the coins into my palm as if it aggrieved her to do so. I closed my fist around the money and shook it a little in the air.

"You would've gotten a tip if you'd let me use the card," I said, then turned and walked out, feeling half vindicated for having told her off for treating me so condescendingly, and half rotten because it wasn't her fault I was in this mess. It wasn't anyone's fault but my own.

Grayson was waiting for me by Hunka, still holding the purse as if it might bite him. I grabbed it out of his hand and tossed it into the seat next to my backpack, then climbed into the car and leaned over to unlock Grayson's door.

He got in just as Hunka roared to life, but put his hand over mine as I clutched the gear shift to get us out of there.

Uh-uh-uh-uh. "We need to talk. What did you mean you're in trouble? Did that Tommy guy get you...?" He trailed off, and even though he was making his throat sound, he looked surprisingly calm. Almost like the old Grayson who made milk shakes in his persnickety way but drank them with a smile.

I licked my lips, trying to figure out how to form the words. He needed to know. I needed to tell him.

"No," I said. "I'm not in that kind of trouble. I'm not pregnant."

"Then I don't get it," he said. "You were at the quarry for no reason. First you say you want to save me. Then you say we're going to the Hayward Fault. And now you say you're in some sort of trouble and that you can't go home. What's the big deal? What could be that bad?"

I swallowed, but didn't know where to begin.

"You remember when that Doug guy kept bothering you at school?" he said.

I looked at him sharply. "Grayson, don't."

But he kept going. "The guy was seriously out of line. Remember?"

I nodded, looking into my lap. Doug Barker was two years older than me. We'd met at a party about six months after Zoe left. He'd hit on me and, even though I'd lied to him and told him I already had a boyfriend, he wouldn't let up. He'd stop by the house on the weekends, show up at the movies when I was there. Constantly trying to get me to go out with him. And when I finally told him that it was never in a million years going to happen, he started saying all these nasty things about me. About my body, mostly. Making it sound as if he'd seen it.

Finally, one night, not sure where else to turn, I knocked on Grayson's door. I told him everything.

The next day, Grayson and Brock waited for Doug in the school parking lot. My brother looked as if he wanted to melt into the concrete, and he kept making that *uh-uh-uh* sound, but when Brock grabbed Doug by the back of the neck and threatened him, Grayson had gathered himself up tall, and they both looked tough. Doug never bothered me again.

"You owe me one," he said. "You said so that day. I'm calling it in."

And I did. I owed him at least one. I'd dragged him into that mess, and now I'd dragged him into this mess. The least I could do was let him know why.

"I cheated," I said. My voice sounded tiny and uncertain, like it might have come from someone else.

"What?"

"My calc semester final. I cheated," I repeated, a little louder. Sounding confident and almost feeling as if I were coming clean, even though I knew I'd only told him part of the story.

"You cheated? Like, how?"

"Someone gave me the answers," I said, also only partially true. "And I used them. And the school found out."

"That's it?" he asked, and my breath got jagged, because part of me really wanted it to be true, that I had cheated and that was it. An even bigger part of me wanted to spill the whole story, but I'd kept it all a secret for so long, the words just would not come out. The part of me that would always remain the Superior Sibling, I guess. The part of me that never messed up, because messing up was what Grayson did. I made the family look good. And part of me couldn't stand the thought of letting that go.

"Yeah, that's it," I said, trying to sound irritated. "I'm going to be in huge trouble. Like, expelled trouble."

"For cheating on a final? I doubt it. You'll probably get ISS, and it'll be over with."

"I wish," I said, remembering Bryn telling me that Chub had been expelled, and how Lia and Shani said that the word was lots of people would be expelled. Getting suspended would be getting off easy, if that was the case. "It doesn't matter now. What's done is done." I put Hunka into gear and started to back out. I could see our waitress kneeling in our booth, an empty milk shake glass in her hand, peering out the window at us, as if she still expected us to do something totally delinquent.

"No," Grayson said, but I backed out anyway. "This is stupid. You're running away because you cheated on a test?"

"It's not just that," I said, pulling out onto the main road again. I turned toward the one gas station I could see. "You wouldn't understand."

"I do understand. I understand that you're running away because of a stupid test." His face started to take on an agitated look, getting red from the bottom up, his eyes getting small and beady. "You're making me...all because of...What are you, Little Miss Perfect now?...It's not right...."

"No, you don't know the whole story, Grayson. Calm down, okay?"

I pulled into the gas station and parked at a pump, ignoring the stares of a woman standing on the other side. Her hair was in curlers and a little boy crouched next to her, making designs in the dust on the ground with his fingers. She watched us pull in and said something to the boy, who looked up and then disappeared into the backseat of her car.

I could only imagine how we looked to strangers—bedraggled and filthy, my bangs still wet from washing my face in the restroom, Grayson red-faced and agitated.

"I don't understand this, Kendra. Why are you doing something so stupid for such a dumb reason?" He was not going to let this go easily. I was going to have to tell him more, like it or not.

"Because it wasn't only one test, okay?" I said. "It was a whole bunch of them. I've been cheating on them since October. And the administrators know. I'll flunk the class for sure. I'll be lucky if they don't expel me. I'll get kicked out of NHS and God knows what else. And there's no way I'm going to be able to face my teachers again, or Mom and Dad. Everything I've worked for. Everything. Basically, I'm screwed."

I opened the door and stepped out into the soft spring breeze that drifted through the air. I ducked into the backseat and pulled more bills out of my backpack, then palmed my cell phone. I felt so embarrassed. Saying aloud what I'd done humiliated me. Admitting being a cheater made me feel so small.

And I still hadn't told him the whole story.

Straightening up, I took a deep breath and headed toward the clerk in the doorway.

I'm so screwed.

And I am definitely not perfect, big brother. So far from it.

CHAPTER
TWENTY-TWO

When I got back in the car, Grayson was working the toes of his shoes in the rocks on the floorboard, and his face had gone back to its normal color. He had rocks clutched in both of his hands, and was rubbing his thumbs across them like worry stones.

I had stocked us up on road trip goodies—candy bars and bags of chips, bottles of juice and soda and water, some smushed-looking sandwiches and little packets of mayonnaise. I set the bags on the front seat between us, then stood by the side of the car, thumbing on my cell phone.

My heart raced as I waited for it to power up. For some reason, trouble didn't seem to loom as large when you were disconnected from the world. I wanted to stay disconnected. To pretend that nothing had happened. To forget about Grayson's outburst and my admission and get back that Grayson who took off his shirt and joked about the restaurants and see if I could make him stay around longer. Most important, I wanted to find Zoe and let her help me fix this. If she could. If she was even there. Why hadn't she answered me?

I pushed the worry away. There had to be a logical answer. Had to be.

I checked my texts first. They weren't as bad as I thought. Looked like mostly people had given up on me. Even Shani, from the sound of Lia's last text:

WTF?! Ur mom showed up @ Shani's house. Shani = srsly pissed. She sez don't call her.

I felt bad, even though I knew I wasn't going to call her anyway. If I was being honest with myself, Shani and I were never close enough friends for me to confide in her about what was going on. She was my stand-by friend. My stand-in friend. The one who would never replace Zoe, even though that's exactly what she was meant to do.

And now I felt bad for getting her into the middle of this. I texted back, knowing Lia would show my text to Shani:

Sorry I didn't tell u guys what was going on.

I stared at the screen, my thumb hovering over the buttons. What else could I say? I was scared? I never really trusted you? I'm a spoiled brat like Grayson says, and the only thing that's ever mattered to me was being perfect and getting some of the attention that he always seemed to get by being sick? That I always just wanted to be better than him; I always just wanted to matter? And that even though I knew those things, I couldn't do a damn thing to change them?

I couldn't say any of those things, so I hit "send" and then deleted all of my texts.

Mom's voice mails were harder to listen to. She was yelling in some of them, crying in others. Some of them were both Mom and Dad together. They'd called the police. They'd been staying up all night. They'd been watching the news. They had talked to the school. They knew about the cheating issue. They had a feeling we were holed up with a friend somewhere and they would find us. They needed to know if Grayson was okay. He needed his medicine. They were worried sick and were so mad at us, but they loved us and wanted us to come home.

I deleted them all and pulled up my text inbox again and opened a new text.

mom we r ok.

I hit "send" and started to press the button to power down my phone, but stopped. There was one more text I wanted to send. I scrolled through my address book, all the way to the bottom.

Zo, u there?

I waited for a few minutes for a response. One came from Mom:

Where are you? Please, honey, call us! You won't
be in trouble!

But none from Zoe.

Seriously, who still has the same cell phone for three years? She probably just got a new number and hadn't had a chance to give it to me yet.

I turned off the phone and shoved it into my front pocket, then hopped back into Hunka and buckled up. Tension was radiating off my brother. The air felt thick in the car.

"I sent Mom a text," I mumbled. "Told her we're okay."

"So we're not going home," he said, staring straight ahead. Not a question. A declaration, as if he expected this information and was reluctantly reconciling it.

I turned toward the highway. "No," I said. "We're going to California as planned. Go ahead and freak out as many times as you want."

"I'm not going to freak out," he said. "Because there's no way you're going to get us all the way to California. You may not want to admit it yet, but this idea of yours is never going to work. There are too many things you haven't thought about."

"Whatever. Just watch."

I punched the gas pedal and steered us down the exit ramp onto the highway. We were both silent, both spent and worried, the only sound the air rustling the bags of food on the front seat and the *scritch* of rocks moving against one another under Grayson's feet. I was going to prove him wrong. My idea was going to work. I may not have been a genius, and I may not have thought it all through, but I'd thought enough through to pull this off. And we'd already made it this far.

CHAPTER TWENTY-THREE

We hadn't talked since I pulled onto the highway. Grayson appeared to be pouting over my refusal to take us home, and I was still thinking about Zoe's unanswered text. What if it wasn't just her cell phone number that had changed? What if she'd moved? What if we drove all the way to California and she wasn't even there anymore?

The thought made me feel panicky, so I tried to bat it away by opening a bottle of apple juice and taking a sip. This was going to be a longer ride than I'd originally anticipated. Maybe it already had been.

"Isn't that the girl from the motel?" Grayson asked, pointing out the windshield.

Walking down the side of the highway was a blonde girl, an overstuffed diaper bag slung sideways across her body, carrying an infant seat in one hand. The muscles of her carrying arm bulged out above her elbow.

I leaned forward and squinted. The straight blonde hair, the baby-blue sweater, the infant seat.

"Rena," I said. "Yeah, it is."

"Where's she going?"

"How would I know?" I took a quick look around. Nothing on either side of us. Fields as far forward as we could see. We were probably five miles away from the motel. She couldn't have been just taking a quick walk to somewhere — not if she was walking this way.

I eased Hunka onto the side of the road behind her and put it into park. She didn't look back at us but must have known we were there, because she started walking faster, her arm going even tauter as her fingers clutched the infant seat handle.

I rolled down the window. "Hey!" I yelled, but she kept going as if she didn't hear me. "Hey, Rena!" At the sound of her name, she finally chanced a glance over her shoulder. "It's Kendra!" I said, fumbling my door open.

Her whole body relaxed with relief as she realized who was yelling at her, and she stopped, turning halfway toward me and setting Bo's seat gingerly in the grass on the side of the road.

"Stay here," I told Grayson, and got out of the car. A passing RV swerved into the left lane, the driver glaring at me as if I were walking down the center of the highway. "What're you doing?" I called, jogging toward Rena.

The wind was whisking her hair across her face. She looked beautiful standing there with the green of the newly budding field behind her, the spring sun glossing the top of her hair. Like she belonged in a soap commercial rather than on the side of a Kansas highway. She stuck her foot under one end of Bo's seat and used it to rock the carrier on the gravel.

"Where are you going?" I asked, slowing as I reached her.

She turned her face to the wind, letting her hair blow back over her shoulder. Her foot moved up and down, but she just stared off across the plains.

I touched her elbow. "Hey. You okay?"

She shook her head. "No," she said, or at least it looked like her lips formed the word "no," but a semi whined past us and I couldn't hear her.

"C'mon," I said, tugging on her elbow. "I'll give you a ride." I bent and picked up Bo's carrier. She grabbed for the handle and pulled it out of my grasp, hooking both arms through the handles and pulling his carrier close to her chest. "Whoa, I wasn't going to do anything," I said, holding my arms up. This Rena was like a totally different girl from the one who'd rolled my tire down the hill to Buddy's a few hours ago. What had happened?

The wind whipped Bo's blanket away and Rena scrambled for it, catching it with one hand, then wadding it up and pushing it back over him. Underneath, he was wearing only a diaper, and his skin looked cold and mottled. He began to fuss, his eyes squinched shut.

"It's too cold out here for him," I said. "You should get in the car."

She looked back over the fields a moment longer, then nodded and walked with me, our shoes crunching against the gravel.

Grayson had pulled my backpack to the front seat to make room in the back. He looked worried as Rena climbed in and I passed Bo to her. His fingers were rubbing the stones, double-time, while he watched Rena strap Bo in. I shook my head tersely at him as if to tell him this was not a good time for that.

I climbed in and turned the heat on full blast, aiming the vents straight back. Bo's fussing was already starting to die down.

We were on the road for several minutes before I said anything.

"Where are you going?" I glanced in the rearview mirror. Rena shrugged.

"I couldn't take it anymore, I guess. Archie."

"What happened?" I realized that Rena was still basically a stranger to me, and I felt kind of like an intruder asking her, but she was in my car, and...well, listening to her talk about Archie took my mind off my own troubles a little bit. Plus, we'd heard the fight. There was basically no way not to.

She shook her head. "I worry that he's gonna hurt Bo someday." She made a soft snorting noise. "The whole reason I married the fat old thing was because he went and got me pregnant, and he's always saying how he doesn't believe the baby is his."

We drove a little farther. I could see Grayson slipping me quick glances every now and then, and I knew exactly what was on his mind: We had picked up a hitchhiker. Really, a total stranger. This went against everything Grayson could possibly believe in. Hell, it went against everything I was ever taught. Yet he wasn't saying anything. Wasn't freaking out. Wasn't even making that throat noise, though I could tell by the look on his face that he wanted to. Mom and Dad would be horrified to know we'd picked up a stranger, but in a way, I was sort of proud of my brother for going along with it.

"So where are you going?" I asked again.

"I don't know," she said, rattling a toy over Bo's carrier. "Away."

"Want me to take you to Buddy's?"

Rena smiled, faintly, and looked out the back window, as if she expected to still see Buddy's shop behind us. We were far enough away now to see nothing but fields, though. "It's best if I just go," she said. "Just me and Bo." Again, she rattled the toy. "Don't really care where. Anywhere that's not here."

We all sat there in silence, the familiar creaks and pops that Hunka always made on the highway the only sound, each of us lost in our own thoughts.

Grayson stared out his window, his lips moving as we passed a long field filled with cows.

Rena had pulled her legs up onto the seat beside her and curled up into a ball, laying her head across Bo and stroking the top of his head with her fingers. She stared at him as if he held all the answers in the world. And she cried, softly, the only real sound her sniffles.

I sat stiff behind the wheel, paying close attention to the RV that had passed us earlier, which I'd caught up with, making sure it didn't make any more sudden swerves. But in my mind I was thinking about what it must be like to be really running away, like Rena.

At least I had somewhere to go. At least I had Zoe out there somewhere. At least I had a home to go back to when I'd gotten everything all sorted out.

Rena had nothing. Just away. What did you do when all you had was away?

Suddenly I was taken back to that last summer, when Zoe and Grayson ran away together.

I remembered sitting on the stairs, watching as Mr. Monett stood shaking in our entryway, Mom and Dad trying to talk him down.

"Rob, you know they couldn't have gotten far. Not with no money and with Grayson's..." Everyone knew what Dad was going to say, but Dad trailed off because he knew that Grayson's *difficulties* was a very sore subject between the Monetts and Mom.

"I think you and Rachel are overreacting," Mom added icily, standing in the dining room doorway with her arms across her chest. But I could see, even from my vantage point on the stairs, that Mom was worried, too. If things hadn't been so changed between them, Mom would've been over at the Monetts' house with Mrs. Monett, making phone calls and wondering aloud if it was time yet to call the police.

"My daughter is fourteen years old, Jonathan, and if that nutcase gets her preg—"

I knew this wasn't going to be good, Mr. Monett calling Grayson a nutcase. I held my hand over my mouth, watching bug-eyed as Dad took two steps closer to Mr. Monett. "I think you'd better go home and help your wife," Dad said. And then when Mr. Monett hesitated, Dad took another step closer. "Now!" he boomed, and Mom and I both jumped. "Before you have to crawl home," he added.

It was an endless cycle, and I never could understand why they couldn't see that. The more they pushed Grayson away, the more Zoe clung to him. The more she clung to him, the more Mr. Monett treated my brother like garbage. The more he treated Grayson that way, the worse Grayson's anxieties got. The worse Grayson's anxieties got, the more my parents jumped to his defense. And around and around it went. It would hardly take a rocket scientist to see how to end the cycle. Just leave Grayson and Zoe alone. But nobody got it.

Mr. Monett inched around Dad and left the house. Half an hour later, a police officer came to our door. The Monetts had decided that nightfall meant it was a good time to get the police involved, apparently. I hoped Zoe and Grayson knew what they were doing.

When Mom started crying and telling the officer that

Grayson needed his medication, I slunk upstairs and shut my bedroom door. Brock and I knew exactly where they were. They were in Brock's dad's brand-new shed—a giant outbuilding with electricity and one end empty and swept clean, perfect for two sleeping bags and the backpack filled with groceries that I'd given them on their way out. A real lovers' nest.

It made me feel weird inside, hiding their secret, but I'd promised Zoe I would tell no one. Even though I knew that their plan to hide out until our parents accepted their relationship was totally unrealistic. Even though I knew our parents wouldn't just "eventually give up." Even though I knew that there was no way a fourteen-year-old virgin and a seventeen-year-old germaphobe were going to have the wherewithal to forage for food and pee in the woods for longer than a day. Even though I knew that by the weekend, probably, Brock's dad would open the shed and find them there, doing God knew what, and would totally turn them in. None of those things mattered. A promise to your best friend was a promise you couldn't break, no matter how ridiculous it was.

Problem was, I wasn't sure how long I'd be able to keep lying to Mom if she was crying. I hated when Mom cried. I felt sorry for her, even though I knew Grayson was fine as long as he had Zoe with him, and that his OCD was never worse than it was when he was with Mom.

They lasted three nights. By the third night, Mom was inconsolable. I couldn't leave my room, the guilt was eating me up so bad. And I knew that by then, after all that time, if I told Mom and Dad that I'd known all along, they'd be livid. Not at Grayson; they'd be mad at me. Story of my life. Grayson making it difficult. Grayson making everyone miserable. Grayson putting me in the position of either pretending to be Miss Perfect and Innocent while holding on to a huge lie, or having to rat out my two best friends and prove myself to have been a liar for the past three days. There was never any gray area for me. All black or all white. Nothing in between.

It happened exactly like I thought it would. Brock's dad went out to mow the lawn and found his son's friend and a girl sleeping in the corner of his shed, curled up together in one sleeping bag.

Both were fully clothed, and both swore that nothing had happened between them. Both were totally shocked to be found. Zoe swore to me, on the bond of our friendship, that she was still a virgin. That Grayson had never even asked her to have sex. I believed her, but her parents didn't.

"I swear to God if my daughter is pregnant, I will tear him to shreds with my bare hands," Mr. Monett bellowed at Dad from across the driveway when everyone got home from the police station. I watched from the front porch — as always, there but not really there. All the attention on my brother. I may as well have not even existed.

"If you'd left them alone, maybe they wouldn't be so desperate," Mom had bellowed back. "You're a goddamned fool! Both of you are!"

They continued screaming insults at one another, Mrs. Mooney from across the street kneeling in her flower bed, watching the scene with curiosity. I watched Zoe and Grayson, who clambered out of the cars, both of them looking sheepish and sad. Zoe's hair hung down in her face. Grayson's fingers were crooked into the counting pose. Their shoulders were hunched, as if to ward off their parents' insults.

I caught Zoe's eye and tried to smile, tried to convey everything I was thinking through that smile. It would be okay. We would get through this. I hadn't told her secret. We were still best friends. She simply wiped her sleeve across her eyes and disappeared into her house.

The next day there was a FOR SALE sign in their front yard.

Zoe had wanted to go away with Grayson. Instead, she was just going...away.

Sort of like Rena.

Would Rena disappear off the face of the earth for someone, too?

Would we?

CHAPTER
TWENTY-FOUR

By the time we pulled into Denver, Bo was getting pretty restless. Grayson still hadn't said a word, but he kept glancing over the back of the seat every time Bo cried. Once, when Rena lifted Bo out of his seat, shushing him and bouncing him up and down, Grayson peered at her nervously, but he still said nothing.

"I think he needs to eat," she said, finally. I looked in the rearview mirror. She had Bo propped up on her knee, facing forward. Her finger was tucked into his mouth and he sucked at it angrily, every so often pausing to let out a little cry of frustration. "I can't let him face me or he goes crazy," she said with an embarrassed shrug.

"Oh," Grayson said, turning around to face front, his ears turning bright red.

"I need to pee anyway," I said, pulling into a Walmart parking lot.

I parked Hunka just as Bo's cries started to crescendo. Rena was turning him to her while lifting up one half of her shirt at the same time. I tried not to look, and then felt stupid for being embarrassed. It was a boob, for goodness' sake. Not like I didn't see two of them every day when I looked in the mirror. Still. What Rena did felt private and made her seem so much older, even though I knew she really wasn't.

"You need anything?" I asked as I leaned over and unzipped my backpack. I pulled out the entire roll of bills and stuffed it into my front pocket. Grayson, who had been watching me, got a shocked expression on his face.

"I don't have any money," Rena said.

"It's okay, what do you need?"

"Well, for some reason, I always crave milk when I'm nursing. If they have any chocolate milk...? You know, like a small bottle."

"That's it?" I asked, holding myself back from asking how many diapers were in that bag. I had a little bit of money, sure. Money that I'd never meant to spend and would most definitely have to account for later. But even I knew I didn't have enough to get me and Grayson to California and take care of a baby.

So how did Rena expect to do it with no money at all?

And why did I care? Bo wasn't my baby. It was up to Rena to take care of him. She just seemed kinda clueless about it.

I got out of the car and stretched, one arm above my

head. The day had warmed up a little, and there was something so clear and bright about Denver's air. I felt good. So good I could almost ignore Grayson, who was glaring at me over the top of the car.

"Come on," I said, heading around the car and toward the store entrance. "Don't let me forget the milk."

"We can't leave her there alone," he said, catching up to me.

"Why not?"

"Because we don't know her. She could steal everything we've got."

I laughed. "She can't steal the car, because I have the keys. The rocks, technically, we stole from her. I have my purse and the money out of my backpack."

"Speaking of. Where did you get all that money, anyway? You've been hounding me for money since we started this idiotic trip—"

"Not idiotic."

"And you have a fat wad of cash in your backpack the whole time?"

"Pretty much." I dodged a woman who was letting her toddler push a shopping cart.

"So?"

"So, the most she could take from us would be about twenty dollars' worth of gas station food. She probably needs it more than we do."

"She could poison the food."

I snorted. "You think she's hiding poison in Bo's diaper

bag? Come on, it'll be fine. Consider it your good deed of the day."

He paused. "So? You never answered me."

"I don't think she's going to poison the food or steal the car or kill us on the highway, okay? She's fine. We're fine. Relax."

I plunged through the automatic doors, feeling the swish of Walmart wash over me—the banging of carts finding a home against one another, the beeps of scanners ringing up sales, the squawk of codes being called overhead, a mishmash of languages and crying babies.

"That's not what I meant," Grayson said as I grunted, trying to pry two carts apart. "The money."

I stopped and looked him square in the eyes. "Is mine. It doesn't matter where I got it, okay?" I gave another yank and the carts separated. I pushed one toward the restroom, wishing what I'd said was true. It mattered, all right. It mattered a lot.

That money was going to be my saving grace. It was going to be the only prayer I had of getting out of this mess I was in. And with every dollar spent, my chances of being able to go home again and look Mom and Dad in the eye got smaller and smaller.

I realized that at some point, I'd chosen this trip over my future. I'd laid all of my problems at Zoe's feet, when I wasn't even sure if she was still there.

As I stood at the restroom sink, it really dawned on me what I'd done. And I couldn't take another step until I'd tried to make it all right. I washed my hands and then backed against the wall, next to the paper-towel dispensers.

Women with little kids whisked past me, pumping towels out of the machines and barking orders while I pulled my cell phone out of my purse and began dialing. A toilet flushed. A baby cried on the changing table. The phone on the other end rang in my ear.

"Ken?" Frantic.

"Hi, Dad."

There was the sound of clothes rustling, like he was walking somewhere, and then a door closing. "Kendra? Where are you? Are you okay?"

"I'm fine, Dad. Gray's fine, too."

"Your mother and I are worried sick." I thought I heard a thickness in Dad's voice, and immediately felt a lump in my throat, too. "Where are you?" His words sounded breathy, as if he was barely hanging on to them.

"Listen, Dad. I can't stay on very long." A woman came in, towing a little boy gruffly by one hand and yelling at him, something about him ruining everything. The little boy was wailing, and once again I had to swallow back the lump in my throat. My parents had never treated me like that. They didn't deserve what I was doing to them.

"The school called. Something about cheating? We told them they had it wrong. But if that's why you..."

"Dad," I said again, wanting to wrap my mouth around that word over and over again: *Dad, Dad, Dad*. My dad always meant safety for all of us. Even if he didn't always know how to deal with Grayson, he always solved the problems, kept us even-keeled. Why hadn't I thought I could trust him to help me? Why hadn't I run to him rather than run away? He was so many miles behind us now. "Dad, I want you to promise me something, okay?" I turned and faced the wall, pressing my forehead against the tile. I didn't care how gross it was, and only distantly worried that the fact that I was thinking of its grossness at all meant that Grayson's thoughts had started to penetrate me at some level, too.

"Whatever it is, Ken, we'll work it out. It'll be fine. Tell me where you are."

"Promise me that you and Mom will go to Italy next year no matter what, okay?"

There was a pause, then in a confused voice, "Italy? What does Italy have to do with...?"

"Just promise. Mom's been learning all those Italian phrases, and I don't want you guys to miss out because of... promise me. Okay?" I knew how ridiculous it sounded for me to be calling about Italy, of all things. But I had my reasons. It made perfect sense to me. My parents were good parents. And they deserved a break. And they were just the kind of parents who would use family drama as a reason not to take one. They didn't deserve that. They didn't deserve me taking their plans away from them like this.

"Kendra. This is silly. Let me talk to your brother."

I flicked a look toward the door. My brother. Grayson was probably freaking out right now, wondering what happened to me. He was probably making a spectacle of himself, counting or making that throat noise or tapping the floor or walking in perfect circles or something. He wouldn't want to get into the car with me, after I'd spent this much time in a public restroom. He'd probably think I was toxic.

But somehow I knew that, even if he didn't want to, he'd still go with me, because that's what Grayson did.

"I've got to go," I said. "I love you. Tell Mom I love her, too, okay? And I'm really sorry, Dad."

"Kendra, don't hang up! Just tell me where you are and I'll come get you. We'll solve whatever this—"

But I hung up and pushed the button to turn my cell phone off again. All I could think as I pushed through the door back into the hustle and bustle of Walmart was *He never promised*.

To my surprise, Grayson was standing next to the cart with his arms crossed, looking very anxious but not doing anything weird.

"What took so long?" he said, practically pouncing on me when I got out.

"I called Dad."

He paused. Seemed surprised. "You called Dad? At work?"

I shrugged, thinking about the rustling noise and the sound of a door shutting. He probably was at work. He'd have to call Mom now and he already sounded so upset. I'd probably totally obliterated his day. "I called his cell."

"What did he say?"

I rolled my eyes. "We talked about baseball. Duh, what do you think he said, Grayson? He wanted to know where we are."

"Did you tell him?"

"No."

"Why'd you call him, then?"

I ran my finger around the rim of a shot glass on a shelf next to our cart. "I missed him, okay? I wanted to hear his voice."

"If you miss him so much, why not just turn around and go home?"

I thrust my purse into the cart seat and pushed down an empty checkout lane, scanning the overhead signs for the infant section. I was feeling very on edge about the conversation between Dad and me—*he didn't promise*—and I just wanted Grayson to stop worrying for one second. If it wasn't the germs, it was the hitchhiker in our backseat or the phone calls to Mom and Dad or…or…or…It never ended. "Have you seen the Hayward Fault yet?" I snapped. "Uh, no. So can we move on? Do you have to pee?"

"I'm not peeing here."

"Suit yourself."

I wound my way through the aisles until I reached the back, where the baby gear was. I pushed into the jungle of clothes, checking tags and sizes. "How big do you think Bo is?" I asked.

"How would I know?"

I shrugged. "Never mind." I pushed past a couple more

racks until I got to a shelf lined with pajamas. They looked warm. I threw a pair into the cart. I wasn't made of money, but I couldn't stand to see that baby's mottled skin one more time. He made me cold just looking at him. I threw in a blanket, too. It was hard to believe that yesterday I was sitting in my car, afraid to walk into school, and here I was, not even twenty-four hours later, buying clothes for a baby I'd never met before, the entire state of Kansas between me and home.

Half an hour later, we were at the checkout. I'd gotten Bo a pack of the cheapest diapers I could find. I'd also picked up a bag of apples, some cheese and crackers, yogurt, granola bars, a big box of Pop-Tarts, six small bottles of chocolate milk, and a little cooler to put them in.

Grayson found a sweatshirt, a toothbrush, a towel, a bucket of antibacterial wipes, and a pack of soap. He also picked up an atlas, which I never would have thought of.

At the last minute, I decided his sweatshirt idea was a great one and picked one up for me, too, wondering if my jacket was still in my locker or if they'd already cleared it out and sent all my stuff home to Mom and Dad along with a letter saying I could never return. I got a small pang in my gut just thinking about it, so I cleared my mind and concentrated on the clerk's hands as she scanned our items and threw them into bags.

When we got back to the car, Rena was standing in the parking lot, bent over at the waist, head lolling, her hair and fingers brushing the ground. She straightened when I opened the passenger door and started stuffing trash into one of the plastic bags. I peeked over the backseat. Bo appeared to be sleeping.

"That was fast," Rena said, sweeping her hair out of her face and then clasping her hands behind her and stretching.

"Got your milk," I said. I dumped the bottles of milk into the cooler and hefted it up on top of the roof. "I also got Bo some stuff. Hope that's okay."

"That's sweet," she said, catching the jammies that I tossed to her over the car. "I'll put them on him later, I guess. He's so sleepy. Didn't eat much." She rubbed the side of her chest when she said it, as if she was sore.

"So I guess we'll get on the road again soon," I said, tying the bag of trash and walking to the back of Hunka to put it in the trunk. "It's twelve-thirty."

"Okay," Rena said, then put her hand lightly on Grayson's arm. I saw him freeze under her touch and wanted to laugh out loud. He didn't like to be touched, especially by strangers. Strangers who were also hitchhikers. "Show me where the bathroom is?" she asked, and to my surprise, Grayson nodded. As they walked away, I could hear his *uh-uh-uh* echoing down the parking lot.

I sank down in the front seat of Hunka, hoping that picking up Rena was the right decision, and I hadn't just piled another mistake on top of all the others I'd already made.

CHAPTER
TWENTY-FIVE

"It's a good thing we stopped here," Grayson said. He was bent over the atlas, his nose practically touching the page. "We have to change highways. Got to get up to I-80."

"Navigate me," I said. My stomach growled and I pawed through a bag on the seat beside me without looking. The traffic was the worst we'd seen since we left home. Twice I'd almost rear-ended the person in front of me. The last thing I needed was to get in an accident and have some cop matching me up to a missing persons report from Missouri.

I pulled out an apple and took a bite.

"That hasn't been washed," Grayson said.

"You got a sink I can borrow?" I grinned and risked a quick glance at him. He was scowling at me.

"You could die from that. They spray those things with pesticide, you know."

"Mmm, pesticide." I bit into the apple again. This time

I chewed for a minute, then opened my mouth and showed him the mashed-up apple inside. "Pesticide is delicious."

"Fine. You'll love *E. coli*."

"Mmm, *E. coli*," I said in the same moaning voice. "Tell me where to turn, Safety Officer Sam."

"I hope you shit your pants," he mumbled, and Rena laughed out loud in the backseat. "Turn off up here."

I hit the highway and headed north. The day had heated up a little, and I rolled down my window a crack, letting that crisp mountain air whip through me. For the first time since we left home, I felt like smiling. We drove out of the city and up where the trees were thicker.

I could see Rena staring out the window, her fingers twisting her little stone earrings round and round. Grayson lined rocks along the highway lines on the atlas, mapping our route to California.

"Holy shit, Kendra, we've still got twelve hundred miles to go."

"That's not bad."

"Not bad? We've already been on the road for nine hours. It's like, another eighteen!"

"See? Less than a day."

He gaped at me, then shook his head and turned to look out the window.

After a long stretch of silence, I turned to him. He was chewing on a cracker. "You don't freak out about over-passes anymore."

"Yeah, I do. I just don't do it out loud," he said. He

swiped the rocks off the atlas and started lining them up on the dash instead.

"Why not?"

He shrugged. "Why do I do any of it? If I had a damn clue, I wouldn't."

"Dude, you can't say 'damn' around babies."

"He doesn't understand what I'm saying."

"How do you know?"

"It's okay," Rena said. "Trust me, he's heard far worse from Archie."

"He's asleep, anyway," Grayson added.

I hit a bump in the road, and the glove compartment door flopped open onto Grayson's knee again. I smiled and took another bite of my apple. This was what those trips to Grandma's felt like before Grayson started fearing overpasses. "Today actually kind of feels like we're just on a road trip," I said.

"It feels like we're running away," Grayson said, slipping another rock onto the dash.

"You sort of owe me a good road trip, since we never got to have any when we were kids, thanks to your overpass issues that are suddenly gone now."

"My whole life was like one big road trip," Rena said, then chuckled softly and gazed out the window again at the passing trees. "One big, stupid, crappy road trip."

"So I'm finally getting my road trip," I added.

Grayson lined up another rock. "Uh-uh. You're running away and justifying it."

"Whatever," I mumbled. "Can't you ever lighten up? Have fun? Just once?"

We drove along in silence some more, my happiness evaporated. Suddenly, all that road trip fun was gone, and it did feel like we were running away. And it felt as though we had so very much to run away from.

Then, very softly, Rena said, "In spring I look gay, dressed in beautiful array."

"What?" I glanced in the rearview mirror.

She turned to meet my eyes, an embarrassed flush creeping up her face. "Oh. It's part of a riddle. My grandma used to tell them to me all the time. Said riddles made you smarter."

"There's truth to that," Grayson muttered. He was slouched forward, using the binding of the atlas to push his line of rocks into perfect formation on the dash.

"Anyway. She died a long time ago, but I still remember some of them." She shifted and fussed with Bo's blanket. "Looking out there reminded me of one of her riddles. It goes like this: In spring I look gay, dressed in beautiful array. In summer more clothing I wear. The colder it grows, I fling off my clothes. In winter I'm naked and bare. What am I?"

I thought about it. I'd never been very good with riddles. They never made sense to me. "A person?" I guessed.

"A tree," Grayson said. He placed another rock just so, then scrubbed his hands with one of his wipes and fished another cracker out of the bag. He popped it into his mouth and turned sideways to look at Rena. "That's the answer, right? The clothes are leaves." He glanced at me. "A person? Really? You run around naked in the winter?"

Rena beamed.

"It was just a guess. I forgot to tell you Grayson is Genius Boy," I said, cutting my eyes to the rearview mirror. "He has a brain the size of Wyoming. Hey, speaking of..." I pointed to a sign ahead, telling us we were crossing over into Wyoming. So many states away from home now. But neither of them seemed to notice.

"Yep," she said. "You got it right."

Grayson grinned as Rena reached over the seat to rummage for a granola bar. "Give me another. I love riddles."

She opened her granola bar, took a small bite, and chewed, scrunching her forehead in thought. "It's been a long time. Let's see...okay. Here's one. "I have two bodies, but they're both joined as one. The stiller I stand, the faster I run. What am I?"

"An hourglass," he shot back immediately. "Come on, that one was easy."

Rena laughed and tossed her granola bar wrapper at his face. It bounced off his forehead and landed on my leg.

"I've got one," I said. "If two nerds drive to Wyoming together, how long before the normal person in the car goes crazy?"

But they both ignored me.

"Okay, okay," Rena said. "How about this? I can't remember the rhyme, but this is close enough. Elizabeth, Elspeth, Besty, and Bess found a bird's nest with five eggs in it. They all took one and left four eggs inside. How did they do that?"

"It was the same egg—they just passed it around," I said, then pointed at Grayson. "Ha-ha, sucker! Beat you to it!"

"Those are just nicknames. Elizabeth, Elspeth, Betsy, and Bess are all the same girl," Grayson said over me, then tossed Rena's crumpled granola bar wrapper at my head and added, "dumbass."

I grabbed the wrapper and threw it back at him. "That's tough talk from a guy whose ass I kicked at the bottom of a quarry yesterday," I said. "And it's a good thing I did. You'd still be there counting if I hadn't." It was barely out of my mouth before I realized I shouldn't have said it. I could see him wilt a little next to me, and I wanted to kick myself for bringing up the one thing I was hoping to help him forget about. After a few seconds, he turned forward again and relined the stones on the dash.

"So what's with all the rocks?" Rena asked.

Grayson swallowed. "Nothing," he said. "I just like rocks." All the playfulness was gone. *Poof.*

"Sorry, Gray," I said after a few more minutes, bumping his shoulder with my hand playfully. "I didn't mean to embarrass you." And even though inside my head I protested—*but he's embarrassed me so many times!*—I was surprised to find that I really meant it. Probably because I knew in my heart that he never meant to embarrass me, either, and if he could have changed it, he would have.

200

He shook his head. "I embarrass myself," he said, then curled up on his side toward the window and grew quiet.

I felt like a jerk. And like I might cry.

I'd never felt farther from home, and Zoe never seemed farther away, and for just a moment, if I let myself, I could almost feel totally lost. Like I'd never get to where I wanted to be again.

CHAPTER
TWENTY-SIX

I left Grayson alone with his thoughts for a while as I took in the scenery of Wyoming and noticed that really every place kind of looks like every other place when you're on the road. But eventually my curiosity got to me. I knew nothing about Wyoming.

"So what's in Wyoming?" I asked, trying to get conversation going again.

"Fossils," Grayson muttered, still pouting.

Ugh. Fossils. Science. Not my strong suit. But I wanted to lighten the mood in the car . . . see if I could get us back to where we were before I brought up the rocks. See if I could get Grayson talking again.

"Cool. Maybe we should pull over and try to find a dinosaur head or something," I said. "Wouldn't that be awesome to come home with a giant *T. rex* head as a souvenir?"

Grayson rolled his eyes at me. "You can't just go find a dinosaur head," he answered. "It's not like they're lying on the side of the road waiting for someone to pick one up as a souvenir."

"How do you know?"

"Well, for starters, when they dug up the ground to lay the highway, they probably would have already found it."

"Maybe. You don't know."

He glared at me. "I do know. It's called logic. You're not going to find a dinosaur head out here."

"If I got out and found one, you'd feel like a real idiot right now," I countered. "How do you think the first guy who found a dinosaur head found it? By getting down on the ground and looking."

"Good luck. And it's called a skull, by the way. Not a head. And a *T. rex* skull would be way too big to take home as a souvenir."

"You have no imagination, Grayson."

"But I have logic."

I made a face at him, secretly delighted at how normal this conversation was. Like a billion conversations we'd had over the years. It felt comfy. It felt like he'd forgiven me for acting like a jerk earlier.

"Jackalopes," Rena said from the backseat.

"Huh?"

She laughed. "Back at the motel, we had these brochures about this place called Douglas, Wyoming. Home of the jackalope."

"What's a jackalope?" I asked.

Grayson rolled his eyes again, as if he was seriously put out about having to explain yet another simple concept to his ignorant sister. But he was also grinning. "Part jackrabbit, part antelope. A rabbit with antelope horns."

"Legend has it they're vicious," Rena said, and giggled again. "A vicious bunny."

"That's ridiculous," I said.

"Seriously? You think you're going to put a *T. rex* head in your pocket to take home, and it's a jackalope that you find ridiculous?" Grayson countered. Then he mimicked in a falsetto voice, "Where's your imagination?"

We drove on for a few seconds in silence. Every so often, Rena would giggle in the backseat. Jackalopes. Granted, I hadn't exactly planned out this trip, but never in my wildest dreams would I have thought I'd be having a discussion about jackalopes. I kind of liked it. Jackalopes had nothing to do with calc or OCD or lost friendships. Jackalopes were just a ridiculous story. Something to talk about to pass the time.

I didn't mind passing a little time. It's not like Zoe was waiting for us or anything.

"Hey, Rena, where did you say this place was?"

"Douglas, Wyoming," she answered.

"Grayson, how far is it?" I pointed to the atlas.

He scrunched his eyebrows up at me as if he couldn't believe what he was hearing. "No way."

"Yes way. How far is Douglas? Lead me to the jack-alope, man!" Both Rena and I cracked up.

Slowly he picked up the atlas and studied it for a few minutes. "It'd be about two hours off the highway."

"That's no time!"

"Kendra, think about it. Two hours off the highway to get there. And then two hours back. Just to see an animal that doesn't exist."

"We have time. Now, tell me where to get off, or I'll start taking random highways."

He sighed, shaking his head. "Fine. Whatever." But he didn't sound as if he hated the idea that much, really. Jack-alopes kinda seemed like something that would be right up my brother's alley.

The afternoon wore on as we drove up the highway toward Douglas. Grayson told us more about jackalopes, proving that, being Genius Boy and all, he knew everything about everything. After a while, his jackalope lecture led to a discussion about unicorns and leprechauns, all of us losing ourselves in legends and myths and stupid stories that nobody in their right mind should ever believe but that have some-how morphed into "true stories" that everyone believes.

Next thing I knew, Rena was pointing over the seat. "Jackalope!"

We gazed up at a hillside, upon which a giant cutout of a jackalope sat, and we all laughed. It looked so ridiculous. Awesomely ridiculous.

"So in the brochure we had, it said something about the world's largest jackalope statue being in the town square, I think."

"Let's find it!" I said.

We drove into town, pointing out the images of jackalopes everywhere, on benches and storefronts. We even saw WATCH OUT FOR THE JACKALOPE signs. It was all so hokey and touristy. I loved it.

"There it is," Grayson said, and sure enough we were coming up on a huge statue of a rabbit with horns. Two other cars were parked nearby, a man taking a photo of two little kids standing in front of the statue.

It was something I'd always wanted and never had—a hokey touristy photo in front of a hokey tourist trap.

I pulled to a stop and grabbed my phone. "Come on, Grayson. I'm getting up on that jackalope."

"What?" he was saying, surprise making his voice squeaky, but Rena and I had already hopped out of Hunka and were gazing at the statue.

Rena kept giggling. "I never actually thought I'd come see this thing," she said, shaking her head.

The family had finished taking their photos and were slowly getting back in their car.

"Take a picture of me," I said, handing her my phone and heading for the statue.

She took the phone and I scrambled up the pedestal that the statue sat on and proceeded to climb up its back. It was a lot more vertical than it looked, and there was nothing really to grab on to, and I kept sliding back down, one close scrape with tumbling to the ground after another.

"Kendra, get down!" Grayson was yelling from his position by the car. "Someone's going to see you."

"So?" I grunted, hoisting myself up again. "I'll play innocent."

Finally, I got some purchase and was able to clumsily wrap myself around the rabbit's back. "Hurry! Take it!" I yelled, and Rena did, while I mugged for the camera like I didn't have a care in the world.

"Got a good one!" she called back, and I started to get down, but had a better idea.

"Grayson! Come up here with me!"

He shook his head, his arms wrapped tightly across the front of him. "Not happening."

"Come on! Look! Nothing happened to me!"

"Yet!" he called back.

"I like it up here. I'm going to stay here until you come up. I think I could probably sleep here." Total lie. I was slipping, and my muscles were trembling and wanting to give.

After a few seconds of thought, he reluctantly started walking toward the statue, looking severely ticked off. "There's a sign right here that says you can't climb the jackalope."

"No, it says you *shouldn't* climb the jackalope. Clearly, I can. I already did."

"That's not what the sign means." He sighed. "Fine. I can't believe I'm letting you talk me into this."

It took Grayson far fewer tries to get up on the rabbit's back, and most of the times he slid back down were because he thought he saw a bug or bird poop or was too put out by the embarrassment of it all.

"Smile," I said as soon as he got up behind me, and Rena took a photo and gave us a thumbs-up.

"Good one!" she yelled.

"Now can we get down?" Grayson grumbled.

"You did it!" I cooed in a kindergarten teacher voice. "Yay, Grayson!" But when I reached back to tousle his hair, he ducked, and both of us slid backward off the rabbit and into a heap at the bottom of the base.

"You okay?" Rena asked, rushing to us, but I was laughing too hard to answer, and Grayson was too busy being angry.

Finally, we untangled ourselves and headed back to Hunka, where Bo was still sleeping in his carrier.

We drove around a little bit more, teasing one another about spotting jackalopes in the bushes on the side of the road or peeking out from behind houses, but as the sun began to slide over the horizon, it became clear that we needed to get back on track.

"Can I stop at that gift shop first, though?" I asked, and nobody argued, so I did.

Inside was a jackalope lover's dream. They even had a stuffed, mounted jackalope head.

"Gross, can you imagine waking up to that every morning?" I breathed.

"I've woken up to worse. I've woken up to Archie's head," Rena joked. We snickered. "Hey, you should buy it. Attach it to the front of the car," she said, her eyes going big. "You know, kind of like a road trip mascot. Proudly leading us to sunny California."

I grinned. A road trip mascot. Grayson would hate the idea. But there was something about Rena's excitement over little things like this that was contagious. "Good idea," I said. "Let's do it!"

"We don't have any money, remember?" Grayson interjected, just as I expected him to.

"We have a little," I countered.

"Not for jackalope heads. Hey, maybe you'll get lucky and find a T. jackalope head on the side of the highway, though."

"Har-har-har."

In the end, Rena and I settled on a small plush jackalope, which I tied to Hunka's grille with my student ID lanyard.

I brushed my hands together and stepped back. We all stared at the poor little thing, antlers trembling in the breeze. "There," I said. "It's Jack. Our mascot."

"I like it," Rena said. "It's cute."

"I think so, too," I said. I turned to Grayson. "Do jackalopes like to eat bugs?"

Grayson grunted and headed back toward Hunka, but his grunt sounded like a suppressed laugh to me.

I got into Hunka and pulled out my cell phone. There it

was, the photo of my brother and me on top of the jackalope statue. He wasn't smiling. But he was there.

We pulled onto the highway and headed back in the direction we'd come from, all of us lost in our own thoughts.

In some ways, it was as though I'd lived a whole lifetime in one day. As though, up until today, I'd been living a pretend life. One where I said and did all the things that everyone wanted to hear so I could be the child who stood out for the right reasons. It was as though I'd spent all of my time molding myself into what everyone else wanted me to be — or maybe even what I wanted myself to be, which was to say entirely unlike my brother — that I never considered being a regular, flawed person, just like everybody else. The kind of person who wanted to do the right things and live a good life, but honestly sometimes fell short. Like everyone else. Not perfect, just... normal.

I kind of wondered if Grayson felt the same way today. He'd been obsessing less, that was for sure. He'd joked a little. He seemed so much more... there. Even if neither of us knew exactly where "there" was at the moment. Maybe my plan would work. Maybe the cure for OCD is to give someone no other choice than to cut it out. Probably, with my luck, it was really dangerous or something and I was messing him up for, like, the rest of his life.

But in some ways, he seemed more like the Grayson that Zoe knew. The uncrushed and unshattered Grayson.

Bringing them back together was the right thing to do. She could fix him. She *would* fix him.

We drove in that easy silence for hours, into the night.

"I've gotta eat," I finally said. "And I've gotta stop driving."

"Pizza," Rena said. "Pizza sounds really good."

"And bed," I added, yawning.

"No motels," Grayson said.

"Don't start."

"Can't we sleep in the car?"

"Oh, yeah, that'd be comfy. Aren't you worried my *E. coli* will surface in the middle of the night, and when I shit my pants the germs will explode all over your side of the seat?"

"Don't say 'shit' with a baby in the car," he mimicked.

"He's heard worse," Rena reminded us.

I sighed. "Okay, I'll tell you what. I'll pull off at whatever the next town is. We'll hopefully find some pizza, and then we'll decide where to sleep."

Grayson nodded wearily. I had a feeling he was too exhausted to argue. He had slept crouching in a chair the night before, after all. And had followed that by spending all day being pummeled by his fears. That had to be tiring.

We found a pizza place—Mama Mio's—right down the street from a ratty-looking motel. Mama Mio's looked as if it had enjoyed its heyday in 1986 and didn't want to jinx success by changing with the times. There were high school football jerseys hanging from the walls, the accompanying team photos showing boys with feathered hair and cheerleaders with giant 'dos and jean jackets. A dusty old pinball machine squatted in one corner, alongside a juke-box filled with songs by a-ha! and Murray Head and Scandal.

We ordered two large pizzas to go and took turns in the unisex bathroom while we waited for them. Even Grayson used the restroom; either he was too worn down to argue or, I hoped, he'd realized that using a public restroom wasn't the end of the world.

We took the pizzas back to the motel, where, fortu-nately, the grungy-looking clerk didn't care if any of us was over eighteen. I used cash to pay for the room, realizing that the wad of bills in my pocket was getting smaller and smaller, but afraid that Mom and Dad would be online, tracking the credit card, and would know that we were somewhere in the middle of Wyoming. The last thing I needed was a door-pounding wake-up call by the county sheriff in the morning.

The room wasn't anywhere near as clean as Rena's motel had been. The bedspreads had rips in them, and there were ashes on the nightstand. There was a hole in the wall where the shower head should have been, and the toilet looked like it hadn't been scrubbed since Mama Mio's was busting out MC Hammer on the jukebox to a full big-haired '80s crowd.

Rena and Grayson complained aloud about the room, pointing out to each other the layer of dust on the TV and the obviously used bar of soap, complete with a few of the previous occupant's hairs, on the side of the bathroom sink, but I was too hungry and too exhausted to care. Truth was, I probably would've slept in the car if Grayson had pushed for it. But I was glad to have somewhere to stretch out. I knew we had a long day of driving ahead of us in the morning, and my back was already sore from sitting behind the wheel for so long. And I was tired and grumpy. But I had Jack the Road Trip Mascot strapped to the front of Hunka, and a scrape on my elbow from falling off a jackalope, so all in all I was pretty content.

I dropped the pizza boxes on the bed and went directly to the bathroom to run cold water over my face.

Rena and I weren't able to get Grayson anywhere near the beds, but with the help of about fifty antibacterial wipes, we finally persuaded him to sit in the vinyl chair by the window and eat a few pieces of pizza.

I flipped through the snowy channels until I found a grainy cartoon station, and we watched that while we ate.

"Your baby doesn't ever cry," Grayson said after a while. "He sleeps too much."

Rena's forehead creased as she bent to look into Bo's carrier. "Not normally," she said. "I should probably wake him up, huh? He's probably just worn out from all the commotion today." She pulled the blanket off Bo and shook the carrier, making soft clicking noises with her tongue. After a few seconds, I could see Bo's little hands and legs start to move around, followed by a squawk.

All at once I was stuffed and so exhausted all I could think about was stretching out and going to sleep. I got up and moved the pizza boxes to the table and crawled up the mattress, landing facedown on a pillow, the floaty and buzzy feeling of sleep pressing in on me. I could hear Grayson's and Rena's voices as I drifted off, but they sounded far away and tinny, as if I were standing at the end of a long tunnel, listening in.

"He's probably hungry…"

"…hope so. You don't mind…"

"*Uh-uh-uh*…it's okay…I'll just go…"

"You don't have to move…"

"He's really cute…worry about germs…"

"…not really…why do you…?"

"I guess I was just made that way. *Uh-uh-uh*…"

"…we all have our issues, I think…"

My arms and legs felt so heavy I couldn't have flipped over had the place been on fire.

And then I was out, feeling warm and happy and like this was any other night, not like I was about to see my best friend tomorrow for the first time in three years and beg her to help me.

If they kept talking, I didn't hear them. I was busy dreaming of unicorns and leprechauns and giant hopping jackalopes, my brother and I happily riding on the back of one.

CHAPTER
TWENTY-SEVEN

I woke up with my stomach growling again.

I looked around the room, which looked no better under the sunlight streaming in between the curtains. Grayson was curled up in the vinyl chair Rena had disinfected for him last night. Rena was sprawled out across the other bed, her head at the wrong end, her arm stretched protectively over Bo's middle. Bo was asleep with his mouth open, his little arms stretched over his head in a victory pose. He was wearing the new pajamas I'd bought him. They were huge on him.

Grayson was right. That baby was too quiet. If he woke up crying in the night, I never heard him. But Rena didn't seem worried about it.

The TV was still on, but the sound was muted. The remote was on Rena's side of the night table. They'd found a news station, the kind with headlines constantly scrolling across the bottom of the screen. I had a pang of homesickness, thinking of the number of times my mom had said, *Those stations make me crazy! I can't decide if I should be listening to the person talking or reading the words at the bottom, and I end up trying to do both. It's exhausting!*

I sat up and rubbed my eyes, squinting at the words at the bottom of the screen, looking intently for any stories about two missing Missouri kids. After a few minutes, I decided maybe we were safe. Maybe calling Mom and Dad had calmed them down. Maybe they figured we were old enough to handle being out alone.

And if that's what I thought, maybe I was still dreaming.

Mom might be okay with me being out on my own, but not Grayson. Grayson was her "sick child"; and as much as I loved Mom, she was way too overprotective of him. She lived her whole adult life waiting for Something Horrible. She must have spent countless days fearing... When would his illness take him away from her forever?... When would he kill himself?... When would he simply walk away, down the highway in that awkward way of his, and never come back again?... When would he be buried under an avalanche of the rocks that he loved more than anything he'd ever loved in his whole life?

For Mom, everything non-OCD-related Grayson did was an accomplishment. Things the rest of us do every day without thinking twice. Did he get dressed in less than two hours? Walk outside and pick up the mail? Make lunch? Any sign that Grayson might be getting a handle on his illness was a reason to celebrate.

Everything else...was tragedy waiting to happen.

If only she could've seen him yesterday. She would have been so happy.

I knew then that no matter how many times I called Mom and Dad, they would not stop worrying. I knew that even though Dad said he was on my side and we could talk it out, when I got home, I would be punished. They would fawn over Grayson as if he were a puppy saved at the last moment from execution. They would tell me I'd let them down. They'd have betrayed quavers in their voices, and I knew that no matter what I did, there would never be a moment in my life when I would make up for this. The time I ran away. The time I thought of myself first. The time I made everyone suffer with worry. Poor, poor Grayson. As if he didn't have enough cards stacked against him, his sister had to go and do this to him.

I reached over and grabbed the remote, pressing the channel button until it was back on the cartoon channel. I left it muted and stared at the fuzzy screen, imagining myself as the characters, being pummeled by giant rocks and having my hands slammed in doors and my tongue run through blenders. Would any of that ever be enough?

Probably not.

After a while, the rumbling in my stomach got to be too much, and I slipped out of bed and walked over to the table where the pizza boxes still sat. The top one was empty, but there was still half a pizza left in the bottom box. I pulled out a slice and scooted behind the curtain to eat it.

The sunlight made me blink and squint, but at least it felt warmer, as if spring had actually decided to really get here after all. In the light of day, the parking lot of the motel revealed a straggly-looking clientele—beat-up cars and pot-bellied men in ripped undershirts coughing and spitting while their dogs peed on tires and rooted around beneath the overflowing Dumpster. I gazed up and down the road as far as I could. Everything had a faded look to it, as if this was a town that had given up.

I heard movement behind me and turned to see Grayson blinking up at me.

"Close those," he grouched, his voice scratchy. "You'll wake up the baby."

As if Bo had heard him say this, he started fussing. I let the curtain drop to a close and now was blinking in the dark room, trying to make out the shifting figures of Rena and Bo on her bed.

"What time is it?" she asked groggily.

"I don't know," I said. "We should get on the road, though. Sorry I woke Bo."

"It's okay," she said. "I'm surprised he slept the whole night. He hasn't ever done that before." She got up and padded around the bed to the diaper bag she'd set on the dresser top. She rummaged around inside and came out with a diaper.

By then, Bo was screaming like crazy. Someone pounded on the wall next to us, and Rena made shushing noises while she wriggled him out of his pajamas and changed his diaper.

Grayson had gotten up and gone into the bathroom. I could hear the water running in there.

Rena finished changing Bo's diaper and pulled him onto her lap, scooting backward to the head of the bed and cozying down under the covers on her side. Bo's cries got more frantic and then were suddenly replaced by slurping noises and Rena's soft singing.

I bent to put on my shoes as the bathroom door opened and Grayson emerged, towel and soap in hand, his hair slicked back on his head. He wasn't wearing his glasses, and he walked with a confidence I hadn't seen in him for...ever.

"Come on," I said, trying not to look too surprised. (Mom would have made a huge deal about this step—probably held a party in his honor—and I so didn't want to act like Mom.) "We can go get gas while she feeds the baby. That way when she's done, we'll be ready to hit the road." I grabbed my purse and dug the keys out of it. Grayson didn't move from where he was standing. "Come on," I said.

He went back to his chair and sat down, rolling the soap into his towel on his lap. "Why don't you go and I'll stay?" he said. "I'm sick of the car. And I want to eat a little." He reached over and fumbled with the pizza boxes.

"Okay," I said, and opened the door to leave.

Grayson chewed, looking straight at the TV, but Rena didn't move at all. I thought I heard a soft snore coming from her bed.

As I pumped gas into Hunka, feeling the early spring

breeze coax goose bumps up on my arm, I remembered the last time I spent the night with Zoe. Her parents had long since stopped letting her spend the night at our house. We always had to stay over at hers, even though she and I would wait until her parents were asleep and would sneak out to meet Grayson in the backyard.

"He's not that weird, you know," Zoe had said, closing her door softly for the third time. She'd been checking every fifteen minutes to see if the light in the den was off yet, signaling that her parents had gone to bed. They were still up. "When it's just him and me, he's almost totally normal."

"I know," I said, even though I knew Grayson and totally normal were a far cry from each other. But Zoe was my best friend and I wanted to support her. And Grayson was my brother, and even though he was a pain sometimes, I still wanted to defend him from people like Mr. and Mrs. Monett—people who think that just because someone isn't like them, there must be something wrong with him. "And he loves you."

"Exactly!" Zoe had said, pointing at me over the magazine she was pretending to be interested in. "You'd think they'd want me to be with a boy who loves me. Especially one who's known me my whole life." She slapped the magazine shut and sighed. "I wish they'd see that he can't help it that he counts sometimes, but it doesn't make him a bad person."

He can't help it.

I knew this. He couldn't help it. So why was I, all these years later, standing at a gas station in Wyoming expecting him to change? Would Zoe be disappointed in me when she found out what I'd been doing to him over the past two days?

I finished filling the tank and stood leaning against the car for a few minutes, my eyes closed, my face turned toward the sun. The wind felt so good.

I pulled out my cell phone and turned it on. There was a text. Eagerly, I opened it, hoping it was Zoe finally responding to one of mine.

It was from Mom.

> We know about the money. We are confused. Come home. We need to talk.

They knew. To my surprise, my knees didn't buckle and I didn't start to hyperventilate. I didn't pass out, and the ground didn't open up and swallow me whole. I didn't even feel like crying.

They knew. And I wasn't going to die from it.

But if I admitted that, even to myself, then I would have to admit that running away had been a complete over-reaction. And I wasn't prepared to admit that. I was too far in.

My call to Dad had probably tipped them off about the money. I guess on some level I knew that all along. Maybe on some level I wanted them to put the pieces together, to find out what a horrible person I was when I was still hundreds of miles away.

That way I couldn't feel anything but the sun and the wind and the rumble of the cars passing by on the highway. That way I couldn't get caught up in the drama of being caught. I was here and they were there and we wouldn't have to face one another with the truth that I wasn't as perfect as any of us thought I was. They couldn't yell at me if I wasn't there; they would have to accept it without understanding it. And, more important, I would have to accept it without understanding it, too.

Maybe I would never go home. Maybe I would stay gone forever.

I flipped through my contacts until I got to Zoe's name and pressed "call." The phone rang three times and went to voice mail.

Hey, yo, you've got Zo! her voice rang out in a singsong. The mere sound of it brought happy tears to my eyes. I laughed out loud, imagining her making her gangsta face while saying this. I could see her so clearly in my mind—lips pooched together, head cocked to one side, making signs with her fingers and crossing her arms like she was tough. *Leave me a message and…whatev. You know.* This last was followed by giggles, but they weren't just Zoe's giggles. Another girl's voice intertwined with Zoe's. *You're a poet and you didn't kn—*, the other voice said before it was cut off. My smile wilted, and a tiny voice nagged in the back of my mind: *That's probably Zoe's new best friend.*

That's probably the reason she never answers your texts or e-mails, Kendra. Zoe's a poet and she didn't know it, and you are yesterday's news.

But I knew Zoe. She was my best friend. Best friends are for life. The girl on the message was probably just some other girl. Zoe's version of Shani or Lia. No big.

The voice mail beeped and I swallowed the lump in my throat.

"Hey, Zo," I said. "It's Ken. I um...I like your voice mail, yo." I forced a laugh, but even to my own ears it sounded like I was trying too hard. How long had I been doing that? How long had I been putting so much effort into making Zoe remember me? "So my number's the same. Give me a call, okay? I have a surprise for you. It's important. Bye." I hung up and stared at the phone for a minute. *You're a poet and you didn't know it.* Why did those words make me feel so rotten inside?

Probably because this was the first time I really felt that Zoe's life had gone on in California. That she wasn't still pining for her best friends back in Missouri. Because for the first time, I had to admit that there was a teeny part of me that worried that she wasn't answering me because she just didn't want to.

I pushed that thought away. I couldn't go there. We were way too far in it for me to start having doubts now. I was being silly. Zoe would be there in California. And she would be happy to see us. She would.

I started to put the phone away, then changed my mind

and flipped back to Mom's text and hit "reply," noticing that my phone had only two bars of battery charge left.

I'm sorry Mom. I promise to fix it.

A car honked behind me and I jumped. A man was idling, in line for the pump. I quickly turned my phone off and stuffed it into the glove box, then started up Hunka and drove back to the motel, wondering why I'd just made that promise to my mom once again.

Why I'd promised to continue to be perfect when I'd already proved that I was far from it.

CHAPTER
TWENTY-EIGHT

Rena and Grayson were sitting on the curb outside the room when I pulled into the parking lot.

"Checkout's at eleven," Grayson said as he opened the back door for Rena. She climbed in, pushing Bo's seat in ahead of her. I noticed that Bo was awake but was lying there, serenely watching the sky with glassy eyes. I still thought he looked funny. Why didn't Rena see it?

We all have obvious things we don't see, my brain rattled in response. *You're a poet and you didn't know it, Kendra.* But I batted that thought away.

"So it must be after eleven," Rena said, "because the maid came in and told us we had to get out or go pay."

Grayson got in on the passenger side. He mimicked in a thick foreign accent, "Dis a-no slop house. You gotta a-pay for da bed!"

He and Rena both cracked up.

"I think she meant flophouse." Rena giggled. "Unless she thought we were pigs." She oinked.

Grayson laughed. "You never know at that place. I'd believe they let barn animals sleep in those beds."

Rena barked out a laugh. "Smelled like it," she said. "The sheets on my bed were sticky."

Bo cried, and Rena pulled the baby carrier's sun visor up to shade his face. Then she rattled a toy over him, and he stopped.

"We a-no clean da sheets at dis a-slop house," Grayson said, adopting the accent again. "You gotta a-pay if you a-wanna da clean sheets on da bed!"

Rena joined in. "You gotta a-pay extra if you a-wanna shower!"

Again, they both laughed uproariously, even though Rena's fake accent was horrible. She sounded like she had a bad cold.

But I couldn't help it; their jokes were contagious. I chimed in. "We have a-no shower! Only sex webcam in dat shower hole!" And we all laughed, even though my accent was worse than Rena's.

"No a-touch da sex webcam! We pay nineteen ninety-five for it!" Rena laughed. "Biiig bucks! Cost a-more dan whole a-room!"

"I no a-touched anything in that bathroom if I could help it," Grayson said, wiping his eyes. "I swear I saw things moving on the toilet seat."

"No a-touch da tings on the towlet seat," I said, shaking my finger at him. "Dose are complimentary breakfast!"

"Ewww," Rena and Grayson moaned together, and we laughed some more as we pulled back onto the highway and headed toward California.

See, Zoe? I said in my head. *I can laugh with other friends, too. I can even make Grayson laugh about germs now.* I wasn't sure if even Zoe was ever able to accomplish that.

We drove for a long time in silence. I peeked into the rearview mirror and saw that Rena wore the same satisfied grin that Grayson had on his face. I imagined mine matched theirs, too. I pushed Mom's text and Zoe's voice mail message out of my mind and drove along, cracking the window and enjoying the whir of the highway under Hunka's tires.

I imagined Lia and Shani back at school, their butts sweating on the plastic school chairs as the classrooms get more and more stuffy as the day warms up. Feeling lucky if one of their afternoon teachers says they can go outside to read their assignments. Girls wearing shorts to school, their legs all white and goose-pimply because it's still not quite warm enough for shorts, but they can't wait until summer to show off their figures again.

Was Bryn at school? What was happening to Chub right now? What about Darian and Tommy and the others? Had they all been expelled, as Lia and Shani had predicted?

A part of me wanted to be there. I wanted to be gossiping

at my locker with the girls and making fun of the kids who were still wearing their winter boots instead of flip-flops. I wanted to be at the honor society meeting. I wanted to be in class, as much as I hated to admit it.

But I knew that would never happen. Not again. I was in too deep. If Chub was expelled, that spelled doom for me. The thought that I'd passed a certain point of no return scared me a little. What would my life look like when I got back? What would happen to me? Would I still graduate, still pack for college in a few months? I doubted it.

I'd promised Mom I'd make it all better, but I knew it was too late for that.

Sometimes I wished I had an excuse, like Grayson. Leaving school early had been no big deal for him. It was sort of expected. Nobody got mad or disappointed. But other things were expected of me. Different things. And staying in school was certainly one of them.

"Can we turn on some music?" Rena asked, leaning forward and resting her chin on the back of the front seat.

"We can try," Grayson said, using an antibacterial wipe as a buffer, fiddling with the radio dial. "Let's see if we can get anything besides static and static."

A few stations tuned in and out again, and then he landed on a song that made Rena suck in her breath and grab his shoulder.

"Leave it there! 'Lullaby'! My mom used to listen to it all the time when I was a little kid. Shawn Mullins." She flopped back against her seat and sang along.

I recognized the song and started singing along to the parts I knew, too, and Grayson seemed to know the whole thing. He even did the talking parts, and before long we were all singing at the top of our lungs.

This. This felt so right. Singing and joking in fake accents and driving in the sun. No sickness here. No perfection to live up to. No hospitals and shrinks and quarries. It was like the song was speaking directly to me—*Yes, Kendra, your life is shit right now. You really screwed the pooch. You've got about eight more levels of hell to go through, probably. But everything's going to be okay. It really will.*

When it was over, an old Savage Garden song came on and we sang along to it, too, and then a Backstreet Boys song that had us dancing in our seats and laughing so hard we could hardly sing.

"This station must be all-'90s-throwback-music-all-the-time," Grayson joked in a radio announcer voice.

As if in answer to what he'd just said, Madonna and Babyface poured through the speakers and we all cracked up, singing along. It felt comforting, singing along to all the songs we remembered from when we were little kids.

Finally, a commercial came on and Grayson turned the volume down a little, then leaned forward and scooped up a handful of rocks and started lining them up on the dash. *Uh-uh-uh-uhuh.*

"What's wrong?" I asked, wondering if maybe something I'd said or done had made him anxious. He'd been fine, and all of a sudden he wasn't fine, and just like the rest of our lives, I wished I knew what made things change for him and, more important...how could we change it back?

He glanced at me, then out the windshield, curiously. "What?"

I pointed at the rocks in his hand. "Everything was going so good. Why are you doing that?"

He stared at the rocks as if he wasn't sure what they were exactly. "I don't know," he said. "It felt like I needed to."

That wasn't good enough. It didn't make sense. It never made sense. I wanted an answer. How could he ever expect to get better without an answer? "But why? I mean, if it's about anxiety, like Dr. St. James said, then why? You weren't anxious five seconds ago."

His ears turned red, and I could see his hands grip the rocks so tightly his fingers went white. "I don't know, Kendra. Why do you always have to be asking me?"

I swerved slightly to avoid a pothole, then looked back at him. "Well, what if it's just a habit?" I chewed my lip. "What if that's all it is? What if you aren't mentally ill. You've got a habit. Like...like smoking or chewing your fingernails or something."

"A habit," he repeated, looking at me incredulously.

"Yes, a habit. You're a rock junkie."

I grinned. I'd meant it to be a joke, but he shook his head and leaned forward to put the next rock up on the dash. Subject closed. His face was so close to the dash that had I stopped suddenly, he would've gone face-first into it.

"I have a question about the rocks," Rena said.

Grayson glared at me as if to blame me for her sudden interest. I shrugged. Not like Rena wouldn't have noticed it if I hadn't said something.

"Why rocks? I mean, why not marbles or matches or pennies, or..."

Grayson paused. Seemed to really consider this, as if maybe he'd never thought about it before. "I guess," he said, "it's because rocks have a story."

"A story," Rena repeated, doubtful.

He nodded. "Yeah. How they were created, where they were created, that kind of thing. I don't know. It's probably stupid, but rocks kind of remind me of people."

"How so?" she asked.

I knocked my fist against Grayson's temple. "Well for some of us, it's probably about hardheadedness. Like granite up here."

He leaned out of my reach. "No. It's just...we take a long time to form, and when we do, we're all different in one way or another, even if we seem alike or came from the same place or whatever. We all have our specific traits, our own histories. And, like rocks, people aren't always as unbreakable as they seem. It's...it's just a theory I have."

She leaned forward and stretched her arm over the seat, pointing at a rock. "So what's that rock's story?"

"This?" Grayson said, picking up the rock she was pointing at. She nodded. "This is quartz," he said. He ran his thumb across the smooth, clear face of the rock.

"I thought quartz was pink," Rena said, turning her hand so it was palm up.

Grayson gave her the quartz. "Sometimes it is. It can be lots of different colors."

"Why is this one clear, then?" she asked, bringing her other hand over the seat. She turned the rock around in her hands, studied it, then held it up and squinted at it through the sun.

"Pure quartz is colorless," Grayson answered, stroking the rock with his forefinger while she held it. "Colored quartz happens when there are chemical impurities in the rock, which I've always thought was really cool irony. Quartz is at its most beautiful when it's been changed by impurities. But this one is pure. That's kind of what I mean by rocks having stories."

"Pure. I like that," Rena said, and a look flitted over her face that reminded me that there was a whole lot about Rena that Grayson and I didn't know. It was a look of sadness, like this girl had some demons in her past. "Can I keep this one?"

"Technically, it's yours anyway," I said. "We stole it from that gazebo."

"A memento," Rena said, closing her hand around the rock. "Of that rock-headed old bastard, Archie. Not pure at all."

"Sure," Grayson said, bending down to pick up another rock, anxiety flitting quickly across his face. He was probably worried that losing this rock meant he had an odd number of rocks left. *Uh-uh-uh.* "Keep it."

Bo started fussing, and I watched as Rena pulled him out of his carrier and nestled him to her chest. She talked to him in a low voice, but he kept squawking, arching his back away from her. She jiggled him and bounced him, but he kept going. She tried patting his back, but that only seemed to make the crying worse. She cooed and sang along to the radio right into the side of his face, but nothing worked.

"Want me to pull over?" I asked, gesturing to an exit straight ahead.

She peered at her baby with concern. "Do you mind?" she asked, yelling to be heard over the baby's cries. "I don't know what's wrong with him. He won't eat. He's not wet."

"Maybe he's sick," I suggested, but Rena didn't seem to register what I'd said.

"Maybe he needs a change of scenery," Grayson said.

"I guess," Rena answered, flipping the baby facedown over her knees and patting his back. He wailed and squirmed like he was being beaten.

I pulled off the highway and down an outer road.

"Pull back there," Grayson said, pointing toward a tree-studded area next to a river. "You should be able to park."

I followed his finger and pulled up onto the grass and parked under a tree. We all got out and stretched while Bo screamed, writhing in agony, his little face beet-red.

"Thanks, Kendra," Rena breathed, streaking past us

and disappearing on the other side of a tree. "I'll make it fast." She spread a blanket on the ground and laid Bo down on it, then sat cross-legged on it and swept Bo up into her arms.

Grayson and I looked at each other and then paced past the tree and to the river's edge. Bo's cries never even so much as slowed down. He was shrieking so hard now some of the cries were silent and would catch in the middle, sounding jagged around the edges. I could hear Rena talking to him, but she still didn't seem all that concerned.

"I wonder what river this is," I said. I picked up a leaf and tossed it in.

"Green River," Grayson answered. "There were signs."

I picked up another leaf and tossed it in, then crossed my arms over my chest. The wind had picked up, as it always does on a riverbank, and I wished I had worn my sweatshirt. Grayson counted softly under his breath. I didn't blame him for being stressed right now. Bo's cries were stressing everyone out.

"Do you think there's something wrong with him?" I asked.

Grayson shrugged. "I haven't been around a lot of babies."

I bumped him with my shoulder. "You were around me."

"I was three."

"No excuse, Genius Boy. When you were three, you already knew all about quartz, I'll bet."

He grunted. "Probably."

"I liked what you said in the car," I said. He stopped counting and looked at me. "About the quartz," I added.

"Why?"

I shrugged and bent to pick up another leaf. "I don't know. I think maybe because of what you said about rocks being like people, you know? It's like we're all born colorless. We all have the potential to be pure. But then impurities creep in, and next thing you know we're...changed. But we're still beautiful. Changed doesn't have to mean ugly. I like that."

He nodded. "Yeah. It's a nice concept. In theory."

"I didn't mean what I said about you being a rock junkie. I was...it was just a thought."

He shrugged. "Would be nice if that was all it was. If I could just stop."

"You're not doing it now," I pointed out. "So maybe you can."

He grunted again but didn't answer.

I sat on the grass and hugged my knees to my chest. Bo cried more at our backs, and Grayson glanced back there, going back to chanting the numbers under his breath. Something about the two things together made me love my brother's illness a little. He was trying to quiet Bo. I knew that to my core. In a way, it was sweet. Frustrating and annoying but sweet.

"What do you think of Rena?" I asked.

Uh-uh-uh-uh. "Twenty-eight...twenty-nine..."

"Do you like her? She seems kind of ... spacey."

Uh-uh-uh. "Thirty-three ... thirty-four ... thirty-five ..."

I reached over and touched the calf of his leg. I wanted so badly to tell him about my plan to go to Zoe's house. I wanted to make him happy, make him relax. "Gray. Do you still love Zoe?"

At first I thought he was going to ignore me, like I'd never said a word. Not like I wasn't used to that. But instead he stood there, counted to forty, and stopped. "Why are you asking me about Zoe?"

"I miss her," I said.

"I don't," he said. "I can't. She was too good for me."

"Bull," I said. "Her parents wanted to make everyone believe that, but it wasn't true. And Zoe never believed it."

"Well, they won anyway," he said. "It doesn't matter."

"Would you ever want to see her again?" I asked, thinking maybe I should go ahead and tell him. Maybe I should come clean now and tell him that my plan was for this time tomorrow to be sitting in Zoe's room making everything okay. That I hoped for him to be as excited to see Zoe as I was. That I wanted for it to be the three of us again, like we were before.

Maybe I was hoping if I hinted hard enough, he'd put the pieces together. Did he even know Zoe was in California? Had she given him a photo with her address scratched on the back? I'd never asked him.

But he suddenly stepped away from me angrily. "This is

stupid," he said, then whirled around and marched toward the tree where Rena still struggled against Bo.

I got up and followed him, jogging to catch up.

"Can I try?" he said, holding out his hands toward Bo.

Rena held the baby up in the air, and Grayson took him, laying Bo's rigid little body against his shoulder and pacing with him. Grayson did what he does best. He counted. Rhythmically. Evenly. In the same steady voice. One. Two. Three. Four. I had a feeling that Grayson would do this forever if he had to, keep going until he reached the magic number that would make Bo better.

By the count of thirty, Bo was calming, his cries turning to hiccups and then to silence. The baby sucked on his fist, watching the light skitter across the water over Grayson's shoulder, the occasional cry-shudder traveling through him.

"Thank God," Rena said, lifting her hair off her neck. "He's never done that before."

"Maybe he's sick," I said again, sitting down with my back against the tree next to her. Rena chewed her lip in response, her eyes searching Bo worriedly.

"I don't know," she said. "He's not been acting right. But he's not, you know, like, puking or anything."

"Maybe he's sick with something else. Like an earache or something," I said.

"He's probably just worn out. He's not used to all this excitement. He'll be okay."

After a few minutes, she got up and went to the car,

then returned with Bo's carrier. She picked up the blanket off the ground and draped it over him and Grayson's chest.

She stood in between Grayson and me, rubbing her arms with her hands and staring out at the river.

"I don't know about you," she said finally, "but that water looks great to me."

Grayson and I glanced at each other. He turned away, continuing to count in Bo's ear.

"Are you kidding?" I said. "That water's probably freezing. It's barely May."

"All the better," she said. She kicked off one shoe and looked back at me, wickedly. "I'm going in."

"You don't know the undertow of that thing," Grayson said between numbers.

"It's fine," she said, and kicked off the other shoe. "Come on."

"Uh-uh," I said, leaning hard against the tree. "You want to freeze, go right ahead. I'm good."

She wiggled out of her jeans and let them drop on top of her shoes, then came over and grabbed my arm. "Come on, Kendra, don't be afraid," she said. "I know you didn't shower today. Dee a-sex webcam was in da way!"

I rolled my eyes, smiling despite myself. "No way, crazy lady."

She pulled my arm harder. "Come on. Come on come oncomeon." Then she started to sing that Shawn Mullins song we'd been singing earlier. And I honestly don't know

238

what happened. Maybe it was that I was so far away from home and had already done so many things Perfect Kendra would never have done. Maybe I wanted to show my brother that I could do spur-of-the-moment things like swim in a freezing river and everything would still turn out okay and nobody would die. Maybe it was something about Rena— motherless, running away, broken, but still spirited—that made me want to let go and live. Maybe I was slap-happy, or it was the jackalope or the song or the long hours in the car or, maybe, it really was just that I hadn't had a shower and I felt gross. Whatever the reason, I did it.

I got up and kicked my shoes off, too, leaving them under the tree next to Bo's carrier. As I pulled off my jeans and tugged my T-shirt so it looked like a short dress, barely able to believe I was doing this, Rena went to Grayson.

"Come on, Grayson," she said. "You know you want to."

Uh-uh-uh-uh. "I'll take care of Bo."

"He's asleep."

Uh-uh. "No."

I laughed, watching Grayson turn a thousand shades of red when Rena, standing in a sweater and underwear, reached out and rubbed his arm. There was no way in a million years she was going to get my brother into that water.

"It'll be okay," she whispered. "You'll wash off the germs you got at that motel. And I promise there aren't any germs that will kill you in this river."

"You have no idea what kind of germs are in that river," he answered.

"And, trust me, he does," I added.

She smiled. "True. But I also know I've swum in a lot of rivers, and look." She turned in a circle, palms up. "I'm still here. Come on. Take it from the girl sitting in the same car with you. You need to bathe."

I held my nose and nodded. "You stink, big brother."

"What if we get caught? You can't just decide to go swimming in a river. The cops will come." He looked pointedly at me when he said the last. "We'll get sent home."

I blinked. That almost sounded like he no longer wanted that to be the outcome to this trip. Maybe he was coming around. Maybe he was even enjoying himself a little bit. "We'll get in and out fast," I said. "We won't get caught."

"Yeah," Rena said. "Just a quick dip." She pried Bo out of Grayson's arms and carried him carefully to the carrier. She pulled up the sun visor, wrapped the blanket around the baby, and rocked the carrier a little to soothe him, but he was already sound asleep.

"Let's go," I said, hopping up and down. "I'm cold already."

Uh-uh-uh. Grayson looked out over the river uncomfortably, as though he didn't know what excuse to make now that the baby was out of his arms.

Finally, Rena stepped in front of him again. "You sure?" she asked playfully. She took off his glasses and handed them to me. I laid them on top of Bo.

"Positive," he answered, but he was starting to get that

uncertain and angry look he'd gotten right before storming over to the jackalope statue.

"Okay, you win," she said. But before he could say anything else, Rena reached out and grabbed his hand, clamping down on it, and started running, pulling him along behind her and shrieking, "You're going in, sucker!"

"Wait! No," Grayson argued, tripping after her, but he didn't fight back too hard, and to me his face looked flushed and happy...and relaxed. And normal.

I followed them, hefting Bo's carrier to the river's edge and setting it on the ground in the shade of a big rock. "She got you!" I called.

They'd reached the riverbank. Rena paused to whip her sweater off over her head, then ran into the river, her bare back looking pale and beautiful in the sunlight.

Grayson shucked off his shoes and jeans and inched timidly to the edge of the water.

"Oh, no, you don't," I screamed, and shoved him from behind, knocking both of us all the way in. I landed on my hands and knees on the shallow river floor.

The breath was sucked right out of me as the frigid water clung to my skin. We came up for air, our T-shirts sticking to us, and cussed and laughed. Grayson's lips were already blue, and my teeth were chattering.

But out in the water, neck-deep and cheering, was Rena. "This is amazing!" she shouted, lifting her arms high above her head and spinning around. "Come out. Marco!"

Grayson and I glanced at each other and then started laughing. "Polo!" I yelled. We both dived in and swam out to her, forgetting about everything but that moment.

After a few feet I paused, the water up to my waist, and stared at Rena's face, bobbing through the sunlight reflecting off the water, her eyes squeezed shut. She was so confident. She didn't need to be able to see us to know that we would all eventually find one another.

For just a second I closed my own eyes. "Marco," I whispered, hoping that across the miles Zoe would somehow hear me, and that I would find her, too.

CHAPTER
TWENTY-NINE

Despite Rena's insistence that the water wasn't so bad and that if we kept moving we'd be plenty warm, it wasn't too long before I couldn't take it anymore. I sludged over the slimy river rock toward the bank and pulled myself out, shivering so hard I could barely stand up straight.

Rena and Grayson stayed out in the river. After a while, my brother disappeared under the surface, then came up with a handful of rocks, holding them with his fingers splayed to let the sediment fall through and back into the water. He and Rena bent their heads over what was left in his hand, him pointing and explaining in that methodical way Grayson does everything.

I could barely believe this was my brother out there, neck-deep in river water, smucking up handfuls of mossy grime, not even thinking about what wildlife might be swimming around his ankles. In some ways he seemed to completely forget his OCD. He seemed more relaxed than he'd been in years. But a part of me wondered how much of that was about my plan working and how much was about me not seeing him for who he really was. Was I just seeing it now because I'd been stuck in a car with him for two days and he was always right there in my face, whereas at home I could isolate myself, pretend he and his problems didn't exist whenever it was inconvenient for me to face them? Or was it because he (or Mom and Dad) had tried to shelter me from his OCD at home? Or was I just blind, forever wanting so much to have the perfect family that I refused to see reality?

I brought Bo's carrier back to the tree. He was still sleeping. I felt a pang of worry. What if there was something wrong with him and Rena never did anything about it? I was surprised by how much Bo and Rena had become part of our trip so quickly. How already I was worrying about Bo and how already I had a feeling that Rena didn't know enough to be worried.

I knew that it wouldn't last—that they'd go their way and we'd go ours. And I wondered if we would even care when it happened. I wondered if I'd forever be worried that she'd never figure out what was wrong with her baby. I wondered if Grayson would care. If he'd be counting for Bo forever, too, instead of just our family.

My shivering died down a little as I sat in the sun, squeezing water out of my hair and thinking how I would never forget this day—the day when I forgot about my problems for a few seconds while swimming in the Green River, which I'd never even heard of before I stepped into it.

I grabbed my jeans and headed to the other side of Hunka, where I peeled off my shirt and underwear and snuggled into my hoodie and jeans. I felt so much better already. I opened the trunk and laid my wet clothes, which were already beginning to stink like moldy river, flat inside it to dry as much as they could while we were driving. I left the trunk open so Grayson could do the same, but by the time I came back around the car, they were both dressed, Rena wringing out her wet underwear by the riverbank, Grayson bare-chested and holding a dripping shirt in a wad in his left hand.

"I told you it'd be fun," Rena called up to me.

I sat by the tree and stepped back into my shoes, making a face at the rocks and grit that stayed stuck to my feet inside them. Yuck. "I told you it'd be freezing," I called back. Bo stirred at the sound of my voice, so I moved toward them.

Grayson was putting on his shoes, looking out over the river. He almost looked as if even he couldn't believe he had done it. "I wish..." he said, but he didn't continue. I waited for him to finish the sentence, but I knew Grayson. He'd never finish it. He'd be too afraid to express a wish out loud. He'd have to count to, like, a billion to keep the wish from being "jinxed." We used to wish on stars together with Zoe. Somehow Zoe must have made it feel safe for him to do that. But this was the first time I'd heard him wish since she left.

"How's Bo?" Rena said, climbing up toward the tree.

"Sleeping. We should go while he's asleep."

She nodded, bending over him and peering into his face, then picked up her shoes and his carrier. "Probably should. Little man won't sleep forever."

We all got settled and back on the highway, none of us saying a word, half for fear that we'd wake up Bo, and half for the endorphins that flooded our bodies. I felt cozy and compact, like my hoodie was a cocoon.

"Where to next?" Rena asked sleepily from the backseat.

Grayson opened the atlas and studied it. "Utah," he said. "I guess Utah."

"Utah," she repeated softly. She shifted so her back was against the door and her legs were resting across the seat. "Never been. We are definitely away from home now, little Bo-bo," she said.

Grayson ate a granola bar, and Rena passed around the leftover bottles of chocolate milk, which were getting warm, even in their cooler. I ate a few pieces of cheese and watched the road. It changed, but not really. Mostly the highway was just the highway, no matter where in the world you were. A grungy gas station here, a rest stop there. Maybe a restaurant every now and then, and sometimes even a whole city, like the one we'd just come out of. Could be anywhere. I guess that's because nobody makes the highway a home.

There's no room for personality on the highway. Everyone is either coming back from somewhere away or going away from somewhere that once was home. Nobody is "here." Everyone is on the way "there."

And where were we on the way to, really? To Zoe? To Grayson's getting better?

That's what I'd been telling myself.

My plan with Grayson seemed to be working. But something about the way he still made that sound in his throat and rubbed the rocks with his thumbs made it feel so tentative.

And besides, even if Grayson did get better, that did nothing to help me. And—I had to face it—I wasn't really running twenty-six hours away from home because of Grayson's problems. I was running away from mine.

I had lots of excuses for why I did the things I did. I was always the ignored sibling. I had to be perfect if I wanted any attention. I never meant for the situation to get so out of hand. I never meant for anyone else to get hurt. I never forced anyone into anything, so it wasn't really my fault what happened to Chub and Bryn and the others. Blah, blah, blah. All cop-outs, every single one of them.

Why couldn't I just relinquish control and admit that, yes, sometimes Kendra the Perfect does screw up?

Why couldn't I let go?

In the small amount of time I'd known Rena, I'd already done things I never thought I would do. Picked up a hitchhiker. Climbed a jackalope. Skinny-dipped in a river I'd never even heard of before. And it all felt so good. I felt so free.

But the freer I felt, the more tied up I realized I'd been for so long. And the thought had begun to creep into my brain in the rattly silence of Hunka that maybe Grayson wasn't the only one who needed fixing. Maybe he wasn't even the one who needed fixing the most.

CHAPTER THIRTY

Bo woke up with another ear-piercing shriek when I stopped for gas. Both Grayson and Rena jerked awake, looking disoriented, their river-wet hair dried in odd angles away from their heads. I stood in the open driver's door, peering over the seat at Bo.

"Sorry," I said to Rena. "I didn't mean to."

"What time is it?" she asked, rubbing her eye with one hand and pulling Bo out of his carrier with the other. He kicked and arched backward angrily.

"I don't know. About three-thirty, I guess."

She sat up straight, like someone had poked her with a pin. "God, he hasn't eaten in a long time." She fought with his buckles.

"Where are we?" Grayson asked, opening his door and stretching out of the car.

"Salt Lake City. I was gonna go farther, but my butt was getting numb. I need a drink."

The wind ruffled his hair as he turned to face the highway, both of his hands pressed against his lower back. "Good thing you stopped. I think it's not much more than desert past here for a while."

The thought startled me. Had I not stopped, would we have run out of gas in the desert, like in the movies? Would we have wandered around out there until we all baked to death in the desert sun, our throats caked with sand?

What does it matter? I told myself. *You're sounding like Grayson now, what-iffing and catastrophizing. You stopped. That's all that matters.*

"I'm going to use the restroom," I said, walking over the pump island. "You coming?"

He wrinkled his nose. "I'll hold it."

"I don't know when I'm stopping again. Desert, remember?"

"I don't have to go. I'll wait."

"I'm sure the restroom is plenty clean, Grayson."

"I said no, okay? Let it go."

I held up my palms, innocently. "Okay. Whatever. But when you're peeing on the side of the highway and a cobra bites your ankle off, don't come running to me."

He shook his head as if he felt sorry for me. "A, cobras are not indigenous to this area. You're probably thinking of a rattlesnake."

"Thank you, Genius Boy, for that little factoid."

"B, it's not possible for a snake to bite a human's ankle off. And, C, if my ankle had been bitten off, how would I run anywhere?"

I rolled my eyes at him. "Captain Literal, permission to go ashore now?"

"Granted."

I turned and walked to the restroom, a smile on my face despite my frustration.

While I was inside, I picked up a few more supplies, including a few petrified-bread sandwiches, since it looked like we'd be in the car for dinner.

I noticed, with a little jolt of panic, that the money wad in my pocket was getting significantly smaller. A lot more singles and a lot fewer twenties. If we were going to make it to California, we were going to have to be very careful. I didn't even want to think about how we'd get back home. Maybe the cashier's refusing Mom's credit card at that diner in Kansas had been a fluke and I could try using it again. I'd think about that later.

Back on the road, Grayson opened the sandwiches and passed them around.

"Did Bo eat?" I asked, taking a bite of mine, even though I wasn't really hungry yet.

"Not much," Rena answered. "But at least he's not screaming anymore." She stroked the top of his head, a concerned crease in her forehead, leaving the uneaten sand-wich on the seat next to her.

"Maybe he should see a doctor."

She seemed to consider this. But instead of agreeing, she turned to him and started singing, her voice velvety and low. We drove in silence until she was finished.

"What was that?" I asked. "Pretty."

"Something my grandma used to sing to us when we were little," she answered. "Church song." When she lifted her eyes to meet mine in the rearview mirror, I noticed tears, tiny and shimmery, clinging to her eyelashes.

"Hey," I said, forgetting about the rearview mirror and looking back over my shoulder at her. "He's fine, I'm sure," I said. "He's just been through a lot of commotion, like you said."

She nodded, curving one finger over her top lip and turning her head toward the window. "I just don't want to screw him up the way my family screwed me up." There seemed to be nothing to say to this, and we all fell into an uncomfortable silence.

I put my hand over Grayson's hands, which were still working the wet wipe, and shook my head. *Not now*, I mouthed. And, to my surprise, he stopped. I made a mental note that sometimes just telling him to stop actually worked. Maybe I should try doing it more often. The sun was setting by the time we reached the desert. Rena's sniffles had stopped miles ago, and she'd sung a few more songs to Bo, then leaned her cheek against the window forlornly.

The desert was like nothing I'd ever seen before. White sand stretching for miles, with little plateaus dotting the distance. It felt like desolation. It felt harsh. Out here, what really mattered? OCD? Cheating? Money? Scholarships? No. None of it.

"I guess I've watched too much TV," I said, taking a sip of my water.

Grayson, who had finally finished his sandwich, looked up from the atlas he was studying.

"I always picture beige sand dunes and camels when I think of deserts," I continued. "This is white and flat. Not a camel to be found."

Grayson was hunched back over the atlas again. "You're thinking of the Sahara. This is Great Salt Lake," he mumbled, tracing a finger over a highway line.

"Duh," I responded. "I'm just saying. I wasn't, like, expecting to find King Tut out here or anything. I guess I was expecting more...brown."

"It's salt deposits. It's really a big dried-up lake we're driving through right now. You sure it wasn't geography you were flunking?"

He grinned. I narrowed my eyes at him but couldn't help grinning a little, too.

I gazed out the windshield, straining to see as far as I could see, trying to picture what it must have looked like back when this was a huge lake. Or, for that matter, back when dinosaurs drank at that lake's edge. Sometimes it seems too surreal that that life really existed. Sometimes I wondered if a future being would find my life surreal, too.

Hell, right now I found my life a little on the surreal side.

"What do you think is out there?" I asked.

"The military," Grayson answered. "And maybe a cobra or two."

We both snickered. I glanced in the rearview, but Rena had resumed staring out to the horizon, saying nothing.

Grayson went back to studying the atlas, mumbling, "It's only about fifty miles across this thing."

Good, I thought, and went back to daydreaming. Something about the desert made me feel unbearably far away from home. I wanted out.

CHAPTER
THIRTY-ONE

The most notable thing about Nevada was that we were starting to see green again. And we were out of granola bars, which, we decided, was okay because we were all sick of granola bars.

And Bo woke up and screamed. A lot.

Rena did everything she could for him. She tried feeding him, but he turned away from her, arching his back and screaming so loud and long you could see his heartbeat in the soft spot on the top of his head.

At a rest stop she paced with him, bouncing him on her shoulder. She rocked him briskly back and forth, taking his breath away, but as soon as he got it back, the screams resumed louder and longer.

She even gave him to Grayson, who walked the entire perimeter of a rest area in small, steady steps, chanting numbers in Bo's tiny ear the whole way. Rena sat on

Hunka's bumper and cried, pressing a balled-up piece of toilet paper to her nose.

I sat next to her and rubbed her back. "I'm sure he's just fussy," I tried, but I didn't sound convincing, even to my own ears.

"What do you know?" Rena snapped. "You're not a mother. This is just a road trip to you. You said it yourself."

I felt my face flush, unsure what to say. Had she seriously not heard me telling her for miles that I thought the kid was sick? "You're right," I finally said, my voice clipped. "I'm not a mother." Neither was she much of one, in my opinion, but I didn't say that aloud. "But you're wrong about this just being a road trip to me." I didn't go on. I didn't need to justify myself to a stranger.

Grayson had paused, out across the lawn, and lifted his foot backward to look at the bottom of his shoe, then resumed his pace, Bo's squeals echoing all the way across the parking lot to where we were.

"I miss my mom," Rena said suddenly, turning her puffy red eyes to me. "As stupid as it sounds, I miss her." She snorted sardonically, then pushed herself up onto Hunka's hood and curved her bare feet around the bumper, her leg brushing up against Jack's antlers. "She'd know what to do."

I bit my lip, unsure what to say. It was hard to stay mad at her when she was crying like that. Plus, as much as it felt as if I knew Rena after the past couple days, there was no denying that I really didn't know her whole story. I didn't know why she really ran away from home. I didn't know how mad her mom was when she left. I didn't know why she was driving halfway across the country with two total strangers.

Still. If it were me, and Bo were my baby . . . I'd want my mom, too.

"You can use my phone," I said, pushing myself up onto the hood next to her. I leaned forward, resting my elbows on my knees. Grayson and Bo were getting closer, and from the sound of things, the walk hadn't helped any.

She shook her head. "Been too long. She doesn't even know about Bo. I can't be all, 'Hey, Mama, I'm in Nevada and you're a grandma! What's up with you?' "

There was a pause, and then finally I asked, "Why not?" And then I remembered how far I was willing to go to get out of talking to my parents about what had happened with the calc final, and added, "Never mind."

We know about the money. We are confused. Come home. We need to talk.

The thought made me sick to my stomach.

Grayson came back and handed Bo off to Rena, who took him and headed toward the restroom. "Maybe if I change his diaper and splash some water on him," she said hopefully.

Grayson was busy wiping his shoe against the grass violently. "Why don't people clean up their dogs' shit?" he mumbled.

I wrinkled my nose. "You should go wash it off."

"I don't even want to think about the diseases," he said, as if I hadn't spoken at all. "Disgusting." He was walking in tight circles now, dragging one foot behind him. I had to press my hand against my mouth to keep from laughing.

"Why don't you go in there and wash it off?" I repeated, pointing toward the restroom.

"Because that would be like adding insult to injury," he said. "I can't go in and touch the faucets in a place like that. And touch my shoe with all this shit and probably maggots on it."

I snickered. Couldn't help it. Maggots? "There are no maggots on your shoe," I said. "You can see that much by looking at it."

"You can't see their microscopic little eggs."

"Okay, if you can't see it, it's like it's not there. Like in the river. So just go wash it off."

"No. I'm not going in there."

"Take your wipes with you."

"No, Kendra, I'm not going in. People have sex in those places. There are probably all kinds of bodily fluids that you can't see with the human eye on every surface."

I was starting to get annoyed. If it wasn't poop, it was maggots. If it wasn't maggots, it was sex fluids. If it wasn't bodily fluids, it would probably be aliens from outer space or poisonous gas clouds or deadly face-eating influenzas. "You're being stupid now."

He glared at me. "Well, if anyone knows stupid..." he said, gesturing at me.

I slid off the hood of the car and stood with my hands on my hips. "Go. Wash. It. Off. I'm not kidding."

"No," he said. "I'm not kidding, either."

"Well, I hope you like it here, then. Because you're not getting into my car with that smell. I'll puke."

"Too bad for you."

He walked over and leaned against the side of Hunka, pulling up his foot to peer at the bottom of it. I sprang forward and snatched the shoe off his foot in one swift pull. He barely had time to register what I'd done before I darted across the lawn to the big brown trash bin at the end of the sidewalk and tossed the shoe inside.

"Hey!" he yelled.

"Looks like it's too bad for you," I yelled back, brushing my hands off. "I'm going to go inside and wash up. Fluids or no fluids!" I turned on my heel and marched into the restroom, leaving him leaning against the car with one foot held up off the ground like an injured animal.

I knew I was letting this go further than I should have. And I knew I probably should have thought it through before I threw Grayson's shoe away. But I was already on edge from the stress of Bo crying, and still stung from Rena snapping at me, and sometimes Grayson was too easy a target. Plus, he'd come so far. My plan was working. I wasn't going to just sit back and watch him go back to the way he was before.

By the time I came out of the restroom, Rena was pacing a finally quiet Bo around the perimeter again, and Grayson was sitting inside Hunka, his head down in a pout.

I got in next to him, just as Rena rounded the last corner and headed toward us. Bo was asleep on her shoulder. Grayson was still wearing one shoe, his other foot bare and resting on top of the rocks on the floorboard.

"That's a good look for you," I said, snapping my seat belt in place. "You should keep it."

"Get my shoe," he said through clenched teeth. His fingers were crooked out in front of him, not in his usual counting pose but like he wanted nothing more than to wrap them around my neck.

"Go wash it off."

"No."

"Then no. If you want it, you're going to have to dig through the trash can to get it yourself. Consider it the best exposure therapy you've ever gotten. Dr. St. James would be proud."

He banged his temple against the window twice, his voice ratcheting up. "You can't go rummaging through public trash cans, you moron," he said. "There could be used hypodermic needles in there. You could end up with AIDS."

"AIDS, Grayson? Really?" I said, tipping my head to one side. I couldn't believe what I was hearing. Lord knows, I'd heard crazier obsessions from him, but this one was definitely up there.

He shook his head, looking out the window at the approaching Rena. "You're such an idiot," he said, then boomed, "Get the shoe!"

"No!" I screamed back, and when Rena looked over at

us sharply, I lowered my voice. "And shut up. If you wake up Bo, I'll throw your glasses away, too."

"Bitch."

"Nutbag."

"God, stop it, you guys. You're acting like little kids," Rena grumbled.

That was the other notable thing about Nevada, I guess. It was the point where the stress started to get to all of us. Rena cried and wished for her mom and called us children. Grayson freaked out over imagined hypodermic needles. And I called my brother a nutbag, even though I felt like crap immediately after doing it.

Rena opened Bo's door and eased him into his seat, rocking it gently when he first startled and then stirred as if he was going to wake and pitch another fit. When she was sure he was asleep, she came around to the other side and collapsed in the seat beside him.

"Let's get to California," she breathed, tipping her head back and closing her eyes.

"You read my mind," I said, and pulled out onto the highway.

CHAPTER
THIRTY-TWO

We didn't make it to California that night, but we got so close I could feel the excitement pinch my flesh up into goose bumps.

"Guys, I'm sorry," I said in a yawn. "But I'm getting tired. I've gotta stop."

"I'm hungry," Rena said by way of agreement.

"Reno," Grayson said, holding up the atlas to see it in the headlight beam of the car behind us. He glanced backward and grinned. "Your brother?"

She blinked at him. "I don't have a brother."

"No, I meant...you know...Rena...Reno. Never mind. It was a bad joke."

But Rena laughed, breathily. "Yeah," she said through her giggles. "It really was."

"He gets it from my dad," I said, and Grayson snorted, nodding. "My dad's the worst joke teller ever. You know his favorite? What should you do if you see a sleeping goat? Call the police! You've just witnessed a kidnapping."

"Har-har-har!" Grayson mimicked Dad's laugh. "Now, don't you kids go telling that one to all your friends and taking the credit," he said in a voice that sounded remarkably like our dad's.

"Like we ever would," I said.

We spent the next few minutes telling all the dumbest jokes we could think of, and I couldn't help feeling a squeeze in my heart for my dad. I missed him. I wished he were with us. He would've swum in the river. He would've laughed when I threw Grayson's shoe in the trash, and he would've known what to do about Bo.

Instead, he was at home, consoling Mom and probably cursing the day I was born for what an ungrateful daughter I turned out to be.

But it was good to hear Rena laugh again, even if the jokes made me a little bit sad. When Rena laughed, it lit up the whole car. Grayson smiled when she laughed, and his hands looked relaxed, and he held back his *uh-uh-uh*s.

I resolved that I would send Dad a text as soon as we stopped. Reassure him that we were both still okay and that everything would be resolved soon.

"Seriously, guys, we gotta look for someplace to stop," I said, rubbing my lower back with one hand. There were a lot of loose springs in Hunka, and after all this driving, my back was starting to feel like I'd slept on a grapefruit all night.

"That's right. Keep your eyes peeled, banana," Rena muttered, and she and Grayson cracked up again.

"That was horrible," Grayson said.

"I know," Rena answered.

"I'm impressed."

"Thank you. Thank you very much."

Grayson chuckled. "Elvis? Is that you? Alive and in Nevada? No way! Who woulda guessed?"

More stupid laughter, and I rubbed my back harder. "Great. Well, I guess I'll find a place myself. You two keep up your little comedy tour. That's okay." I tried to act put out by it, but I couldn't help grinning. There was something about the quirky way my brother was telling stupid jokes that reminded me of why I loved him so much.

I finally saw the perfect place—another in a long series of beat-up and nasty motels—and pulled into the parking lot.

"I'll go see if I can get us a room," I said. "You can stay out here with Bo. C'mon, Gray, come with me."

My brother sighed, all the fun and games draining out of his face instantaneously, but he didn't argue. He grabbed two rocks out of the pile on the floorboard, stuffed them into his pocket, and got out.

"Picked another winner," he muttered, taking in the dead bugs stuck to the outsides of the room doors and the taped bullet hole in one window. The flip-flops I'd bought him at the last gas station to replace his missing shoe whacked against the ground.

"I know. I'm sorry," I said. "I'm going to owe you big-time when this is over, huh. Like a presidential suite in a Hyatt somewhere?"

He shook his head. "Anyplace where strangers take their socks off and walk around with their dead skin cells leaking into the carpet is gross. No matter how posh. Athlete's foot knows no socioeconomic bounds."

We turned the corner to the office. "So, basically, I'll never make it up to you."

He let out a deep breath, stopped for a second to peer at the office door, then said, "Kendra, you don't have to. It's not like that."

"What's it like, then?"

He pulled one of the rocks out of his pocket and studied it, rubbed it with his thumb a few times, then closed his fist tightly around it. "I know what you're trying to do," he said.

For a second I thought that meant he knew about the money. Or maybe he'd figured out about my plan to find Zoe. My skin grew cold. The last thing I needed was him ruining my plan after we'd gotten so far. "What?" I croaked. "What am I trying to do?"

He dipped his head. "Make me normal," he said to his feet. "But it's not about me."

"Of course it's about you. And I don't know if you've noticed, but you've gotten better."

He made an impatient face. "No. That's not why you're doing this. You want to make me better so I'm not always causing problems for you."

"That's not true," I croaked.

But it was true, in a sense. I'd wanted to run away to get away from my own problems, but I also wanted to get his to go away, too. I wanted to cure him. But was I really doing it for him? No. And I think I'd known it all along. Probably before we even left Missouri. I wanted to cure him for me. How could I deny that I wanted to change him into someone "normal," someone who fit my life better?

It was true, and I felt like the biggest ass in the world for it. The worst sister ever.

What a spoiled brat. I couldn't just love him for who he was. I couldn't just be happy that I had a brother who loved me in a family that loved one another. I had to focus on the fact that he was somehow...I don't know...less than me. That he was broken and that I, perfect little Kendra with all the answers, could fix him. What a crock of crap.

Not to mention what an egotistical jerk I was. Thinking I could fix him. That I could do something as messed up as I did, and instead of facing it, I could step in and shine up my brother, and everyone would think I was a hero. That's what I wanted, wasn't it? To be a hero? To be a hero so big Grayson's recovery wouldn't be about him at all? God, how could I be so self-centered?

When it came down to it, I was running away, plain and simple, and I had only talked myself into believing that I was doing something great for Grayson at the same time. But no. I was using him as a crutch. As an excuse. Just like always. Excuse at school, excuse at home, excuse for why I didn't face things I didn't want to face or do things I didn't want to do. As long as Grayson was in charge of my life, I didn't have to be. How very convenient.

I ran my palm over my forehead, blinking back tears. Grayson was rubbing the rock with his thumb again, not meeting my eyes. Around us, the sounds of night went on like normal—bugs ticking against the flickering globe lamp outside the office door, car doors slamming in the parking lot, wind sighing through bushes.

"God, what am I doing?" I muttered.

"It's okay," he said. "I wouldn't want to live with a freak like m—"

"No," I said, interrupting him. "Stop. Grayson, just stop. It's not about...God, I can't believe...First of all, you're not a freak, okay? You're not." But I didn't know how to go on from there. I blinked, and two tears streamed down my face, the breeze pushing across them and leaving two cold streaks behind. I had to tell him. I had to tell him everything. That's all there was to it. "It's not about you. It's about me. I didn't just cheat," I said.

But I couldn't get any more out, because Rena was coming at us from the parking lot, running at full tilt.

"Help," she coughed out when she reached us. She grabbed Grayson's arm, jarring him so that the rock fell out of his hand and bounced on the sidewalk at his feet. She had a terrified, wide-eyed panic set in her face, and her skin was red and bulgy. I heard my brother gasp.

"What's going on?" I pulled at her hand, which had so

surprised Grayson he got that full freak-out hollow to his chest that I'd seen so many times before. But Rena wouldn't let go of Grayson, wouldn't tear her frightened eyes away from him. "Rena," I said, and pulled again, wrenching her free.

"It's Bo," she said, her voice coming out in a panicked rasp. "I can't get him to wake up!"

"What?" I asked, but I had already let go of her arm and was sprinting down the sidewalk back toward Hunka. I ripped open the door to the backseat and, sure enough, there was Bo, eyes closed. I reached down and shook his belly. Nothing. I jiggled him harder. Nothing again.

"Hey," I shouted, unsnapping his harness and pulling him out. It was the first time I'd held him, really, and I was shocked by how heavy he was. How alive he felt—nothing like the little dolls Zoe and I had played with under her picnic table. "Alive," I whispered, when the thought entered my mind. He wasn't pale, and he was definitely breathing. But he was hot as fire, except for his hands, which were cold, and when I held him up in front of my face and jiggled him, his eyes fluttered open and then shut again. His head lolled.

Rena was pulling at his hands and feet, her breath rushing into the side of my neck in harsh, hot gasps. Grayson had come up behind us but was still standing on the sidewalk, his arms crossed over his chest. He was moaning and making that *uh-uh-uh* sound and shifting his weight.

"He's okay," I breathed. "He's okay."

Rena grabbed Bo away from me and cradled him. "He's not okay. He won't wake up. That's not okay."

"Okay," I said, because I seemed to be stuck on this one word, my mind whirling and my chest feeling tight. *Okay* was all that would come to my mind. *Everything's okay. Everything's going to be okay.* In my periphery I could see Grayson, squatting now and wrapped around himself in a little ball, and could hear Rena yelling Bo's name, telling him to wake up, and all I could think about was that I didn't know what to do. That I was scared and that, for the first time in three days, I wanted my mom.

She always knew what to do. She always had a calm head. She'd been through so many crises with us over the years and had never looked rattled—not when I broke my arm doing a cartwheel on Zoe's trampoline. Not when Grayson needed stitches after running his bike into the back of a parked car. Not when she came home from work and found him, naked and freezing, in the hallway shower, having been there for somewhere around nine hours. She always dropped into some calm zone, said "Let's get to the hospital," and saved her breakdown for later when she was alone and everyone was somehow, miraculously, still alive.

"Let's go," I said, pushing Rena's back toward the car. "Grayson, get the atlas and find a hospital. Bo needs a hospital."

Rena raced around toward the other side of the car and slid into the backseat, still clutching Bo, but Grayson stayed where he was. He moaned a low moan.

"No," I said, pulling on his shirt, trying to get him to stand. "You can't do this right now." But he refused to move. "Grayson! Dammit!" I yelled, tugging some more. By now, there was a family standing outside their room watching us, whispering to one another. I looked around wildly for something that would help me get my brother to move. I could hear Rena shouting "Hurry up!" in the car.

Then I saw it. The rock. The one that Grayson had been holding when Rena grabbed onto him. It had bounced onto the sidewalk and rolled a few inches, but it was still there.

I rushed to the rock and picked it up, then rushed back to my brother and tucked it into the crease where his arms held tight against his chest. "There," I said. "You have two now. Okay? You're even. That means everything is going to be okay. Let's go." I pulled on him again, and still nothing. "Please, Grayson, I'm begging you." I squatted next to him and rested my forehead against his shoulder. "Just please be normal this one time," I whimpered, knowing that I had just negated what I'd said to him earlier about this trip not being a way for me to make him normal. The thought brought the tears that had been so absent in all the chaos, and I squeezed my eyes shut, letting them soak into my brother's shirt.

After a few seconds, which seemed like hours, I felt his shoulder move. He had shifted the rock into his hand and was staring at it. I pulled back and looked directly into his eyes. "Let's go to the hospital," I said.

Slowly, we both got up, and somehow I managed to fold

my brother into the car and shut the door behind him. I wiped my eyes on my forearms and walked on noodly legs to the other side, then slid in.

Grayson had the atlas open in his lap. *Uh-uh.* "Take a right," he said. "It's not far, actually. You'll probably see—*uh-uh*—signs as soon as you—*uh*—turn." And then he shut the atlas and turned toward his window, his throat working *uh-uh-uh*s and his fists furiously clenching two rocks apiece.

CHAPTER
THIRTY-THREE

By the time we reached the hospital, Bo had whimpered softly a couple times, so we knew for sure he wasn't dead, and even though none of us said so, I knew what had been on all of our minds at first—that Bo could have died while we were skinny-dipping and telling stupid jokes and climbing on a ridiculous jackalope and laughing it up like this was some fun summer road trip.

For the few minutes while we drove toward the hospital, all of us seemed to kind of be in our own heads. Rena held Bo against her shoulder and was whispering and singing into his ear. Grayson stared out the window, and I was busy following the blue H signs and trying to pinpoint where exactly I'd gone most wrong over the course of the past week. Or month. Or, hell, I don't know, my whole damn life, from the minute I popped my perfect little head into Grayson's imperfect little world and called him the messed-up one.

God, I was so stupid to think he was getting better. So blind.

I pulled up to the emergency room entrance, let Rena out, and then parked, taking so many deep breaths to calm myself I started to get dizzy and my hands started to feel numb.

When I opened my door, Grayson didn't move. I paused. "You staying here?" I asked, not wanting to push him any more than I already had. "You don't have to come in."

He nodded slowly, then, even more slowly, opened the car door and stepped out. I waited while he tucked handfuls of rocks into each pocket, not saying a word, and then we walked through the parking garage together.

"He's gonna be okay," I said, not sure why I was feeling the need to say this out loud. "He's just sick."

Uh. "We should've taken him to a doctor yesterday. Or the day before."

"We tried. And we're not his parents. Rena is."

"We shouldn't have ever left home," he said, his voice sour. "We should be home right now instead. With *our* parents." The automatic doors swooshed open in front of us, releasing that unmistakable hospital smell. "We shouldn't even be here," he continued, pausing before stepping across the threshold. "God knows what kinds of diseases we'll pick up here. Probably get influenza and die in California.

Nobody will know who we are. We'll just rot in a Dumpster somewhere."

"Cheery," I said, doing my best to ignore him by gazing around the waiting area for Rena.

There were two old ladies sitting side by side, clutching each other's hands, and a teenager across the room whose finger was pointing the wrong direction. In another area a baby cried relentlessly, but it wasn't Bo, and nearby a little girl lay limply across her mother's lap, staring at a TV screen and sucking her thumb.

No Rena.

"Excuse me," I said to a passing nurse. "We're looking for our friends? A blonde girl and a little baby? We were parking the car."

She looked confused for a moment, and then recognition struck. "Oh! Yeah, they took her back right away. I'm sure she'll come out as soon as she can."

So Grayson and I sat in the same room as the old ladies and waited.

And waited.

And waited.

Hours had gone by. God only knew what time of night it was. I started feeling drowsy, but I couldn't rest because my stomach was rumbling too loudly.

I flagged down another nurse. "Um, we were waiting to hear something about the blonde girl with the baby? Um, Bo? And Rena?"

"They're in with the doctor right now," she said.

274

"Can we go back?"

The nurse pressed her lips into a thin line. "I'm sure she'll come out as soon as she knows something. Might take a while."

I sat back. My stomach growled again. I felt washed out, and, as much as I didn't want to admit it, I wished I were home, sleeping in my own bed, wearing clean underwear and texting Shani about her stupid love life. For a minute, the urge was so strong, had Grayson asked one more time to leave and head back to Missouri, I wouldn't have hesitated. I would've driven all night long.

But unlike Grayson, I knew that the life I was imagining back home wasn't going to be the life waiting for me when I got there. What waited for me was lots of explaining, lots of crying, and lots of grounding. Lots of disappointment. Lots of people hating me.

My stomach cramped up again.

I couldn't take it anymore. "I'm going to get something to eat. Want anything?" I asked, standing up. Grayson had finally made himself comfortable in our little area. He'd laid Kleenex across the arms of the chair, and the two little old ladies had disappeared behind the emergency room doors. I had changed the TV to Discovery Health, and he was absorbed in some story about a little girl with a bleeding disorder. He wasn't going anywhere anytime soon. "I'll bring it to you. You can wait here for Rena."

He nodded. "A sandwich or something?"

"I'll see what I can find."

It felt good to be up and about again. Something about sitting still and waiting made time seem insufferable. Not knowing what the doctor was telling Rena about Bo was driving me crazy, and I had to fight the urge when I walked past the ER doors not to storm in there and look for her room, so I could find out what was going on.

Instead, I took a left and pushed through the doors underneath a sign that read HOSPITAL. The hallways were dark, buttoned up for the night. I wasn't sure which way to go, so I took a right and kept moving, past outpatient offices. There was silence. My shoes made echoed clopping sounds down the hallways. Twice I heard the hum of machines and followed the noise, hoping to find a vending machine, but only found a squat ice machine or a mini fridge with a coffeemaker on top.

I turned a corner and walked some more, coming up with nothing but more empty waiting rooms and dark alcoves. It was as if nobody ever got sick in this town. Finally, I happened upon a cafeteria, closed for the night, not to open again until six A.M.

For a minute I stood there, my palm pressed against the glass window of the cafeteria, and looked longingly at the bags of chips and cinnamon rolls and bananas sitting on the counter. I wanted to cry, it looked so good.

Finally, I turned and went back the way I'd come and headed toward a door to the outside I'd seen when I left the ER waiting room. I'd never been this hungry in my life. Not eating was no longer an option. I'd just swing out and get something real quick.

I grabbed my keys and patted the money in my front pocket and trotted out to Hunka. Surely someplace would be open all night.

Rena and Grayson wouldn't even know I was gone, much less miss me.

CHAPTER
THIRTY-FOUR

Half an hour and what felt like a hundred stops later, I plowed through the doors into the empty hospital corridor, juggling three bags. I'd driven around forever looking for a place where I could get Grayson a sandwich, but no place was open. So I'd finally found an all-night grocery store and had gotten stuff to make our own sandwiches. My plan was to stake out a clean-looking corner in one of the empty main lobby waiting rooms, drop the food off there, then go get Grayson and let him go to town with the new anti-bacterial wipes I'd bought. We could picnic in the dark, and then maybe stretch out in the shadows for a free night's sleep.

But no sooner had I stepped inside the building than I saw a ripple of blonde hair in a baby-blue sweater stepping off an elevator down the hall.

"Rena!" I shouted, much too loudly in the silence, and she turned.

"Kendra? You're still here?" she said, blinking at me.

"Of course. I mean, I just got back. I brought sandwiches." I held up the bags. "Didn't Grayson tell you where I was?"

She shook her head confusedly. "I didn't think you guys even came in when you dropped me off. They admitted Bo hours ago. I've been upstairs."

"Admitted Bo? Is he going to be okay?"

"Yeah," she said, and for the first time I noticed how tired her eyes looked, as though she were way older than she appeared to be. "He got some virus, and you know how he wouldn't eat much? Well, he got dehydrated, I guess. But they've got him on an IV now, and they said he should be fine."

I held my hand over my heart, relief washing through me. "Thank God." But Rena was sort of swaying, and I reached out to steady her. "Hey, you okay?"

And that's when the tears started for real. Her bottom lip quivered and then crumpled completely, and her face scrunched up, and she started to look like she was going to buckle at the knees. I put the bags on the floor and grabbed both of her arms, stepping in close. "Hey," I said, over and over again. "Hey, are you okay?" because that's all I could think to do.

"I should've known," she cried. "A good mother would've

known. What if they take him away from me? He's all I've got." She leaned into me. Bent and laid her forehead on my shoulder lightly. I smelled the funk of the river and sweat and sleep, but underneath a sweet smell, like oranges or something citrusy, and I felt the weight of her against me and I realized...I hadn't been leaned on—literally leaned on—by a friend since the day Zoe whispered in my ear not to forget her and then moved away.

So I leaned back. And I closed my eyes. And breathed in. And I wished with all my heart that I were minutes away from Zoe's house rather than hours, and I wished with all my heart that I'd tried really letting Shani or Lia in, rather than holding them out to keep plenty of room for a memory. And I mostly wished that I hadn't been spending the past three years building a wall around myself, because once I felt Rena's warmth, I realized I'd been cold for so, so long. I rubbed her back and pulled her hair out of her face, and after she was done crying, I used my fingertips to wipe the tears off her cheeks.

And I told her that all mothers make mistakes sometimes and that nobody's perfect and now she knows to take Bo to the doctor right away in the future. And I told her about my mother, about how she was all about my brother most of the time and I felt so ignored and alone, but that I never once, not in my entire life, doubted that she loved me as much as she loved him. That the love was different, but it was inescapably there, and that's what makes a mother good. And I told her that I knew she had that love for Bo because I could hear it when she sang. And all of that was true, even if I wasn't sure Rena would ever really get it.

And by the time I was done talking, I was crying, too, because I missed my mom so much. Grayson got all of the attention, but he never got all of the love. There was enough of that for both of us. I never could have doubted it. I should have counted on it, leaned on it, rather than run away from it.

Rena smiled and wiped her eyes and kissed me on the cheek and said, "I called my mom."

I stared. "What'd she say?"

A couple more tears slipped out, and for a second I thought she was going to break down again. "She cried. She said she'd been looking for me. She divorced that jerk she was married to. She can't wait to meet Bo. She's coming here."

"Omigod, that's great!" I cried, and hugged her. "I told you!"

"Yeah," she said, looking flushed and smiling sadly. "I guess."

And then we went and got Grayson, and when he saw Rena, he stuffed the rocks he was holding back into his pocket, and the Kleenex fell off the armrest of his chair and he didn't even notice.

Instead of going to a dark corner in the lobby, we followed Rena up to Bo's room, and Grayson ate his sandwich wearing rubber gloves and poking the pieces up under a surgical mask, and we laughed at him softly so as not to wake up the baby, and then we laughed about that, because just hours before all we wanted was for the baby to wake up.

After a while, Rena stretched out on a cushioned bench next to Bo's crib, and Grayson pushed together two chairs for himself. I found a pillow in a drawer and curled up with it on the floor. A nurse came in and glared at us, but we must have looked really tired because she left without saying anything and then came back with a blanket for me. I was just happy to finally see Grayson lying down, even if he did seem tense, as if he were lying on a bed of broken glass.

The whir and hum and beeps of Bo's machines began to lull us all to sleep, and pretty soon the spaces between our hushed conversations were getting longer and longer. The last thing I remember hearing was Grayson whispering, "I have a tough one for you. As I was going to St. Ives, I met a man with seven wives. Every wife had seven sacks, every sack had seven cats, every cat had seven kittens. Sacks, cats, kittens, wives. How many were going to St. Ives?"

And Rena giggling, then whispering back, "That's Mother Goose, you dork."

And then drifting and drifting into a world where brick walls were falling and opening up to the sun, which bore down on my face and made me smile.

CHAPTER
THIRTY-FIVE

I awoke to the sounds of a baby crying and lots of rustling going on. At first I was really confused. I was lying on a cold tile floor with a flimsy blanket wrapped around me. But it didn't take long for my brain to catch up, and I realized the crying baby was Bo, and the rustling going on was a nurse and Rena changing his diaper and chatting happily about how much better he looked already.

I sat up and blinked, looking around for a clock. But when I turned my face, I found my nose practically touching-distance from my brother's, which was poking out from under the arm of a chair. He was sleeping with his mouth open, acrid breath drifting out at me. I grimaced but inwardly smiled. I was glad he was finally getting some real sleep.

"Hey," I whispered to Rena, pulling myself upright. "Bo's awake."

She nodded, smiling. "And his fever's down. He woke

up wanting to nurse." She finished changing his diaper and snuggled him until his cries died down.

"What time is it?"

She looked over my head and I turned. There was the wall clock. "Almost ten," she answered. "I guess we were all pretty tired."

"I guess so," I said.

I pulled myself up off the floor and stretched, then walked over to Bo and tickled the side of his cheek with my finger. Grayson snorted and began stirring.

"I'm so glad he's better."

"Yeah," Rena said, caressing the back of his head. "Nurse said he'll probably need to stay here today, but if he keeps improving, maybe I can take him home tomorrow." She was silent for a minute, then shrugged. "Wherever home is."

"Won't your mom take you home with her?"

She shrugged again. "Maybe. We'll see."

And we were both silent then, because we both understood what this meant for us. Wherever home was, it wasn't going to be in Hunka anymore, sucking down granola bars and warm chocolate milk and challenging one another with riddles. Even though I hadn't planned on Rena, I sure was going to miss her.

"You want us to wait for you?"

She shook her head. "You guys go on ahead. I'll figure something out."

As if on cue, Grayson sat up and wrung his hands, looking worriedly toward the bathroom. He didn't even need to open his mouth for me to know what he was thinking. I leaned over and rummaged through one of the bags I'd brought in last night and pulled out the tub of antibacterial wipes. Wordlessly, my brother took it and headed to the bathroom.

Rena watched the door close behind him. "He's a good guy," she said.

I stuffed my hands in my pockets and stared at the door, too, as though we would find some great truth about my brother there. Behind the door I could hear muffled *uh-uh*s.

"A little quirky sometimes, but...good," she said, and when I looked back at her she was staring at Bo, tracing his ear with the tip of her finger. "It's good to know that good guys still exist out there somewhere, you know? They're not all like Archie or my mother's jerk husbands or Sal."

I sank into one of the chairs Grayson had slept on the night before, and stuck my finger under Bo's curled hand, wiggling it so he'd make a fist. It sure sounded like Rena had known a lot of bad guys over the course of her life. Grayson, who seemed like a real pain to me, must have looked like a dream to her.

"You're really lucky to have him," she added.

I glanced back over my shoulder at the bathroom door. I could hear water running and Grayson muttering rhythmically. I swallowed. "Yeah," I whispered, "I guess."

We both touched and jiggled the baby for a while, soaking up his contentedness, and after what seemed like a really long time, Grayson came out of the bathroom, his hands so washed he looked like he was wearing pink gloves. He stepped over the door's threshold several times counting. Great. A new compulsion. Well, a new *old* compulsion. He'd done the doorway thing before but had kicked it in treatment two years ago. That was the thing about Grayson—you never knew when a new compulsion would crop up or an old one would reappear. You never quite knew what to expect. It wasn't even worth commenting on.

I untangled my finger from Bo's hand and stood up. "Listen, why don't I get us some breakfast?" I said. "I saw cinnamon rolls in the cafeteria last night. Can't get 'em out of my head."

"Sure," Rena said.

I turned to leave, tugging on Grayson's filthy T-shirt as I passed him, forcing him to stop. "Come with, Grayson. I'll need extra hands if we want coffee." I wasn't really sure I would need extra hands, but for some reason I really needed him to stop going through that doorway. I really needed him to be Rena's "good guy" for a while longer. Especially since I had a feeling it wouldn't last.

He stepped through the doorway another nine times (great, he had me counting now, too), and then into the hallway and back into Rena's room another thirty-six times, and then, reluctantly, as if this number wasn't high enough and he wasn't sure it would do, followed me.

"Why thirty-six?" I asked while we waited for the elevator.

"Huh?"

"You went in and out of that door thirty-six times. Why thirty-six?"

The elevator door opened, and I stepped in next to a nurse in pastel purple scrubs with lambs on them, but Grayson looked inside with wide eyes, panicked. I sighed, stepped back out, pulled his shirt again, and said, "Stairs."

By the time we got into the stairwell (thirty-six ins and thirty-six outs) and down the stairs (thirty-six ups and thirty-six downs), I was beginning to think we'd be buying dinner instead of breakfast. He never did answer my question, which told me he pretty much had no idea why thirty-six. I let it drop.

Grayson stayed out in the hallway while I went in and ordered. Three cinnamon rolls, two coffees, and a bottle of chocolate milk for Rena.

We were heading toward the stairs when a nurse came out of the ER doors, jacket on and car keys in hand.

"Oh, there you are," she said, and at first I thought she was talking to someone behind us or something. But she kept coming straight at us. "I've been looking for you."

"Oh," I said awkwardly, but she was heading for Grayson instead. She put a hand on his shoulder and leaned down to talk to him.

"We were able to get a hold of your mother last night. She gave us the prescription and insurance information we needed, and as soon as the pharmacist gets the okay from insurance, you'll be good to go. Do you know where our pharmacy is?"

Grayson shook his head, stepping away from me and clearing his throat so softly it almost sounded like the beginning of a word. *Uh.*

She pointed down the hallway, but I honestly didn't hear anything she said. I was still trying to process what I'd just heard: *We were able to get hold of your mother last night.*... I gripped the bag holding our cinnamon rolls so tightly my fingernails turned pink. The hospital had called Mom.

Which meant...

Our parents knew where we were.

After the nurse left, Grayson wouldn't look me in the eye. Instead, he stared at his bare toes, white from hospital chill, poking out the bottom of his jeans. I turned on him, trying to keep my voice level.

"You had them call Mom? What..." For a minute I was afraid I wouldn't be able to speak at all. The lump in my throat had swollen, and I feared air wouldn't get past it. That maybe I'd end up in the ER, gasping for breath, having a tube shoved down my throat. But confusion welled up in me so great my vision started to get grainy, and I clutched at that paper bag with everything I had. "What the hell, Grayson?" I hissed.

And I started walking because that was the only command my brain could take in at the moment. Walk. Burn energy. Burn it off before you burn up. I pounded through the stairwell doorway, not even bothering to wait for my brother, but somehow knowing that he was coming behind me anyway.

It was over.

So close—so close!—and he'd ruined it all. Mom would be coming. She'd probably already booked a flight to Nevada. She'd probably already called the cops. I was this close to seeing Zoe again, and everything had come crashing to a halt because of my brother. Of course. As always.

He'd been looking so good. So changed. I was a fool. He would never change. I was stupid to think he ever would.

"I can't believe..." I said, stomping up the stairs, my mind racing. I turned back after reaching the top of the first flight, and gazed down at him. He was stepping through the doorway again—in, out, in, out. I couldn't deal with it. If I tried, I was going to blow up on him. I turned and walked up the second flight of stairs, leaving him to follow me.

At the top of the second flight, I paced and waited for him. When he finally appeared at the top of the steps, he looked behind him as if he wanted to go back down and up again, but seemed to think better of it.

I whirled on him. "Why?" I asked. "Why would you do that? What were you thinking?"

And it was then that I saw the tears. Big ones, rolling down his face. His mouth was wet, too, and super red, like he'd been chewing on his bottom lip.

"I need my medicine," he said in this helpless little voice, gesturing weakly with the coffees, as if even he was disappointed with himself. "You were gone forever getting those sandwiches, and I started to worry that something had happened to you, so I started counting and...and the nurse could see that something was..." He swallowed, his throat clicking. "...wrong. So I asked her to call Mom so I could get my medicine."

"You've been fine without it," I countered. "We were almost there. We were almost..." I trailed off when I realized how not almost-there we were, at least in terms of Grayson being cured. Or my situation being any better. The only "there" we were almost was almost there to Zoe, but I couldn't tell him that, and I especially couldn't tell him, or maybe even tell myself, that my faith in what Zoe could do for us was waning. I paced over to the wall and pressed my forehead into the cool brick, my mind reeling over what options were left for us.

We had to leave. As fast as we could. Tell Rena and Bo good-bye and go. If we weren't too late already. That was our only option.

"You don't understand, Kendra. You can't...force someone to be who you want them to be."

"We're so close," I said, squeezing my eyes shut and feeling the breath of my words puff back into my face.

"You don't understand," he repeated.

"No," I said miserably, and turned and pressed my back to the wall, then sank to the floor, letting my head flop forward between my bent knees. "You don't understand."

"What?" he said exasperatedly. "What is it that I don't understand? That your life is oh-so-hard? That you really wanted to take a road trip and who cares what anyone else needs? That...what, Kendra? That you cheated and you're scared of not being perfect?"

My head snapped up. "How about that I didn't just cheat?" I cried, then rubbed my forehead with my hand, willing the headache that was starting to go away. "Okay?" I mumbled. "I didn't just cheat."

He was silent for a minute, his flip-flops swishing against the concrete floor as he shifted his weight. "What do you mean?" he asked quietly.

But I squeezed my eyes shut again, so hard I could see purple inside my eyelids, then opened them and took a deep breath, picking up the cinnamon roll bag and standing up again. "She's probably already on her way," I answered. I pushed through the door and into the hallway and headed toward Bo's room.

What did it matter anymore that he didn't know the whole story? Why bother to tell him the rest now? Everything was going to fall apart. We were going to be forced home. He would find out everything soon enough.

I walked into Bo's room, where Rena was sitting in a chair, bent forward watching Bo sleep in his crib. Her face brightened when she saw us, then folded into a frown. "What's wrong?"

I set the cinnamon rolls in her lap, then pulled the bottle of milk out of my pocket and handed it to her as well. "Ask

Genius Boy," I said. "I've got to use the bathroom before we hit the road." I walked past Grayson and into the bathroom, leaving the two of them to talk.

"You're leaving right now?" I heard Rena say, and then I turned on the water and drowned them out.

By the time I came back out, Grayson and Rena were both eating their cinnamon rolls, as if nothing had ever happened. I'd run cold water over my face, and I definitely felt better, but I was still so mad at my brother I wished I'd left him in the quarry that day after school. Wished I'd hopped back in Hunka and gone to see Zoe myself. I didn't need him to get to Zoe. Why did I ever think I did? She was my best friend, too.

She was my best friend *first*.

We even had our own special handshake, Zoe and me. We'd lock thumbs and make fists like we were getting ready to arm wrestle, but instead would pull each other close and bump hips while snapping the fingers of our other hand. We came up with it when we were seven. It was our way of reminding each other we were sisters at heart, without ever saying a word. She never did the secret handshake with Grayson. Only me.

She didn't only love him. She loved me, too. Sometimes I thought she loved me more. But nobody in either of our families ever seemed to remember that. Nobody even seemed to care. But I cared. I remembered. I'd never forget. Because I promised her I wouldn't.

And Zoe had made that promise, too.

Rena held up the paper bag holding my cinnamon roll and shook it. "Before you go," she said.

"You can have it," I said. My stomach was in knots over the thought of Mom—or the cops—being on their way, and there was no way I'd be able to keep anything down until I was over the California state line. I missed my mom, but getting to Zoe was something I needed to do, and until I'd done it, I wasn't ready to face Mom. "C'mon, Grayson. We need to leave."

He swallowed and looked sincerely confused. "What about my medicine?"

I sighed and threw up my hands. I'd had enough. "Mom is on her way. You want your medicine? You'll have to stick around and wait for it yourself. You can go home with Mom when she gets here. I give up. I'm going to California."

"You can't go by yourself," Rena said. She stood and walked over to me. I felt sick about leaving her, especially after last night, and wasn't sure how to say good-bye to someone I'd met only a couple days ago but who already felt like a friend.

"I'm not waiting around. No way is my mom going to leave us here," I said. "If he's going to wait, I'm going without him."

"Kendra, come on, this is stupid," Grayson said, sounding whiny and agitated.

He was probably right, but I'd gone too far now to go back. "So be it," I said, and leaned in to hug Rena. She smelled like icing, which made my stomach twist all the harder. "Take good care of Bo," I said. "He's going to be one of those good guys someday. I just know it."

She hesitated, pulled back to look at me, then hugged me, resting her chin on my shoulder. "Thanks," she said. "Be careful, okay?"

I nodded, feeling stupid that my eyes were welling up. We'd only known each other for two days. It wasn't like she was my best friend or anything. But she could've been. In a different situation. In a different time. Rena and I could've been friends. And as silly as it made me feel, I was going to miss her.

I grabbed a pen off the side table by the bed and wrote my cell number and e-mail address on a napkin. "Let me know where you end up," I said.

She nodded, and I turned and walked out the door.

"You can't let her go by herself," I heard her say, and my brother said something back, but I was beyond caring at that point. He'd blown it. He'd ruined the plan. He could deal with it.

I stepped into the elevator and pushed the "close door" button with my thumb impatiently until the doors closed. He was officially off the hook. On his own. I'd call Mom as soon as I got in the car. I'd tell her he was waiting for her. He'd be fine.

The elevator stopped and I was walking out before the doors were even all the way open, turning my shoulders sideways and brushing against the doors as they groaned slowly ajar.

Forget him, I told myself. *Let him have his way. Get to Zoe yourself. You'll be fine, too.*

I repeated these things on a loop as I walked down the hallway, veered through the ER waiting room, and then broke into a jog as I hit the parking lot, digging in my front pocket for my car keys as I went.

I wasn't going to waste any more time. I was ready to call this done.

With or without Grayson.

CHAPTER
THIRTY-SIX

My backpack had been crammed under Grayson's seat. It took me a few minutes to dig it out, and I eventually resorted to shoveling handfuls of rocks from the floorboard to the parking lot blacktop. Screw Grayson's stupid rocks. If he wasn't going to go with me, I had no use for them anymore. They were just more evidence of how I'd tried to make this work for him, and how he hadn't tried to make it work for me. I didn't need them.

Finally I got hold of a shoulder strap and pulled the backpack free, then dumped its contents on the passenger seat, my cell phone bouncing off the seat and onto the floorboard below. I picked up the phone and dialed.

"Kendra?" Dad's voice. "You're in goddamned Nevada?"

I closed my eyes and slid into the car, shutting the door softly behind me, as if I had to keep the other people in the parking lot from hearing me get yelled at. Dad hardly ever blew his stack. This wasn't going to be good.

"I'm sorry, Dad."

"You should be sorry. Do you have any idea how much hell you've put us through with this stunt? I can't even believe you would do this! You've been gone for three days. We thought you were hiding out at a friend's house somewhere, but...Nevada!"

"I didn't mean to—"

"Now what are we supposed to do? Your brother is in crisis, calling us from a hospital, for Chrissakes, needing his medication that he's not taken for days now. Your mother is inconsolable. Her sick son calling her from a hospital across the country, and her daughter nowhere to be found!"

"We weren't at the hospital because of Grayson," I said weakly. "Rena's baby got sick."

There was a pause. I imagined Dad standing with his head down, one hand on his hip, like he always did when he was trying to control his temper. "Who the hell is Rena?" From the sound of his voice, it wasn't working. He was definitely not in control of his temper.

I sank down in the seat, knowing how this must sound to him. "Nobody. Just someone we met."

"So you're picking up hitchhikers, too? For the love of Pete, Kendra, I can't believe you of all people would do this!" *You of all people.* Translation: How dare you not be Little Miss Perfect?

"I'm sorry, Dad. Is Mom there? I don't have much battery left."

"No. She's not. She's actually at Dr. St. James's office, trying to figure out what to do. The police have already informed us that at seventeen and twenty you're not considered runaways, so we're kind of at a loss here. What do we do? Do we fly to Nevada? Come get you? Wait for you to come home and pray that nothing horrible happens to you? Send someone else after you and wait here at the same time? What? You tell us." His voice squeaked at the end, like it'd been strained.

So Mom was at Grayson's therapist's office. Ordinarily, I'd think this was good news. Dr. St. James was constantly telling Mom to back off and stop enabling Grayson's OCD. He'd probably be trying to persuade her to let us be. I'd normally be breathing a sigh of relief that we could keep going and maybe Mom would listen to Dr. St. James. But no. Grayson was freaking out instead. I needed to let them know that Grayson was waiting for her here. That she'd need to come get him.

"So are you coming home or what?" Dad asked again, the squeak gone and the nothing-but-pissed sound back.

I cleared my throat. "I still have something I need to do. But—"

A knock on the window startled me and I bolted up straight. Grayson was standing outside the car, holding the cinnamon roll bag in one hand and a cup of coffee in the other. He motioned for me to open the door.

"Hang on, Dad," I said, and opened it.

298

"Get out of my seat," Grayson said matter-of-factly. "I can't drive, remember?"

"What are you doing?" I hissed, covering the mouth-piece of my cell phone with my thumb.

"Going with you," he said, as if this was totally expected. But he didn't look happy about it. In fact, he looked about as happy as Dad sounded.

We regarded each other solemnly for a few beats, until he began to look impatient and waved the bag and cup in the air again.

I slid out of Hunka and tried to hide my smile. He was coming with me. Without his medicine. He was looking past himself and doing something for me. As he got in, unceremoniously shoving all of the things I'd dumped out of my backpack onto the driver's-side floor, I held the phone to my ear again.

"Dad?"

"But what?"

I took a deep breath, gazing up at the bank of windows on the second floor of the hospital. Rena would be behind one of those windows, cradling her baby, maybe watching Grayson go to the car and go with me, just as she'd told him to do. I probably owed her more than I even knew.

But Grayson is staying. He needs Mom to come get him, I was going to tell Dad.

But Grayson wasn't staying. He was fussing with the cup holder and my coffee, waiting for me to get us going back on the road.

"But we'll be back soon, okay? Just wait for us. We'll be fine. We have each other," I said. And, I realized, this was the truth. We really did have each other...in our own weird way.

"This is unacceptable," Dad roared, that squeak coming back again. "You need to consider what your actions are doing to others, Kendra. You need to consider your brother." How many times had I heard some version of that sentence? *You need to think about Grayson. You need to consider your brother.*

When have I ever not? I wanted to say. *When has it ever been okay for me to just act without first considering my brother?* But at the moment the thought had no real conviction, not with my brother sitting in the passenger seat of Hunka, still holding my cinnamon roll in his lap, ready to follow me to wherever I needed to go, whether he thought he could do it or not. With or without his medicine. Trusting me.

Dad was right. I hadn't been thinking about Grayson.

I knew what had changed between my brother and me over the past three years. It wasn't that he'd left me. It wasn't that he'd gotten too sick. It was that I'd left him. That his illness had suddenly mattered too much. And now I missed those times when it was just the two of us, laughing over something stupid, making fun of each other's quirks. I ached to have our relationship back. And there was no reason why we couldn't get it back. I didn't need to cure Grayson; I needed to cure *us*. And that I knew I could do. It was not too late.

"I'm sorry, Dad," I said. "I really didn't mean to hurt you guys. But this is something I need to do. I love you. Tell Mom I love her, too. Gotta go."

And before he could get another shot at trying to talk me home, I ended the call. My battery light was flashing now, and I knew that pretty soon dodging their calls and texts wouldn't matter anymore. My phone would be dead, and it would officially be just me and Grayson out here alone. I didn't even bother to turn it off before shoving it into my pocket this time.

I walked around Hunka and opened the driver's door. The stuff from my backpack was strewn all over the floorboard. I didn't say anything, just stuffed it back inside the backpack and flung it onto the backseat.

I heard a rattle and looked back to see that the backpack had fallen on one of Bo's toys, forgotten by Rena in her haste to get him into the hospital last night. I started to reach for it but decided to leave it there, sort of as a memento. Proof that they existed.

"Rena talked you into it, huh?" I said as nonchalantly as I could while I got myself situated and Hunka roared into life.

Uh-uh-uh. "No. I decided. I'm supposed to protect you. It's what Mom and Dad would want."

His words reminded me of when we were little kids and Stu Landry had been hassling me on the bus. Calling me Chicken Ankles and pulling my hair, stealing pencils out of my book bag and throwing them at kids in the front of the bus. I must have been in kindergarten, and by then Grayson was so filled with anxiety, he basically scrunched down in a seat at the front of the bus every day and prayed that nobody would bother him. It was right about that time that he started making the *uh-uh-uh* noise. I remember because Stu Landry liked to tease him about it.

But one day Stu stole the little sparkly pink teddy bear I'd brought for Share Day. And he wouldn't give it back. Tucked it down the back of his pants and sat down on it with a smug smile on his face. And it stayed there, no matter how many times I asked for it.

I came home crying, my teddy gone, and ran straight to Mom.

"And what were you doing when this was going on?" she asked Grayson, who stood in the kitchen doorway, bug-eyed, listening to the story.

"I wasn't sitting back there," he said, and his voice sounded so plaintive, so weak, I knew, even then, that he was embarrassed that he had to sit at the front of the bus with the shy kids while his baby sister and Zoe were sitting in the back, braving Stu and his gang.

Mom made a skeptical noise, and then later, at the dinner table, Dad chimed in. But rather than console me about my bear being gone, Dad turned on Grayson. "You're her big brother. You're supposed to protect her from stuff like that."

"I didn't know."

"Then you make sure you know from now on."

Subject closed.

The next day, Grayson followed me to the back of the bus, making that new *uh-uh-uh* sound and twitching beside me. When Stu got on, Grayson stood up.

"Give my sister's bear back," he said, staring down at Stu, even though Stu was older than Grayson, and bigger, and Grayson would've been scared to be staring down a preschooler.

"Shut up," Stu answered.

"You took it yesterday. You owe her a new bear."

"Shut up, idiot," Stu said, so Grayson stepped closer.

"Give it back!" he said, and then his tic took over. *Uh-uh.*

And Stu looked at his friend Geoffrey, and the two of them cracked up and started mimicking my brother. "*Uh-uh-uh! Uh! Uh-uh!* Graytard!" they shouted, and the bus jerked into motion, and the bus driver told Grayson to sit down, so he did, and he was crying.

"I tried," he said.

But I was too embarrassed of him to thank him.

Zoe had reached over and grabbed my hand, gripping it tightly, but had leaned forward and said, "They're jerks anyway," and I nodded, but I realized it was Grayson she was talking to, refusing to be embarrassed by him, even if I was.

Sitting in Hunka, it occurred to me that nobody was telling him to do it this time. He was protecting me on his own. Even if he was scared.

"C'mon," I said, opening the car door. "Let's go get your medicine first."

"Wait," he said. "Before you go anywhere."

I stopped.

"You need to tell me everything. What did you mean when you said you didn't just cheat?"

"Gray, let's go, okay? It's nothing. Really. Come on. Before Mom decides to come out here." And I started to inch out the door again, but Grayson put his hand on my arm.

"If you don't tell me, I'm not going with you. Take your pick."

I glanced at his other hand, which had wrapped around the door handle and slowly started to pull. He was amazingly steady when he was threatening me.

I sighed and closed the door again. "Okay, okay." I swallowed, trying to figure out where to start. "I bought the test from Chub Hartley," I said, then reconsidered. "Tests, actually. More than one."

"You bought tests."

I nodded. "He's Mr. Floodsay's senior T.A. And he's in my study hall, and one day we were talking and I was telling him about how I wasn't getting calc, and he offered to sell me a test ahead of time so I could get all the answers and memorize them. For ten bucks. So I bought it. And...and every test after that. Including the semester final in December."

"That's it? That's what's so bad? You paid ten bucks for some tests, and we're running away because of it?"

I leaned my head back against the seat and closed my eyes. "I wish," I said. "But no. After the final, Chub started to get afraid he was going to get caught. So he tried to quit doing it. But I was so far in by then, I couldn't quit or I'd fail. So I talked him into keeping our deal, but he would only agree if I paid fifty instead of ten. Which I didn't have. So I had to borrow."

Grayson nodded, then bent to pick up one of the remaining rocks. He rubbed it thoughtfully. "So now other people know."

I nodded. "Yeah. I borrowed from Bryn Mallom, because she sat behind me and I could see her test scores when Mr. Floodsay handed them back, so I knew she was totally failing, too, and I figured I could get her in on the deal. So I borrowed twenty from her, photocopied the test, and gave it to her to keep her quiet."

"But she didn't stay quiet."

I shook my head, remembering the day that Tommy and I broke up. I'd walked into calc and he was sitting at my desk, and two of his idiot buddies were standing around looking smug.

"What's going on?" I'd asked, and Tommy had narrowed his eyes at me and answered, "Someone's been naughty," and then he'd demanded that I make copies of the tests for him and his friends or they would tell Mr. Floodsay and I'd be busted. I'd told him no way and we were done if he was okay with blackmailing me like that, and we'd fought for the whole rest of the week and it had gotten seriously ugly, so eventually I gave in and cut him in on the deal.

"But Tommy still told Chub," I told Grayson.

"And Chub was pissed, I'm sure."

"Yeah. Totally. So with year-end finals coming up, he told me the only way he'd give it to me was if I paid three hundred dollars for it."

Grayson let out a low whistle and gazed down at the rock in his hand.

I felt a tear roll down my cheek, and started to swipe at it but decided to let it roll. I was so ashamed. Saying it all out loud only made it worse.

"So did you go to Bryn again?"

I shook my head, directing my gaze out the window away from Grayson.

"Where, then?"

"Mom and Dad's Italy money. Mom's been socking it away in that metal box in the back of her closet. I took it out of there."

Grayson's eyes bored into me. "You stole from Mom and Dad?"

"Yes," I cried, "but I planned to pay it all back!"

And then I launched into what was probably my dumbest plan ever. How I'd realized that if I didn't photocopy the final, a lot of people were going to fail. And how they all knew that. And how, at this point, they couldn't tell on me or they'd be busting themselves, too, so they were in the shit as thick as I was, and the only one sitting pretty and safe was Chub. Or so I'd thought.

"So I sold the photocopies," I said matter-of-factly. "For twenty bucks. And there were more people doing it now, and people in other class periods wanted in, so I ended up actually making money on the deal. And I was going to put Mom and Dad's money back and graduate and nobody would ever know, but...someone must have said something, I don't know."

"The money you've been using this whole time is...?"

I nodded again. "Yeah. I never replaced it. And now we've spent almost all of it, and it doesn't matter anyway because Mom and Dad know and I've probably been expelled for orchestrating this huge cheating ring, and my whole future is ruined, which is why..." I trailed off. I'd gone this far. He needed to know the rest. He needed to know everything. Now was the time. I didn't want to, but I had to say it. I had to tell him. I turned to him, licked my lips, and started over again. "Which is why I'm taking us to see Zoe."

At this point, I turned and faced my brother, whose face went totally white.

But before he could say anything, I whipped my door open and headed into the hospital to get his medicine.

Next stop: Zoe.

CHAPTER
THIRTY-SEVEN

It seemed as if we were hardly on the road at all before we came up on Citrus Heights. My heart started beating faster, and my palms were slick on the steering wheel. I couldn't wait to see Zoe. If Hunka had crapped out on me right then and there, I would've been able to sprint to Zoe's house, I was so full of adrenaline.

I pulled into a gas station and showed the attendant Zoe's address. He got out a map so old it was ripping along the folds, and traced directions with a gnawed and crusty-with-oil-and-grit fingernail. I wrote what he was saying across the back of my arm, grabbed two packs of doughnuts—the chocolaty kind that sticks to your teeth— and hurried back out to Hunka, where Grayson was up to 1,567. A bad number. Not only odd, but with three consecutive numbers in a row. Omen city. I wouldn't dare interrupt him now.

Grayson's reaction to the news that we were going to Zoe's wasn't at all what I'd expected. I'd expected him to yell at me, start pulling on the steering wheel again, order me to turn around, berate me for lying. Instead, he'd simply sat in the passenger seat, the glove box door open and lying on his knees, and begun counting while I picked up his prescription in the hospital pharmacy. His eyes looked far away and sad, as though he was remembering things he'd rather not remember, and I felt bad for him, so I went ahead and let him count.

Was that what Mom would have done for him? Probably.

Did it really matter at this point? Not really.

It turned out that Zoe didn't live far from the gas station where I'd stopped. After a few minutes I was pointing Hunka down a tree-lined side street, my whole body buzzing with anticipation. Days on the road. Riddles and jokes and river water and cow skulls. Meltdowns and sick babies and pizza in nasty motels. Daydreams and memories and fear. All of it had been leading up to this. This moment.

I watched the house numbers slide by, slowing to let a couple of baggy-pantsed boys move their homemade skate ramp out of the middle of the street and stand, leaning against their upright boards and glaring at us. And then we were there: 555 Clark Street. I pulled to the curb and turned off the car.

I peered out Grayson's window. I could see his reflection as he stared at the house as well.

There was a swing on the front porch. There were the numbers, brass and shiny. There were little statues and tidy bushes keeping sentry on each end of the front porch steps.

And there.

Right by the front door.

Was a hand-painted flower pot. The one Zoe made in third-grade art class. The one that had always sat by their front door.

"We found it," I breathed. I nudged Grayson, who had stopped counting but didn't seem to have anything to say. "We found it!" I repeated, louder, and then laughed. "We found Zoe's house!"

And for the first time since I ran face-first into his chest in my kitchen doorway back home, I forgot all about my brother. I darted out of Hunka and bounded up the front porch steps, not even caring if he was following.

It took a long time for someone to open the door. So long, in fact, I started to worry that nobody was home. I was prepared to sit in the porch swing and wait for her to come home, but what if they were out of town or something? It was possible. Maybe that's why she hadn't e-mailed or called me back.

But there was a skinny rectangular window next to the door, and the curtain stretched down the length of it moved slightly to the side, and I could hear murmuring going on inside. My heart leaped. They were home!

So why was it still taking so long for them to answer?

Why wasn't Zoe bounding out the front door just as I'd bounded up the steps?

I heard a shuffle behind me and turned to see my brother standing on the sidewalk. He'd kept his door open but had ventured a few steps away from it, his hands crammed in his jeans pockets, his flushed face turned to the door curiously.

Finally, the door creaked open, and I couldn't help myself—I did a little hop on my toes, clasping my hands together in front of me.

"Zoe!" I cried, but it wasn't Zoe who opened the door. It was her mom, looking rankled and as if she'd been interrupted while doing something important.

She pushed the screen door open a few inches. "Kendra," she said. A statement, not a question or an exclamation. Just as matter-of-fact as if she were reporting who was at her door. She didn't look at all surprised to see me, which was weird. But I tried to hold on to hope. Maybe it meant that all had been forgiven.

I smiled. "Hi, Mrs. Monett. Long time, huh?"

She craned her neck through the opening and peered at Grayson, then frowned. "So Jonathan was right. You two were headed here. All the way from Missouri."

I nodded. I should have known Dad would think of calling Zoe once he figured out we were in Nevada. He probably had the white pages pulled up on his laptop the minute the hospital phoned. "I wanted to see Zoe. Is she home?"

And when Mrs. Monett turned her frown on me, my heart started to sink. This was the same woman who'd let me borrow her swimsuit and given me chocolate chip cookies and picked me up from school when Mom was running late. This was the woman who was so happy when I was born she requested my bassinet be placed next to Zoe's in the nursery. The woman who kissed me on the forehead and told me good night at sleepovers.

This woman loved me.

She did.

Once.

I knew it.

But this woman who once loved me was now looking at me like I was some sort of criminal and was barely cracking her door open to talk to me. Frowning at me as if I were soiling her porch. And I knew just as sure as I once knew she loved me...that she wasn't going to let me see Zoe.

My best friend.

After all these years. Even though I'd done nothing. No forgiveness. No gentleness. No pity or mercy. None.

It wasn't me. It was my brother. Why could nobody see that I was not an extension of my brother?

The thought made me panic, and I reached out and clasped the edge of the door, as if I could turn this around if I just kept that door from closing.

She shook her head and glared down at my fingers, as if she thought I was going to hit her. "You shouldn't have come here. If my husband finds him here..." She trailed off, gazing out at Grayson once more. "We left our home because of..." But she couldn't seem to wrap her lips around the right words and instead clamped them tight and breathed heavily through her nose.

I took my chance, wishing I could just tear open my chest and let her see how my heart would break — for the second time — if she did this to us. Wanted to open up my brain and show her the memories I had of her being wonderful to me, and how those memories competed with the ones in which she was so horrible to Grayson. How they seemed to come from two separate lives, and how I wanted to pick up where the wonderful life left off and try again. "Please, Mrs. Monett. Please. We came all the way out here. I need to talk to Zoe."

She shook her head again. "I don't want him on my property. I don't want him anywhere around my daughter. And neither does she. She's moved on, and you two need to do the same. You should not have come here. Not with him. She does not need some mentally imbalanced stalker following her across the country. And the fact that you brought him here lets me know that you're as imbalanced as he is."

"Please," I begged, desperate. "He'll stay in the car." I was so fraught I barely had time to register the guilt I felt at pushing Grayson aside like that. I just felt that if I could get them to listen to me, I could talk them into letting him in, too. Could tell them all the amazing things he'd done over the past three days, and how he was here because he wanted to protect me, and get them to see that it didn't matter anymore what was wrong with him as long as you loved him and were willing to see what was right, and that it had taken me seven states to figure that out, but I had learned it, and if I could, surely they could, too.

She started to pull the door closed, out of my grasp. "You need to leave," she said firmly. "Zoe doesn't want to see you." And she shut the door.

Just like that.

At first I simply stood there, uncertain what to do next. Was she telling the truth? Was that really what Zoe wanted? Never in my plans had I considered what I would do if Zoe didn't want to see me. I had been so sure this would work.

I could hear Grayson behind me—*uh-uh-uh*—and when I finally turned, I could see the defeat in his face, as if he wanted nothing more than to dissipate into nothingness. Like he wanted to dissolve into the ground or...or become a rock and be kicked into a gutter somewhere.

Slowly, slowly, I walked down the porch steps, my mind reeling. What would we do now? What was left to do?

I passed Grayson on the sidewalk and headed around to my side of the car, and it wasn't until I started to pull it open that I noticed his gaze had been drawn upward. I followed it and there she was. Zoe. Standing behind a window above the porch, looking down on us, the curtains splayed out over her shoulders, her face drawn down in a mixture of curiosity and regret.

My breath caught, and all I could think was, *Her hair is so thick and curly and her eyes are as beautiful as before and her skin so cocoa, and she looks like I always imagined she'd look—gorgeous and sleek and exotic and her cheek-*

bones are higher and her face slimmer, but she's Zoe stand-
ing up there. My best friend is standing right up there.

I lifted one hand and waved.

And she just looked at me. Then shook her head sadly, as if she wished it could be like it was before but it wasn't. Then turned away, letting the curtains drop closed.

My hand dropped, too, and I opened Hunka's door, too numb to even cry.

My phone vibrated in my pocket. I pulled it out and almost laughed at the irony: The text was from Zoe. Finally. After all this time, she answered me. Her text read:

U shouldn't have come here. Please go.

It was over.

All of it.

All this way, and it was over.

Suddenly I couldn't pull up a single memory of my child-hood with Zoe. No swing set. No school bus. No sleepovers and magazines and warm homemade caramel. All of it, gone. It was as if she never existed, as if we never existed. And, God, she was so important to me for so many years; if she never existed, I couldn't even remember who I was.

Grayson got in next to me. Just got in, no theatrics, the seat squeaking under his weight. He shut his door, and we sat there together in silence for what seemed like a lifetime.

"I'm sorry," he said, breaking the silence. "It's my fault."

I turned my head to look at him. His eyes were droop-ing at the edges, and he had them pointed at the dashboard, as if he were too ashamed to even make eye contact with me. His shoulders slumped and his right knee shook ever so slightly, and he looked like the most dejected, saddened, guilty person to ever walk the earth.

Seeing that look on my brother's face, I got it. I understood Mom's and Dad's rage toward Zoe's parents. It washed over me, threatened to pull me under like a wicked tide. I could feel myself fighting it, arms and legs flailing and grasping for solid ground. But instead all I got was mouthfuls of bitterness and a clarity I wished I'd had three years earlier. Maybe even further back than that. Before the swing set and school bus and warm caramel.

How dare they? How dare they do this to him?

He was a good person, and he never did anything but love Zoe.

"Bullshit," I said, and scrambled back out of Hunka. I raced to the flower garden by the front porch and scooped up a handful of rocks. Then I backpedaled until I could see the window Zoe had been looking out of. "Come back and face him!" I screamed, and threw a rock. It went wide and *thunk*ed against the side of the house. "Come back and face *us*, Zoe!"

I threw another rock, and this time it hit. But the rock was small and my throw weak, and it was a barely audible *tick* against the glass. So I palmed a heavier one and threw it with all my might. *Gong!* It smacked the window, and I saw the curtains flutter like someone had moved away fast, but nobody appeared at the window.

"Come on, Zoe, you coward! It's not his fault, and you know it! It's not his fault! You said so yourself! Get out here!"

I threw another rock, and then another. Again the curtains fluttered, but nothing, so I turned my attention, instead, to the window by the front door. It was skinnier, a harder target to hit, but I didn't care. I got closer, scooped up another handful of rocks, and threw them in rapid fire— *zing! zing! zing!*—all the while screaming everything I wished I'd ever said to the Monetts and never had the guts to before now. All the things that had swirled through my head as I'd watched from the stairs or the driveway or the swing set. And not just to them. To everyone who ever treated Grayson as though he were subhuman. To everyone who ever treated our family like we were somehow not good enough because of my brother.

"You uncaring bastards!" *Smack!* "How could you do this to him? You had no right! You *have* no right!" *Swack!* "You're not so superior! Do you hear me? You're not better than him!"

I was sweating and breathing hard, and in the distance I could hear my brother saying something, calling something, but I was so blinded by my rage at that point I didn't care.

"You don't stop being a best friend!" I cried. "You can't just stop that! You said you'd never forget, Zoe! You promised you'd never forget me! You'd never forget us!" *Zip!* "How could you?"

I'd run out of rocks, so I bent to pick up another and found my hands wrapping around a decorative rock, about the size of both of my fists together. *What kind of rock is this?* I imagined Rena asking Grayson, her eyes big and eager. *Sedimentary*, I imagined him answering, and imagined him turning it in his hands to show her, but the only answer I had was *the kind of rock that gets a point across.*

Even though I was spent, I heaved that rock with everything I had, with a mighty roar, or maybe a growl, or probably more like a screech, releasing three years' worth of anger and frustration and grief and worry and fear. They had no right. They had no right to treat him like that. They had no right to treat anyone like that.

Somehow I hit the target.

I knew as soon as I heard the *crack!* that I'd hit it. And almost at the same time, the front door opened, Mrs. Monett storming out onto the porch with a phone in her hand. Zoe stood in the doorway, staring at the shattered glass on her front porch, her hand over her mouth.

Mrs. Monett's mouth was moving, but all I could hear was myself screaming over her, over everything. "He's not a freak! He loved you! He loved you more than anyone will ever love you! And you know what? You don't deserve him! He's too good for you, Zoe! Do you hear me? He's too good for you! You destroyed him, and all he ever gave you was the best he had! Screw you, Zoe! Screw you and your stupid parents!"

"Kendra," Zoe was saying, "you should leave…please… oh, my God…you're crazy…we aren't kids anymore… you can't just show up at someone's house…"

I felt a hand go around my middle, and I felt my feet

leaving the ground, and I saw myself being pulled away from the house, but it did nothing to stop me. I kept screaming. I saw Mrs. Monett bark something into the phone, but I didn't care. I didn't care about anything but proving that they were wrong.

That they'd always been wrong.

About Grayson.

About us.

Zoe had betrayed me. She'd said she'd never forget, but she did.

My brother carried me across the lawn, bawling and cursing and kicking and flipping off my former best friend in the world. He dumped me into the passenger seat of Hunka, my knee jabbing painfully into the corner of the stupid glove box door, and before I could do anything but continue to blubber—"How could you do this to him? He's a person, too, you know..."—he slid behind the steering wheel, and Hunka roared into life.

I watched my best friend's face—contorted with tears, hand still in front of her mouth—as we pulled away from the curb, then curled into myself and cried seventeen years' worth of tears while my brother sped us away.

While he rescued me.

CHAPTER
THIRTY-EIGHT

It seemed like we drove forever, but when the car finally came to a stop and I uncurled myself and squinted through the sun, we were in the parking lot of a little playground not far from the gas station where I'd stopped and asked for directions earlier. There was nobody else there. The swings drifted lazily back and forth in the breeze.

The graininess of the world through my tear-soaked eyes, combined with the sight of the gas station, gave me a sense of déjà vu, and for the slightest moment it was as if none of what had just happened had happened at all. It was as if I was about to march inside and get directions to Zoe, and then everything would go according to plan.

But it didn't go according to plan at all, did it?

I knew it didn't, because my nose was plugged up with snot from all the sobbing I'd done. And because I could still hear the *crack!* of the window beside Zoe's front door breaking. And because I could still see the words of her text: *Please go*. And, most important, because when I turned my head I could see my brother in the driver's seat, his hands trembling on the steering wheel.

"Good thing you didn't get pulled over," I said. My voice was scratchy. My throat felt raw. "No license."

He shrugged. "I had to get you out of there. She was going to call the police." He peered at the dashboard through the holes of the steering wheel. "This car is dusty. You're lucky you don't have asthma."

I couldn't help myself. I laughed, accidentally snorting at the end of it. And then the snort made me giggle. And the giggle made me laugh harder. I threw my head back against the seat.

"What?" he was saying. "Asthma can kill."

Which made me laugh even harder. All that we'd gone through...all that Mrs. Monett had said about him...all of the driving that he'd just done, probably scared to death the entire time...and he was worrying about dashboard dust giving me asthma.

Only Grayson.

Only my brother.

God, I loved him.

Pretty soon I was laughing so hard I was crying again, and I'm not so sure my body really knew which one it was supposed to be doing, because the sounds coming out of my mouth were half-guffaw, half-sob. I ended up sounding so ridiculous, even Grayson started to tip the slightest smile.

After the laughter died down, I wiped my eyes again and took a deep breath. "Well, that was a bust," I said.

The seat creaked as Grayson shifted. "So, now what?"

Good question. Really good question. What would we do? What did people do when the friend they'd put all their hopes on left them twisting in the wind? What did they do when the secret they'd been keeping was laid bare, and their hopes were dashed, and they were days away from home and had no money? What did they do when the only solution they'd ever seen to their problem ended up being no solution at all, but just another problem? Nothing had changed. Nothing had been solved. I still faced loads of drama back home. Grayson was still counting. I still had no idea what would happen to me when I got back. Only now, I didn't even have enough money to get back. So *what now* was sort of the question of the hour.

But one thing was clear. Clearer to me than it had been in…maybe forever. Whatever *what now* was going to be… I was going to have to be the one to make it happen.

No, actually, *we* were. We would have to trust each other and finish this out ourselves. But the funny thing was…even though every plan I'd made turned out to be as stupid as Grayson said it was, and even though he was no better than three days ago when I'd found him in the quarry, and even though I was no less busted than I'd been when we left Missouri…after all we'd been through, I had a feeling we could do it. We could make it just fine.

"I'll tell you what we do now," I said, opening the door. "We swing."

I grabbed his tub of antibacterial wipes and then got out of the car, taking a deep breath of fresh air through my clogged nostrils.

To my surprise, Grayson followed me, no argument, no counting, no stopping to tap his toe or touch the ground with his finger. Maybe he could see my new take-charge attitude. Maybe I was fooling him, because I certainly wasn't doing the greatest job of fooling myself.

He caught up with me as I stepped up into the grass and headed for the empty swing set.

"How much money do we have left?"

I rummaged around in my pocket and pulled out the small cluster of bills that were left. I counted. "Forty-six dollars."

"How are we going to get home on forty-six dollars?"

"I don't know."

"We can't get home on forty-six dollars."

"I know that."

"You really didn't think this whole thing through."

"I know that, too."

I stepped over a railroad tie into pea gravel and sped up a little. I had no clue why this idea had made sense to me at all, but somehow I knew that if I could just make this one decision and execute it properly, everything else would fall into place. Grayson's flip-flops struggled through the rocks beside me. He didn't say anything more about money; he sank to his knees and began sifting through the tiny stones.

I eased into a swing and let my feet leave the ground as I pulled back on the chains to get myself going. Pretty soon I was soaring through the air, letting my mind go blank.

We didn't talk about my spectacle at Zoe's house. We didn't talk about the broken window or the dwindling money supply or my dying cell phone battery or any of that. We settled into a comfortable silence that was only occasionally interrupted by small talk.

"What do you think Rena's doing right now?"

"I don't know, Gray. Probably still at the hospital."

"Think she'll call you?"

"Maybe. I don't know....Did you make any friends in treatment?"

"Not really. Everybody kind of keeps to themselves in those places."

"Were you scared in treatment?"

"Sometimes. Why?"

"Just wondering."

"It's really warm here." *Uh-uh-uh.* "Not like home."

"Yeah, I know. Would be awesome to live here..."

But eventually we ran out of easy topics.

"You going to call Mom?" Grayson finally asked. He didn't look up.

I thought about it. I basically had no other choice at this point, right? But I'd put her through so much, I almost couldn't even bear to think of talking to her. "I don't know," I said. "I honestly never thought what I would do if the Zoe thing didn't work out." At the mention of her name out loud, my stomach flipped again, and I paused, let my swing slow.

My brother picked up a pebble and studied it. "Why were you so sure she'd help us?"

I thought about it. "Because we would've helped her," I said. "Because she said she wouldn't ever forget us." I thought some more and sighed. "Because everything in my life always has to be perfect. I even have to have the perfect lifelong friendship."

Grayson glanced up at me. "Nobody's perfect."

"Trust me, I know that now."

He went back to his rocks, mumbling, "Must be nice."

"What does that mean?"

He shrugged. "Nothing. It…must be nice to be just now figuring out that you're not perfect. I had pretty much figured out that I was a total screwup by the time I was ten."

I rolled my eyes. "Grayson, you're not a total screwup. Check it out. You even drove a car today."

"Still. I would've rather been as not-perfect as you any day."

I swallowed, let my swing slow to a stop. It had never occurred to me before that my brother would want to be like me. I'd always been so worried about how who he was affected me; I'd never stopped to think how who I was affected him.

"Well, you wouldn't want to be me right now," I said

around the lump that had formed in my throat. "I think I have perfected being not-perfect at the moment."

"Overachiever," he joked, and we dropped back into silence.

Overachiever. Sounded about right.

Only it didn't feel like an insult. Or pressure. It felt like acceptance.

■ ■ ■ ■

We didn't stay at the park much longer. Neither of us had much to say. My mind was reeling with everything that had happened. It wasn't supposed to be like this. It was supposed to be me saving Grayson. It was supposed to be Zoe saving both of us. It was supposed to all work, and it hadn't.

Instead, I'd driven eighteen hundred miles with a sick brother whom I couldn't fix and a total stranger who let her baby almost die, just to reach a best friend who'd forgotten about me and moved on. I was the biggest chump in the world.

I had nobody to blame but myself.

All of it was my fault.

It was my fault I'd gotten busted cheating. It was my fault we ran away. It was my fault we were out of money. And it was my fault we were stranded in Citrus Heights and all we had to show for it was some broken glass and a text message telling me to go away.

So I sat on that swing with my self-blame and misery

and didn't even try to stop it when I felt it gnawing through my stomach. I deserved it. I deserved to feel like crap, and I deserved to have nothing to show for the money I'd stolen. I deserved it all.

It wasn't until we'd gotten back to Hunka and I'd driven down the street and put the last of the money into the gas tank that Grayson finally spoke again.

"How far do you think that'll get us?" he asked, opening the atlas and flipping to the Ns. "At least to Reno. We could stop at that hospital again, if you want. Bo's probably still there." He reached down to the floorboard and scrabbled up two little rocks that had escaped my fingers back in the hospital parking lot. He lined them up on the highway line on the map. "We could call Mom from there," he said.

"Yeah," I said, putting the car into drive and feeling totally defeated. I'd have to call Mom. Tell her I was going to have to use the credit card to get home. That was a no-brainer. But I didn't want to. I wanted to come back a hero. The daughter who saved their son. Instead I would be slinking back as a failure.

I couldn't cure Grayson for them.

It took more than a stupid road trip to cure someone like Grayson. I should've accepted it, like Mom, and caved. Let him count his rocks and...

Wait.

The rocks.

California.

Of course.

I couldn't cure my brother.

And without Zoe, there was no way I could get us back to the threesome we used to be.

But I could still give him something.

I stalled before turning onto the highway, and a car behind me honked. But I couldn't make my foot press the gas pedal, couldn't make my hands turn us back toward home.

"What're you doing?" Grayson asked, glancing back at the line of cars behind us as I sat at the exit ramp, totally still. *Uh-uh.* "This is the right turn." He pointed toward the exit ramp, like I was a complete idiot who couldn't see the obvious right in front of her face.

I was shaking my head. No. I couldn't go back that way. Not yet.

Instead of turning onto the exit ramp, I flicked on my blinker and swung back out into the other lane. Cars were honking like crazy now, and one guy was shaking his fist at me like a cartoon character, but I barely even noticed any of them.

"What are you doing?" Grayson was demanding, but I'd started giggling, sounding a little unhinged, I knew, and veering off into the left lane to catch the highway going west. He was punching the atlas with his finger, holding it up for me to see. "You want east. This is west."

But I ignored him.

Pressed on the gas pedal and eased onto the highway.

Sure of myself.

I didn't need Zoe. I didn't need her help or her plans. I didn't need her to save us. I didn't need Rena or Mom or Dad or Bryn Mallom or stupid Chub Hartley. I could do this myself. It wasn't the plan that I'd made, but that was the thing about plans—when they got screwed up, you made new ones, and sometimes the new, imperfect plans turned out to be far better than the original, so-called perfect ones.

I couldn't cure Grayson for my parents.

I couldn't cure Grayson for me.

I couldn't cure Grayson at all.

But, by God, I could see this trip through.

Grayson was still freaking out in the seat next to me. "What are you doing? You're going the wrong way!"

I shook my head. "Nope. For the first time, I'm going exactly the right way, big brother. We have a change in travel plans. We are going to the Hayward Fault."

CHAPTER
THIRTY-NINE

Grayson didn't freak out like I expected him to. Didn't even argue. He made this moaning sound and turned toward the window and rubbed those two rocks he was holding. Rubbed, rubbed, rubbed them with his thumb until I was sure he'd rub the skin right off. He'd started counting, this time by twos.

I was a little surprised, to be honest. Surprised that he didn't give me a lecture about money or some guilt trip about Mom and Dad or point out to me that Zoe's mom had probably called the police when I broke their window, and that she'd also probably called our house and that would be one more headache I'd laid on Mom and Dad. Normally, that is exactly what Grayson would do. He could lecture almost as well as he could wash his hands.

But I was too over it to think this meant any progress on my brother's part. We'd gone too far during this road trip. I had no delusions that maybe this meant he was more relaxed or that he was having fun or liked the idea in any way. And I especially didn't fool myself into thinking that maybe this meant he wasn't thinking about all those things, plus a hundred or a thousand more dismal others.

More likely, he'd given up arguing with me. He'd probably figured it would be wasted breath.

So we drove in silence, and I squinted into the sunlight, feeling like I was driving out of cold, gray early spring and into paradise. Feeling like I could drive forever and just pretend that life was nothing but sunny and beautiful.

I turned on the radio and searched until I found a song I knew, then sang along, nudging my brother's shoulder a few times.

He ignored me. *One hundred twenty-two.... One hundred twenty-four...*

"Hey, Gray, remember this one of Dad's? What's black and white and red all over?" I paused. "A newspaper! Now don't you kids go stealing that one."

Nothing.

When we started seeing signs for San Francisco, I knew we were getting close, but didn't know where to go from there.

"Hey, Gray," I said, turning down the radio volume. "Can you get out the atlas?"

No answer. He wasn't even counting anymore.

"Grayson." I nudged him again. "We need to look at the map."

Nothing. Just that incessant rubbing, rubbing, rubbing.

We were getting closer. Traffic was picking up. And I wasn't sure where to go, but I felt sure that if I stayed in this lane on the highway for much longer, I'd miss it. I'd miss everything and then I'd run out of gas and would be stranded somewhere in Cali-freaking-fornia and I was so sick of this, so sick of this, and God I couldn't even get this one thing right!

"Dude, come on! Where is this thing?" I practically shouted. Hunka swerved and a car honked. I smacked Grayson's shoulder, and when he slowly turned to look at me, I could see his lips, pulled together in a tight line across his teeth, like a dog giving a warning growl. But his eyes didn't look angry. They looked watery and searching behind his glasses. They looked afraid. It was a look I'd seen before. "What's the matter?" I asked, trying to sound forceful, but it was tough getting the words around the lump that had suddenly formed in my throat.

And that's when it happened.

Official full freak-out mode.

Just like on the way to Grandma's house all those years ago.

My brother started screaming and pounding his head back against the seat, kicking the bottom of the dash with his feet, his fists clenched, shrieking, "Stop! Stop! Stop!" and I don't care how many times you witness something like that, it scares the holy living shit out of you every single time. You never get used to someone coming completely unhinged and shouting in your face. You never get used to someone you love acting crazy, acting like someone you've never seen before. Acting like a total stranger.

"Okay!" I yelled, reaching out with one hand in a useless calming gesture. With the other hand I plunged Hunka in and out of lanes, cars slamming on brakes and people yelling behind their steering wheels, until I was clear over on the right and could pull off the road. "Okay, okay, see? We're stopped!" I said, putting Hunka in park and turning to hold both palms out toward my brother, like, even though the one-hand-out gesture didn't do a damn bit of good, maybe the two-hands-out gesture would.

And more than anything in the world, I wanted Mom and Dad. I'd witnessed Grayson's freak-outs before, but I was always only that—a witness. I could close my eyes if I wanted to. I could go to my bedroom and lock the door. I could pretend I didn't hear him, didn't see him, that he was normal, that we were all normal. I could go to school and forget all about him. But my parents never could. They were front-row ticket holders to Grayson's freak-outs. They couldn't close their eyes or go to their rooms or pretend.

I didn't want to be in the front row.

The front row was scary and loud and made my chest hurt.

His screams of "Stop!" had turned to just plain screams now, his voice bouncing off the windows and driving into my eardrums.

"Okay," I said, still holding my hands out defensively. "Okay, okay. I stopped. Look. I stopped, Grayson. We're stopped." But my voice was carried away on top of his, like the words were being yanked out of my mouth and crushed before they could even form into sounds. It felt horrible, as though, if he kept it up, I wouldn't be able to even think straight and then I would have no choice but to start shrieking and crying, too, and as awful as it felt to think this, I couldn't help myself thinking it—*I don't want to turn into him. Please, God, please don't make me turn into my brother.* I didn't want to become a scary person, too.

I tried to think of what Mom and Dad would do in this situation. What had they done before? Hold him down? Yes, sometimes. Yell at him? Only when they were at the bottom of their bag of tricks and nothing else had worked. Let him go on until he was screamed out? Only Mom did that, and only if Dad wasn't home.

But I couldn't let him go on. My head already felt full to bursting with his wails. And I didn't think I could really hold him down. Not when he was like this.

So I tried yelling.

And for a while it was both of us yelling in that car, him flailing around and me with my eyes closed, and it must have sounded like *screech*dammitGrayson*wail*shutup*squeal*we're stoppedlookaround*shriek* . . .

And we must have looked nuts in there, but if we did, nobody seemed to notice—they were all busy heading off to their normal lives while we created chaos out of ours.

But then, all of a sudden, Grayson seemed to come back to a semblance of reality, which ordinarily would have been a good thing. But this time he looked around wildly, his arms and legs flinging out and clutching the seat, one of the rocks flying out of his palm and thwacking me in the chin. He took in an enormous gasp, like you would expect to hear out of someone who has just seen a zombie pop up out of the ground at his feet, and before I could even react, his hand scrambled for the door handle and out he went, rolling onto the grass beside the highway and sprawling there, his fingers curled into the grass, clutching for dear life.

"What the...Gray?" I called, peering out the door, which he'd left open. I could see him, a couple feet away from the car, and I was scared, yes, and I wanted to be sympathetic—I really did—but something about the way he was lying there, looking like a freak for all the world to see, was the last damn straw.

I let out a howl of my own, pounded the steering wheel a few times with my fists, checked the side mirror, and then, when the coast was clear, darted around Hunka into the grass on the other side, seething.

I was so done with this.

I was sick to death of embarrassment. Sick of not going to Grandma's. Sick of not being able to do anything when he was around, forever a prop in *The Grayson Show*. Sick of losing everyone to him—Mom, Dad, even Zoe. Everyone tiptoed around my brother. Everyone wanted him to be normal, not even bothering to see that I was better than normal. I was damned perfect. It was all about him, all the damned time, and I was so sick of it I wanted to scream.

"Get up!" I yelled, when I got around to the grass. He didn't budge. "Get up!" I repeated, halfheartedly kicking the dirt next to his right arm. "I'm not kidding, Grayson. Get up!"

He turned his head just enough to show one eye, glasses half-on, and his mouth. "I can't," he breathed.

I held both arms out at my sides, gesturing to the highway stretching out on either side of us. "There aren't any overpasses. Get back in. You're acting like a freak. Everyone is staring." Which, by the way, was oddly *not* true. Nobody even seemed to notice.

He swallowed. "What if today's the day?"

"The day for what?"

"The big one. Today could be the big one."

"The big what? You're acting ridiculous."

But then I understood. All those afternoons in the backyard, Grayson running around, pulling Zoe and me out of upended wheelbarrows, our bodies limp, him crying, *Oh, the humanity!* It was one of our favorite games to play. Our little Hayward Fault rescue game.

Only to my brother, it wasn't a game. It was practice.

I crouched down next to his head. "You've got to be kidding me," I said. "You're worried about an earthquake?"

"Studies show earthquakes with a magnitude of six-point-seven happen twenty times a year worldwide, Kendra!"

"That's stupid."

He lifted his head. "You're the one who brought us here. You're the one who had this brilliant idea to go to a fault

336

line that's famous for the possibility that it could cause a hugely devastating earthquake any day, and you're blaming me for thinking an earthquake is possible? Who's the stupid one?"

"You are!" I yelled, knowing full well that we sounded like a couple of little kids. I think even I wasn't sure if what was coming out of my mouth wasn't the six-year-old me, wanting to yell at him to stop playing this idiotic game of fear and sadness and put the coins away and stand up to the big boys and stop crying all the time and just be normal.

"Well, that's rich," he said, "coming from you. I never had to cheat."

"At least I made it past my junior year," I shot back.

"At least I was smart enough to take the tests all on my own."

"How the hell would you know? You spent all your class time counting how many times your teachers blinked."

"At least I never dragged you into my messes," he said.

I glared at him, barely believing what I'd just heard come out of my brother's mouth.

"Oh, didn't you?" I said, my chest feeling like it might explode, I was so angry. I started to pace, little staccato steps around his head. "How many times have I had to stop what I was doing to climb down into that quarry for you, huh? How many times did I have to listen to Mom cry because you were back in the hospital? How many nights have I sat alone in the kitchen at dinnertime because Mom and Dad were too busy discussing what next to do with you? What about my birthday party that was canceled because you were having a rough time and Mom and Dad didn't think you could handle company in the house? And the time that we never got to Grandma's at Christmas because you couldn't handle an overpass? What about my best friend who had to move away because you couldn't be normal? You think this is all about *you*, Grayson. That this sickness of yours is *your* problem, but you drag the whole family through your problem. Every. Single. Day. So don't even talk to me about dragging *you* into *my* problem. My whole life has been about *your* problems. So my advice to you, Genius Boy, if you don't like being dragged into my mess? Deal with it. I have. My whole life."

"Whatever," he said into the ground, his voice sounding as if he was crying, or at least on the verge of it.

"And you really think that hanging on to a few blades of grass is going to save you from 'the big one'?" I made air quotes with my hands. "That's as stupid as thinking that counting to a zillion will keep us all from dying, or any of the other ridiculous rituals you do." I was on a roll now. "Haven't you ever noticed that normal people don't do those things? That you have the whole family totally wrapped up in your crap? It's like you—"

"Shut up!" he cried, pulling his face up from the ground. His glasses had totally fallen off, and there was a piece of grass stuck to his beet-red forehead. His face was covered with sweat and snot and tears. He took a deep, ragged breath. "You have no idea what it's like to be me."

"And you have no idea what it's like to be me," I yelled. "Always living under your shadow. Always having to be perfect to make up for you, but nobody ever noticing me at all until I screwed up. Always worrying that I might become you. That I might someday wake up and I won't be able to get out of bed until I've recited every color I could think of or some other stupid, crazy obsession. You have no idea what it's like to be me. It's worse than any earthquake, because this. Never. Stops! Never!" I swiped my hair, which had caught a breeze, out of my face. Anger was pulsing through me so strongly I could feel it in my eyeballs. It had been such a long day, so filled with emotion. I felt raw and ragged.

Grayson was still staring at me, but the red had faded a little bit. He was breathing hard, though, and his voice was weak from all the screaming. "Poor you, you've got it so hard," he said. "How do you stand it?"

"You have no idea," I repeated, shaking my head.

"I don't, huh?" he said. "Let me tell you something, perfect little princess. I have every idea. You don't think it killed me every time someone treated you like there was something wrong with you because of me? You think I didn't notice when your friends' moms wouldn't let them come around our house because of me, or that one time when that one girl's mom wouldn't let you come inside her house because she thought whatever I had made you trashy?"

"Kathy," I murmured. I'd forgotten about that. How could I have forgotten? We were in sixth grade, and her mom refused to let me any farther than the front porch. I'd sat on the porch and told her I understood, but later I'd cried and had hated my brother with every ounce of energy I had. For doing this to me.

Never had I thought what it might have done to him.

"I'm not blind," he said. "I see what I do to the family. I see how Mom and Dad look at you. How they joke with you and laugh and relax. They can carry on a conversation with you without ever once looking at your hands. Did you notice that?" He paused, and the blade of grass fell off his forehead. "Because I noticed. Did they ever once make a big deal out of something good that I did? Did they ever once just treat me like a member of the family? No. I'm always the sick one. The one who struggles. The one with difficulties. The one to blame for everything that doesn't work out. And every time you did something great, I had to act happy for you, when all I could think was how much I hated you for not being sick like me. How much I wanted to be you. Just for one day." He took a deep, quivering breath. "So, yeah. I think I have a pretty good idea what it's like to live in someone's shadow."

A car pulled up behind Hunka, and a woman opened the passenger door, sticking her head out.

"Y'all okay?" she asked, a Southern twang to her voice.

I nodded, brushing my hair away from my face again and trying my best with a confident smile. "Fine," I called back. "He gets carsick."

"You need us to call someone?"

"No, thanks," I answered. "I've got a cell. He'll be fine in a couple minutes anyway." But in my head I was thinking, *Will he? Will we ever be all right?*

The woman nodded, eased back into her car, and shut the door, and they pulled away. I felt relief, but also worry. I had to get my brother back in the car before someone thought I'd murdered him, and called the police.

I sighed and lowered myself to the ground, my back against Hunka's open door, my feet at Grayson's head. I could hear him make his muffled *uh-uh* sound. He sounded miserable.

As miserable as I felt.

I'd done it. I'd said everything to my brother that I'd always wanted to say. So why didn't I feel any better?

After a while, I reached inside Hunka and pulled out one of the rocks, which had rolled under Grayson's seat along with about a dozen others.

"What is this?" I asked, holding it up and squinting at it. "One of those metaphoric ones?"

Grayson lifted his head slowly, one eye closed. "Metamorphic," he corrected, "and no."

"Well, what is it? One of those sunstones you were talking about?"

He gave me a look. "No. Do you see any glitter in it?" He sounded irritated, but I noticed his hands loosen their grip on the grass. His arms slowly worked their way in until he was able to prop himself up on his elbows. "It's a rock."

I dropped it back on the floorboard and pulled out another. "This one looks like the same thing."

He nodded. "It is." And then, acting extremely put out, he proceeded to tell me about how a sedimentary rock is formed, which led to a more relaxed lecture on how rocks are classified, which led to a comfy little soliloquy about lava rock and why we should be able to spot plenty of it around where we were right at that moment. And as he talked, slowly, slowly, he pulled himself up out of the grass, until he was sitting next to me, his back against Hunka's side panel.

I pulled out another rock and then another, until all that was left was a long, thin, flat rock that felt so delicate I could crush it with my fingers.

"That's mica," he said, pulling it out of my hands. "See those lines in it?" I peered, nodded. "Those are the cleavage lines I was telling Rena about. Mica breaks cleanly. So you could hold both pieces of a broken mica together and they would fit perfectly."

"Sort of like us," I whispered, without even realizing I was speaking out loud. I could feel my shoulder brush up against my brother's. "Broken and way messed up but not destroyed. Not ruined."

He glanced at me but didn't answer. We sat in silence for a few moments, nothing but the noise of traffic *whoosh*-ing around us.

I leaned my head on his shoulder. "I'm sorry, Gray," I said, and I felt his shoulder dip a little, but surprisingly he didn't pull it away.

"For what?" he answered. *Uh-uh-uh.*

I thought about it, felt a tear slip out, and watched it soak into his jeans. "I don't know. For my shadow, I guess."

"Yeah," he said, but he didn't say any more, and neither did I, and maybe that was because we both knew that everything else kind of fell under that. It was both of our shadows that hurt. His mental illness, which seemed to take over everything about our lives, and my perfection, which made him disappear.

Those shadows were how we'd ended up here. How we'd ended up driving across the country, counting rocks and running from consequences. How we'd ended up breaking Zoe's window and lying facedown in the grass off the highway. Everything, if we were to trace it all back to the beginning, started with those shadows.

And on some level I knew we were lucky, because we both knew the shadows were there. We'd acknowledged them, accepted them. Everybody has shadows. And I don't know why it took all of...this...for me to understand that, but it did. And maybe it took all of...this...for my brother to understand it, too. I don't know. I'll probably never know when he decided that living in my shadow was sometimes not all that horrible. I just know when it happened for me. Right there, by the car, I realized that sometimes you don't have to say you love someone for it to be true. Sometimes you just have to hang out in that person's shadow and be okay with it.

I didn't need to tell my brother that I was sorry for

trying to fix him. And he didn't need to tell me he was sorry for trying to make me turn around and go home. And, miraculously, I didn't even feel so sorry about the calc final anymore. I was ready to face the consequences, full on, head up, just as my brother had faced the road ahead of us.

Another car pulled up behind us, and another woman asked if we needed help. We kind of laughed after she left, because she seemed super pissed that we weren't dying or anything and were just being "dangerous teenagers."

But after she pulled away, we decided it was time to get back in the car.

"You still wanna go to the fault?" I asked after we settled in and I started the engine.

"No," Grayson answered. He still had lines on his forehead from pressing it so hard into the grass.

"Okay."

"But we should."

A pause, then, "Okay."

And we did.

CHAPTER
FORTY

The stadium was huge. I don't know what I'd been expecting—probably something along the lines of my high school football field—but I hadn't been expecting this. I allowed myself a moment of daydreaming—that this was my campus and I was going to my first football game with my new friends from the dorm. That I was a little bit worried about a poli sci test that I'd taken earlier that day, but that I was excited to flirt with the cute senior who worked at the reference desk in the library.

That life was good and as it should be. That I'd never messed it up at the eleventh hour.

The thought was too depressing.

Grayson's face was practically pressed up against his window, staring out at the field. I watched him. Was he trying to be still? To detect the slightest tremor in the earth? Or was he, like me, simply daydreaming? What-iffing?

Imagining a life where he was whole and normal and feeling possibility?

Finally, I found a place, pulled over, and turned off Hunka. I rolled down my window, letting the fresh air, the smell of exhaust, and the sound of distant cars and birds fill the car. Grayson didn't move to open his.

I wondered if he was remembering all the times we played that game in our backyard, or if his brain was flipping through all the possible catastrophes that could happen, like a file cabinet of Scary Scientific Knowledge.

Those games we played—Grayson, Zoe, and me—they were fun. Grayson acting the superhero and rescuing us over and over again. But he always saved me first. Not Zoe. Me. Always. And that had never occurred to me until right then, watching him stare out the window at the stadium.

"Come on," I said after a while.

He didn't move.

"I didn't come all the way here to look at it through Hunka's gross windshield. I came here to experience this thing," I said, even though I knew that wasn't true. I didn't come here to step on the Hayward Fault; I came here to fix my brother and fix myself. And I already had done those things, in a way. Or rather, I'd let us fix each other. "Well, I'm going."

I opened the door and stretched in the sunlight, then walked around to the chain-link fence that stood between us and the stadium. I peered down inside. Nothing but an empty football field.

"Hey!" I shouted over my shoulder. "I don't see any crack in the ground."

My brother's eyes flicked to me, and then back to the stadium.

"Are you sure this is the right place? I thought you said it ran right down the middle of the stadium. Goalpost to goalpost, remember? Why can't I see it?"

Grayson rolled his eyes this time, and his door opened. I'd said one stupid thing too many. But he didn't correct me. He was too busy trying to put one foot in front of the other, his legs visibly shaking.

I jumped up and down a few times, my sneakers *thunk*-ing on the ground. "Solid as a rock," I said. "No quakes today. You're good."

He finally reached the fence and looped his fingers through the lattice. I smiled, proud of him, and turned to look down onto the field again, looping my fingers through the fence next to his.

"Can you imagine playing football on this field?" I asked.

He shook his head. "Never."

I leaned my cheek against the fence and looked toward campus. "Can you imagine going to school here?"

He shook his head again. A pause, then, "But I can see you doing it."

I sighed. "Maybe I could've. But not now."

He glanced at me. "Kendra," he said. "Your life is not over. You'll get this worked out."

"If by worked out you mean not getting into any college."

"You'll get into college."

"You think?"

He nodded. "Yeah. You messed up, but you didn't ruin your life or anything. You made this way bigger in your head than it really is. Five years from now, you'll probably look back on what you did and laugh."

"I don't think so."

Another pause, then a chuckle. "Yeah, probably not. But I will. The point is, you're not going to be expelled. You'll fail calc. You'll probably get suspended. And you may have to choose a different college that you'll still be awesome at. So what?"

For the first time in days, my heart lightened. Maybe he was right. Maybe this would cause a ton of problems in the short run, but in the long run everything would be okay. "Maybe you're right," I said. "I hope you're right."

"But..." he said, then paused.

"What?"

"Nothing." He turned his eyes back to the stadium.

I let go of the fence and nudged him. "No. Say it. But what?"

"But. Don't take calc. Or if you do, have your brother help you with the tests. He is a genius, after all." A smile crept up the corners of his mouth.

I barked out a laugh. "Jerk," I said, nudging him again. I'd never even thought of that before. What would things have been like if I'd done that in the first place? If I'd trusted my brother and asked for his help and not tried to be so... above him all the time? I turned back toward the fence. "Let's climb it," I said.

His eyes grew wide behind his glasses. "What? No!"

"Yeah, come on. Let's climb it. Don't act like you haven't climbed a fence before. Plus, you climbed a jackalope, and those are notoriously vicious."

"I'm in flip-flops. I can't climb a fence in flip-flops."

"Oh. You're right. I wouldn't want to ruin your pedi."

"We'll get busted."

"Like that's ever stopped you before. Come on. We came all this way."

We stared at each other, Grayson's jaw working, contemplating. Finally, without saying a word, he moved his hands up a few links and pushed his toe into a link at about knee height. Grinning, I did the same.

Fingers here, toes there. Watch the sharp, clipped edges of the fence at the top. Swing over the right leg, balance, swing over the left leg, balance, and then push off. But not too far—you didn't want to tumble, ass over teakettle, as my dad always used to say, onto the sidewalk below.

We landed on the other side, my brother's legs still shaking, but a brightness to his face that I hadn't seen in a very long time. We began walking—more like skulking, hoping nobody would catch us and tell us we had to leave—and talking about nothing, really. Grayson told me about how they'd just finished remodeling the whole stadium, how it had shifted on the fault line. I told him about the football games I'd gone to at school and how I couldn't wait to start going to college games. We talked about Dad and Mom. And about home. We both missed it. Even though I knew what awaited me, I still missed it.

I was startled by a vibration in my pocket. I'd forgotten about my phone.

I pulled it out and opened the text I'd just gotten. It was from Zoe.

> Sorry about what happened. You should have warned me. You still in Cali?

I laughed out loud when I read it. I should have warned her? How many calls had gone unanswered? How many e-mails had she ignored? How many texts unreturned? I should have warned her? She should have let me know she'd moved on. Or maybe we both should have let go three years ago. Actually, yeah. That was what "should have" happened. That was definitely what was going to start happening now.

"Who is it? Mom?"

I shook my head, thumbing a reply:

> Sorry, wrong number.

"It's nobody," I said. "Nobody that I know, anyway." And that was the truth.

We kept walking, the two of us side by side, Grayson making his nervous *uh-uh-uh* noise in his throat.

When we'd walked around the whole thing, I bent and

picked up a rock off the ground. Small and gray, nothing pretty or interesting to speak of at all. Maybe, technically, a pebble. But I picked it up and handed it to my brother anyway. "A memento," I said.

He took it, nodding, turned it over between his fingers, and stuffed it into his jeans pocket. Then bent and picked up another and stuffed it in there, too.

I laughed. Of course. Two of them. How could I forget?

And we stood there for a while together at the top of the stadium. I felt the breeze against my forehead and smelled the chalky dust of rocks being ground up all around me. I listened to my brother count softly next to me and felt that somehow we had come full circle. This was a good place to be.

"Ready to go home?" I asked after a while.

He nodded.

I handed him my cell phone. "Here, you can call Mom."

He stared at the phone, shook his head. "We'll call her later."

Instead, I turned the phone to face us, scooched in close to my brother, and stretched my arm around him. "Say cheese," I said, then smiled and took a photo, with the stadium behind us.

We hustled back to where we'd climbed the fence before and lifted ourselves back over. I gave Jack the mascot a little pat on the head, and we hopped back into Hunka. Grayson picked up the atlas and I pulled into traffic, trying to figure out how to turn around and get back to the highway.

Suddenly, my brother started chuckling.

"What?"

"I can't believe it," he said, shaking his head as if he was totally mystified.

"Can't believe what?"

"I can't believe you actually got us all the way to California. Your stupid plan worked."

I mulled it over, smiled. "Well," I said, "I am perfect, you know."

"Oh, I know. Believe me, I know," he said. Both of us were laughing now.

"Besides," I added, "the real miracle will be if I can actually get us home."

I turned Hunka, and the sunlight shifted across the seat. Hunka's glove compartment door swung open and hit Grayson on the knee. He grunted and slammed it back into place.

We'd get there. No problem.

ACKNOWLEDGMENTS

Grayson had his rocks, and when it comes to making novels, I have mine. The following people were my *Perfect Escape* rocks, from sturdy foundation and support to beautiful gemstones to decorative marble, and each of them deserves thanks.

A special thank-you to my agent (and friend), Cori Deyoe, who always has my back (even when I don't know my back needs having!), who never seems to mind reading rough drafts and making suggestions, and who tells me I'm great even when I don't ask her to.

Thank you to Julie Scheina, my very patient, incredibly thorough editor, and all of the Little, Brown team, especially Leslie Golden, Leslie Shumate, Diane Miller, Barbara Bakowski, and Erin McMahon.

Thank you to the following for the feedback, the information, the willing ear, the sturdy shoulders, and the hand-holding: my critique partners, Susan Vollenweider and Melody O'Grady; the 2009 Debutantes, who are always there to help a girl out; and my writing friends Cheryl O'Donovan, Laurie Fabrizio, and Nancy Pistorius.

Thank you to my brother and sister, Steve Gorman and Lynn Smith, for providing the inspiration for writing a sibling story.

Paige, Weston, Rand, you are my diamonds. Thank you for shining.

And, always, thank you to Scott; you are the other half of my mica.

AUTHOR'S NOTE

I am the youngest of three siblings. I have a brother, who is eight years older, and a sister, five years older. Being a sibling—sort of like being a wife, mother, daughter, author, stay-at-home mom—is something that defines me.

The sibling relationship is one of the most intimate and complex relationships that could ever exist. Who else in your life can you have, over a lifetime, utterly despised, thrown shoes at, tattled on, cried over, laughed with, taken baths with, shared clothes with, cussed at, fought with, and loved?

Throughout my life, there have been times when I've been frustrated by my siblings. Times when I've been extraordinarily proud of them. Times when I've argued bitterly with them. Times when I've wanted them to just go away and leave me alone forever. And times when I've clung to them.

No doubt about it, I am a different person when I am with my siblings. And different yet again when I'm alone with just one of them. My relationship with each is unique. With my sister, I've been known to cuss like a sailor and party into the night. With my brother, I've been known to wage board game wars and laugh so hard my stomach hurts. When we're all together, I'm the baby. The artist. Nobody takes me all that seriously, and that's my role, and I'm happy enough with it.

Think about it. Your siblings are the people in the world who will likely know you for the longest span of your lifetime. My siblings knew me long before my husband and children came around, and they will still know me after my parents are gone. These are two people who hold my story and can even tell parts of it that I can't. Parts I can't remember. Parts I misremember. Parts I never knew. They hold my history in their hearts, and they know me — not only the Jennifer With Her Best Face Forward me but the Jennifer at Her Worst me, too. And they love me anyway, just as I love them at their worst.

When I call up memories of my childhood, some of my favorites are those god-awful family road trips we used to take before my parents divorced. We drove everywhere. To New Jersey, to Texas, even to South Dakota. During those car trips, we really got to know one another, and at times it felt more like torture than vacation. Yet we always find a way to laugh at them now (and sometimes we laughed at them then, too).

There's something special about a road trip with your siblings. Something about the way the sides of your legs rub up against each other's for hours on end. Something about the way you discover a new idiosyncrasy of your sibling, whether it be the way he chews or the way she hums or the way they both smell. Something about the way you share a secret chuckle over something completely stupid or private or both that brings you and your siblings closer, whether you want it to or not. To this day, the phrase "Well, if the platform shoe fits..." brings me to tears in a fit of laughter, not because the phrase itself is funny but because the road trip was long and it was a respite of silliness among hours of dullness.

It was with my two siblings—"Sleeve" and "Leonard," as I call them, and have since I was a child—on my mind that I wrote *Perfect Escape*. Because if any two people know as much about being a sibling as I do, and about all that it can encompass—the love, the tears, the forgiveness, the hardship, the prayers, the grudges, the name-calling, the hugs, and the road trips—it's those two people.

We have hung out in each other's shadows, and at times those shadows have felt cold and lonely and impenetrable. At times the shadows have felt isolating and impossible. And at times they have been dark, dark shadows full of secrets none of us would probably care to share. But over the years we've hung out in those shadows long enough and resolutely enough that I dare to say we've gotten comfortable with them. We expect them and we wait it out, and as

Kendra points out in *Perfect Escape*, sometimes that's all that's needed to let someone know that you love them.

Like Kendra and Grayson, my siblings and I are not perfect people. We are not perfect siblings.

But also like Kendra and Grayson, we've got each other's backs, and we know we don't have to be perfect to be... there. And in the end, "there" is really all that matters.

What inspired you to write this book?

The idea for *Perfect Escape* came to me, as story ideas so often do, pretty much out of nowhere. One day the first sentence—"I was six the first time we found Grayson at the quarry"—popped into my head, and I envisioned this little boy hunkered down against a pile of rocks, miserable. That vision stuck with me, and I mulled it over for several months before finally sitting down to write this story. I wanted to pinpoint exactly what I was trying to say with this novel. Was it really about a boy with OCD? About a girl who cheats? Or was it about their relationship? In the end it was the complexity of the relationship between two siblings, one with a mental illness, and the complexity of sibling relationships in general that really drew me to this story.

I have long wanted to write a story exploring the relationship between siblings. In *Hate List*, Valerie has Frankie, and the two of them enjoy a solid, rich friendship, one where each can be honest but where love is the overall feeling. In *Bitter End*, Alex has Celia and Shannin, and her relationship with her siblings is almost the polar opposite of Valerie's relationship with Frankie. Alex and her sisters share nothing, they don't understand one another, and their relationship is rife with conflict. In both stories, I briefly shone a light on sibling relationships, but neither enjoyed the spotlight that I truly believe sibling relationships can and should endure. I wanted to write a story that was all up under that spotlight.

Why did you choose OCD for Grayson's "difficulties"?

I chose OCD because it is estimated that two million to three million adults in the United States have it. That's a lot of people! But I also chose it because OCD is an anxiety-based disorder, and I think a great many people—especially teens!—are struggling with, and can relate to, anxiety. OCD is repeated and unwanted thoughts (obsessions) causing severe anxiety. Often, the person experiencing these thoughts will perform "rituals" (compulsions) to make them go away. Everyone has some unwanted thoughts and rituals, but OCD is defined by how much those thoughts and rituals interfere with their daily lives.

But the thing about OCD is that while it can be a struggle, it can also be overcome. People with OCD who work to get control of it can live totally happy, healthy, productive lives. And I wanted Grayson to see this. He is so wrapped up in and freaked out about his mental illness—I wanted him to see that even pretty severe OCD is something he can get past. I wanted Kendra to see this, too. I wanted her to understand that her brother isn't perfect, and never will be, but that doesn't mean he isn't worth having a relationship with.

But truth be told, *what* makes his shadow loom so large in Kendra's life wasn't as important to me as the fact that they get past it and see that each of them has shadows for different reasons. Kendra always felt like she was stuck under the shadow of Grayson's problems, but Grayson felt like he was stuck under the shadow of her perfection. And this was the important message to me. We all have something to live under or live up to when it comes to our families, friends, schoolmates, whatever, but we can all get past that and be the really great people we were meant to be.

Do you do a lot of research before writing your novels?

Depends on the novel, but overall, yes. For *Perfect Escape*, not only did I do a lot of research on OCD, but I also had to research other things. I researched rocks so I could make Grayson's obsession with them seem real. I also had to research the Hayward Fault, the Great Salt Lake Desert, Cal Memorial Stadium, riddles and jokes from the 1800s, rattlesnakes, dehydration in infants, the Green River, and even jackalopes! I wrote with Google Maps pulled up on my laptop next to my desktop and with an atlas in front of me the entire time. Kendra and Grayson's route is mapped out in Sharpie on my atlas, with stars here and circles there, hours between stops notated, the whole thing a mess of lines and stops.

But honestly, the most important "research" behind my novels is life lived. I do tend to write what I know, and I know what it's like to be trapped in a car for hours on end with a sibling you may or may not be getting along with. I know what it's like to feel the need to be perfect. I know what it's like to feel that your sibling gets all the attention. I know what it's like to meet new people and make new friends. And I know what Kendra's stubbornness is like, too. That stubbornness has gotten me into a lot of trouble over the years...and has also gotten me to some really good places...such as writing novels about stubborn, perfectionist girls!

■ ■ ■ ■

RESOURCES

Living with a mentally ill sibling can be stressful, painful, unpredictable, confusing, and at times frightening. Sometimes you can feel like your needs always come last, like your sibling gets all the attention, and like you can never predict what's going to happen next. You may feel like everyone in the house is sad, nervous, or anxious all the time, and like others are judging your family. You may also be embarrassed by your sibling sometimes, or feel overprotective of your sibling. You may even feel guilty for all your conflicting feelings and have a profound sense of wishing your life was just "normal." You are not alone. Here are some resources, current as of the date this book was written, to help you learn to cope with living with a mentally ill brother or sister.

WEBSITES

National Alliance on Mental Illness
www.nami.org
NAMI Information Helpline: 1-800-950-6264
"Coping Tips for Siblings and Adult Children of Persons
with Mental Illness": www.nami.org/Content/Content
Groups/Helpline1/Coping_Tips_for_Siblings_and_Adult_
Children_of_Persons_with_Mental_Illness.htm

National Institute of Mental Health
www.nimh.nih.gov

Sibling Support Project
www.siblingsupport.org

BOOKS

Being the Other One: Growing Up with a Brother or Sister Who Has Special Needs, by Kate Strohm (Shambhala, 2005)

Mad House: Growing Up in the Shadow of Mentally Ill Siblings, by Clea Simon (Doubleday, 1997)

My Sister's Keeper: Learning to Cope with a Sibling's Mental Illness, by Margaret Moorman (W.W. Norton & Company, 2002)

The Normal One: Life With a Difficult or Damaged Sibling, by Jeanne Safer (Free Press, 2002)

The Sibling Slam Book: What It's Really Like to Have a Brother or Sister with Special Needs, by Don Meyer (Woodbine House, 2005)